Away From Home Season

Away From Home Season

*The story of a Vietnamese volunteer
veteran in Cambodia*

A Novel

By Nguyen Thanh Nhan

AWAY FROM HOME SEASON

© Nguyen Thanh Nhan 2010

(Contact: tieusu@gmail.com)

ISBN 978-0-557-77276-6

To my comrades in the 4th Regiment,
5th Division, Front 479 in Cambodia
and my beloved Khmer people

"When does the spring come? – I never know.
My homeland winds can't reach this place.
I wait in my endless sorrow
For the day this war goes away."

ACKNOWLEDGEMENTS

I would like to express my sincere thanks to my adoptive aunt, Mrs. Diana E. Backhouse (Yorkshire, United Kingdom), for her great encouragement and support and Mr. Frederick Lipp, author of *The Caged Birds of Phnom Penh* for his honest comments. For me, those supports are invaluable gifts in my discouraged times.

For some details in this book, I am grateful to Mr. Aki Ra, one of the CNN Heroes 2010, the founder of Landmine Museum in Siem Reap, Cambodia for his permission.

I would also like to thank the staff of Lulu, who gives me a great chance to publish my work and fulfill my long-time desire.

Last but not least, my warm gratefulness is also sent to my old comrades Nguyễn Phong Nguyên, Nguyễn Ngọc Ánh and many other ones, the late poets Nguyễn Khương Bình and Nguyễn Trung Bình, who have read the Vietnamese edition of this book and contributed their opinions for the amendments in this edition.

CHAPTER 1

The days near *Tet*[1] in the jungle pass slowly. The mornings lengthen. The middays linger. The afternoons come languidly and leave hesitantly. And every night seem to be endless.

The forest is lonesome and desolate. Only some gloomy wind whispers in the distance. The whole space is conquered by an absolute quiet. Now and then, sounds of AK double shots echo from somewhere so far. It is spring now, but the forest is quite dull and dreary. The little buds seem still asleep somewhere behind the old axils. The birds seem to entice each other to wander elsewhere, not come back yet. The old trees, with their dark brown or mossy-green or grayish trunks, patiently put on their sallow leafy coats, standing side by side in silence. Occasionally, at one or another, a dry branch grills itself suddenly and then down off the trunk in a whirlwind. For a moment, the leaves on the high level rustle mournfully, as if they like to say farewell to their buddies who have just left.

Sometimes, peals of thunder suddenly echo in the deep night. A rain is falling at some far off distance – a capricious thunder storm appears once in a while in the tropical jungles. In the daytime, the air is sultry; even the rare winds are just like the steam rising out from a huge kettle of boiling water.

The temperature from twilight forward decreases steadily, and since 9 p.m. on, a cold rushes up amazingly – a sort of numb cold. The weather here always changes severely and capriciously. The spring – the warm, generous and tender one – does not come yet. However, the young soldiers feel that some unknown things are wriggling silently, evolving excitedly inside the rocks, over the old trunks or under the warm ground. Natural objects seem ready to rush out and bloom up, showing their liveliness, singing their dauntless and wordless songs to praise the wonderful and eternal life.

The transport company encamps at a corner of the forest. Their tents added a bit of funny and strange hilarity to this dull still landscape. They look like some casual paintbrushes that break out the monotonous layout of clusters of green pale trees and dry sallow grass cover.

These tents, rather, these tiny huts, are built very simply; each one has four small posts – their size about a grown-up's wrist – two long and two shorter, forming a sloping frame. Four sides of the huts are empty. The roofs are made by connected raincoats, and covered upon with branches and thatch. From a far off distance, they look like the dollhouses that rural children often build to play wedding and cooking. Once in a while, some gray sparrows flying over the forest suddenly make a prompt stop and goggle amazingly. They perch on a thick branch, hiding themselves under the leaves and quarreling stridently. As if they ask each other, "What odd things appear down over there?" They loudly and worriedly discuss and wonder which strange big birds have come and built those ugly nests. At last, after a peal of frightened and high-pitch whistles, they fly away; leave the tiny branches who are rocking slightly in wistfulness and sulkiness to such hurried buddies.

The huts of Platoon 2 are set under a cluster of three ancient keruing trees. Occasionally, the keruing flowers fall whirly down when a wind rises up, sprinkling many brown dragonfly wings all over the sallow grass. Huy sits in front of his hut, being absorbed in writing. Sometimes, the flowers softly land down again on his shoulders. Chi 'pheo'[2], Deputy Head of platoon, sits nearby sharpening his machete on a semicircle-shaped stone. He stops working and looks at the machete, nods his head with satisfaction.

"Well, it's about to my fourth *Tet* away from home… Goddamn it! What a *Tet* in this hell jungle!" he says idly.

Huy looks up at Chi. His statement makes him somewhat sorrowful. The next day will be *Tet*, he thinks, and looks out over the scattering bush and empty moor to the dull dark green jungle in the distance. There is not any slightest hint of the spring! The spring surely loses her way and cannot come here!

Huy recalls his early day abroad. He has left the General Command Front Station and gone straight to the borderline through the way of Samraong, crossed a forest in the west, half a day of walking from Samraong. Its edge was full of old mountainous ochna integerrima plants then. It was early spring, so the flowers filled the branches and became golden in the sunshine. These glorious flowers always remind the away-from-home sons of the springtime in their homeland. He pockets his pen and sits stupefied. A stream of thoughts and images floods his mind.

This season, in the suburb gardens, the ochna integerrima plants must be transplanted into pots and trimmed off one more time and transported for sale in the city center, along the pavements or at the bazaars. Tet markets now must be at a chance of bustle and mirth, with all colorful flowers and fruits.

Look! Blossoms of white, yellow, violet and bluish daisies are lying by red, pink dahlia. And haughty roses are rustling in early sunshine side by side with simple and familiar marigolds; and blooms of carmine peaches and colorful peonies and gladiolus. And tuberoses of snow-white and royal blue... There are perhaps up to hundred kinds of flowers showing their beauty and fragrant. And so many kinds of cake and confectionery and jam, so many kinds of fruit which are competing to show their attraction and sweet taste too...

Oh, Sweet Home! What a nostalgia of the boulevards and bazaars and markets where gather so many bright eyes and rosy lips of young picture-like girls; of the early spring breeze slightly touches over the dress-laps and rustling green buds and fresh leaves; of the sweet smell of thousand of flowers and confectioneries; of the hair fragrance wafting back from some pass-by girls. What a nostalgia of one boisterous Saigon at the end of year; of the familiar or unfamiliar people whose eyes are brighter and whose smile glimmer, expressing a new hope and new belief in a luckier and happier tomorrow...

***

Huy went back eastward some miles yesterday to look for a branch of blossoming ochna integerrima for the New Year Eve. He went on and on searching around and found nothing but a yellow color of withered leaves. "Oddly," he wondered, "there is nothing here, though this place just some twenty miles away from Samraong. Does it need to walk forty miles to and fro to get only a bunch of flower?"

He came back at last, thought that the moment of changing between the years would be much less warm and holy without flowers and the tender smell of burning joss sticks.

"Nevertheless," he thought, "what else can be done? You are a soldier, right now staying in a jungle, ready for a new battle, so you should be pleased with things you get now... Anyway, my first New Year eve away from home still promises some extremely attractive things. Every division has strong liquor. How talent the old fellows are to manage for the matter! Every squad gets a four-littered yellow can full of liquor. Tonight, I will take the masculine pleasure, fraught with generous satisfy, like the heroes in the old martial Chinese books, with a B52 bowl[3] full of strong spirit, I will take a long swig to experience a buoyed, dizzy feeling."

Huy does not ever drink liquor. He has just heard about the strange feeling it might have brought to people and quite liked it. "Tonight, tonight I will be like the warriors of the old times, holding up a bowl of liquor and loudly reciting the tragic, heroic verses of Wang Han[4]:

> *The luminous jaded-bowls*
> *are full of fine wine.*
> *[we] just want to drink,*
> *yet the pipas call for marching.*
> *Don't laugh at me*
> *who lie down from drunk*
> *onto the sandy field.*
> *From the ancient time forward,*
> *how many people would be able*
> *to come back from war?*

Moreover, there will be another interesting thing that every soldier of the three battalions and the regiment headquarters companies has secretly concluded together: launching fireworks to welcome the New Year Eve. The fireworks and crackers here, in this very battlefield, will be made of variety of tracer bullets. The tracer bullets will weave lots of flowers in the sky, and the warriors will be no longer homesick. Gunshots of AK rifles and other big machineguns will replace peals of small, middle crackers, and the roar of the 60mm and 82mm mortars shell will become very impressive blow-up sounds of the big ones! This is an extremely serious violation of army orders, because wasting and abusing ammunitions are strictly forbidden. Anyway, are we all warriors? So we must play mighty thus sometimes."

This transport company has sixty men. This number is much bigger than the real power of the direct combat companies, especially in the campaign season now. It is partly because its number is rarely changed, moreover, the company was given supplements at the end of last year to serve better the combat companies.

Huy was sent to this company right on the day he joined the regiment. Thai, head of company, was pleased to receive him, and temporarily appointed him as the deputy head of Squad 3, Platoon 2. He told Huy some details of his responsibilities and the company's role before the latter's crestfallen eyes. Huy felt disappointed to know that he could not join a direct combat unit, but just an army service one, in such a great battle. En route, staying at the station in the town of Battambang, he had met an officer on his way on leave. When he knew Huy would join Division X, the officer remarked that it had been granted "The Heroic Army Unit" title for two times. "It'll be rather hard for you, I have been serviced one of its battalions for a few years, I know that," he added.

Huy had imagined of the brave and vehement battles just like in some long ago seen famous historical movies – the romantic startling great battles, fraught with blood and flowers. He had imagined, almost desired that he himself might have taken some feat of arms, just some little one, and got some little wounds as well – wounded but not "completely lost" a leg or an eye – so that he would have had some scars for memorial! But how can it be now?

Thai realized at once his thoughts, he consoled him:

"Now listen! Don't think it's a simple and easy work. It's rather hard and dangerous indeed, and moreover a significant one. From where can the units get supply for fighting? Who'll carry the dead and wounded to the rear? In fact, it'd be rather boring than in the direct combat units. But we are soldiers; we need to know that no matter where we stand and what we do, the important thing to judge us is our spirit, not the form. In addition, you've just come; you're not accustomed to the conditions and have no experience. They liked to make you familiar to battlefield conditions and give you some more experiences. Be sure! Sooner or later, you will be sent to one direct combat unit. I am just afraid that you then are too discouraged to do your duties."

Huy carried his rucksack to Platoon 2 thus, and experienced his first battle in this company.

***

In the nearby hut, Sergeant Major Truong, Head of Platoon 2, just finishes his plan for the New Year days. He arranges all the available food and other stuffs – some dozen of canned fish from the booties gained at Ampil Base, the domestic canned-meat, dried fish, shredded-salted fish, cakes, candies, tobacco and cigarettes from the home front – so that the stuffs are available for the guests during the festival days, as well as left a bit for the later days.

He steps out of the hut and calls Nhu, the platoon cook, who is sitting to pick out the bad rice, gives him a piece of paper which he has carefully listed the stuffs.

Chi 'pheo' loudly orders Nhu to come near, snatches the paper and reads it, and then shouts at Truong, "How can you be so bloody far-sighted? A fighter means no limit, just play at his will, then he'll not regret anything if he would die tomorrow! Nhu, don't take his way, you just cook all of things for the festival, remember my words!"

Nhu looks at Truong, and then at Chi 'pheo'. He does not know whom he should obey. "Well," he thinks, a little inclined to Chi's side, "each of them has his reason. Yet I just know things of today on today, no need to think much of it."

Chi 'pheo' grunts a bit more, and then shouts, "Where're the chaps on duty? Follow me!"

As assignment on the meeting yesterday, Hoa, Huy, Phuoc, and Danh have to collect wood for the campfire to welcome the Lunar New Year Eve tonight. They take their axes and machetes and gather in the front of the hut. Chi shouts again, "Let's go!"

Truong looks at them departing and smiles, as if he has not any annoyance. He understands Chi 'pheo' pretty well, even his nickname too showing clearly his characteristics. Chi is a light-hearted fellow, not ever remember any of his words. He appears somewhat fierce, yet he is really a kind and sensitive man.

After they have arrived at Phnom Srok district a little time, he and Chi once went out to pick up bamboo sprouts, suddenly a stray shot pierced through Truong's left leg muscle. The injury was only on soft fresh, not too dangerous, but bleeding so much. Chi pulled quickly some wild climbing plants and pulled from his pocket a handkerchief, which was his lover's present, to bandage the wound. Chi was very fond of this handkerchief; he always put it in his pocket and never used it. Yet it was too thin, so the blood continuously flowed and wetted Truong's trousers. They were about two miles away from the base then. Chi helped him to go some two hundreds yards more, then found that his blood still flowed, he said, "Well, let me carry you on my back. If you keep on walking, lot of blood will be lost. It'll be very dangerous." And he lifted Truong onto his back, carried him pickaback to their base.

Another time, Phuoc was attacked by violent malaria. His body so convulsed that no one could keep back his pity for him. Chi lay embracing and pressing him down, tears and snots wetted his face. Chi loved and looked after Phuoc very carefully indeed. Both of them were orphans when they were too young, having the same hardest life, so they easily felt sympathetic to each other. They would so many times lie side by side and talk in low voice all night that Truong had to shouts, "Hey, you two fellows'll live together too long and long, it's not only one day to so talkative. Get your sleeps and let the others sleep!"

At this, Truong suddenly finds himself so depressed, remembering further things. For over two years he hasn't got any home news. His parents died long ago. One of his brothers has come up to Cao Bac Lang to do woods exploitation; the other entered Central Highland to plough new land. He knows nothing about their lives now. And An, the girl of Thanh Hoa province, whose black eyes are brighter, whose cheeks blushed seeing him when they have just got acquaintance, after her last letter – with swerved, ambiguous words that implied to tell him to forget their old days – was silent, gave no reply to his worried, questioning letters.

"Where is she now? How is her life? Is there any time she look at the golden ripe rice fields and remember the evening that both sides swore to live together forever?" he wonders.

Factually, he has no reproach to An. Certainly she has reasons. Moreover, Truong himself too has wanted to cease their love before her hurting letter. There were the moments of terrible shock and emptiness after a big battle in which many men have got wounded and died. He would imagine her extremely painful feeling if she might get some bad news from his comrades. And then he wrote short letters with unreasonable and dry sentences, sometimes rather offended too, so that she would be angry, and forget him.

However, when he was calm down later, Truong tore to tiny pieces those letters. An had become his non-detachable part that made his heart full of happy and love and sorrow. He was unable and discouraged to hurt her because of something did not come yet and might never come. He was just miserable because she hadn't given any reason to help him not to worry. He knew that she had things too difficult to speak. He knew that he shouldn't wonder any more and accept a plain truth: he had lost her, and the best way was to forget everything. But the conflict in his heart was just like the eternal conflict in human heart: to be aware very well what the best way is to heal one's wound, yet just does the contrasting way, just himself makes it deeper.

Truong takes a groaning sigh and shakes his head violently as if he wants to sweep out his heavy thoughts. He enters the hut, takes out a machete, and heads for the heap of woods. He chops into pieces the dry branches, until the heap is almost done, and his faded green coat is soaking wet with sweat.

***

They have collected a lot of wood; all are firm branches of keruing and chengal trees. Into two bundles they bind their gaining and carefully tie them, then each one pick up a straight branch for the shoulder pole to carry the bundles home.

Huy staggers like a drunk. Chi 'pheo' looks at him and chuckles. He wonders why they have recruited such a little and feeble student-like fellow, who is maybe possibly as weak as a kitten, into the army. He is even a fire commander too!

"With this bearing, this chap would be bloodless to shoot a half of 12.7mm cartridge belt!" he thinks, and begins to mock at Huy.

"Hey, Huy, don't know why the hell they chose a student-like guy like you to be trained of machine gun and all. Well, it's not enough yet. Your appearance is nothing of a soldier. With your appearance you can only get one way: to be a pen-pusher!"

"Well, don't judge a book by his covers, my brother Chi." Huy retaliates, "Yours too is nothing of a soldier. With your appearance, it is most fashionable for you to get back to Vu Dai village to cut yourself your face to claim damages!"[5]

Suddenly, Hoa laughs whinnyingly, he turns to Chi and asks, "Hey, Chi 'pheo', do you remember the bloody taste of tea this fellow Huy made the day he just joined us? Hehehe... That is what we call making tea according to the model of 'generals and soldiers are like fathers and sons.'"[6]

Huy bursts into laughing. So do all the others.

That day, Chi 'pheo' gave him a pack of tea, told him to make it. He boiled a big pot of water, and then poured all the tea into the pot.

At the other end of the camp, Chi yelled, "Huy, where are you? Why do you take too long time with just a little tea?"

Chi 'pheo' was startled when he saw Huy bringing the pot with a serious manner. "For what you bring this pot here, Huy?" he asked.

"You ask me to make tea, don't you?" replied Huy imperturbably.

"You make a little tea with that whole big pot!" Chi's eyes wide opened, "Damn it! You're really a stupid!"

"Then how to make it?" Huy asked angrily.

"Well, Hoa, you must train your subordinate again. If it's like this next time, you won't be forgiven. Hm! This pack of tea then really a waste," Chi pulled a face, "Now, let me see the pot!"

It turned out that making tea here was different from making tea at his house! Here, the soldiers were accustomed to the *trà quạu*[7] which was very strong. The tea pack of Chi needed only one third of bidon, yet Huy poured into the pot two liters of water!

Obviously, in the warrior life here there are so much new strange things that Huy has not yet known. He is bewildered with the strange words of the old soldiers; among which there are some serious ones, and there are also slang words that the old soldiers usually use to tease the brand new ones.

When he just entered the platoon's house, his clothes were still sweaty, and all the old soldiers noisily gathered around him. This guy looked at him like people looked at a haughty cockerel to assess whether it would die easily or become a proud cock with the ability to lead the whole flock of hens. The other one crushed Huy's arms and legs with his fingers and then curled up his lips and shook his head with contempt. His pride boomingly arose. Anyway, for all nine months, he has been training days and nights until his skin was sunburnt-black like coal; his flesh was sinewy like iron, not a breakable one. Only that he was a little short of stature and thin! Then a guy who had an audacious face and a shaggy beard and hair – later known as brother Chi 'pheo' – grinned and winked at him in a mischievous way, showing his teeth which were blackened by *thuốc lào* (pipe tobacco) smoke.

"Did the regiment pay you the 'sok-lo' money?" the guy asked.

"What is the 'sok-lo' money?" Huy was really bewildered.

"Well, that is a sort of subsidy for the newcomers. Go and ask the regiment financial board tomorrow," Chi played act, "Strangely! They should have paid you already!"

The soldiers burst into laughing. Huy looked at them, as helpless as a kitten up a tree. He asked over and over again, but no one wanted to give him a clear answer, they just said vaguely that it was an extremely attractive sum of money, and that if one misses it, a half of his life is surely wasted. In the meeting that afternoon, once again Huy got a surprise when Truong reminded.

"Remember to turn your watch on time, my comrades. Don't swindle five or ten minutes to fall out with each other…"

Huy looked around, no one had a wristwatch. "There is no wristwatch here, how can we know the exact time?" he asked.

"We will look at the stars to guess the time. Gradually, you'll be used to that. For example at nightfall it is six thirty, the evening star rises then. We take a mark to compare with the star, for instance a treetop. In one hour, the star will move away from the beginning position about a span…" Truong explained.

"A span?"

"That is to say you stretch out your arm and stretch out your fingers to measure."

"Well, well…" Huy nodded interestingly.

Another time, a few days later, Huy felt uneasy and strangely sleepy. They were concealing troops to wait for their D-Day then, so there were not so much duties to do, he slept all the time. Chi 'pheo' hurriedly waked him up. "Don't sleep so much in the daytime. If you feel uneasy, find something to do and get sweaty. To sleep so much in the jungle will make you feverish…" he said.

Generally, such small and simple knowledge always makes Huy surprised and interested. Everyday, he learns some new and strange things.

Walking, talking, and teasing at each other, they soon reach the camp. Everyone brings his bidon[8] out to refresh his body to welcome the eve. This water is fetched from a far place, so they have to economize by the way of "one-bidon-washing". That is to say they wash their bodies within that limit of water. Firstly, they put the bidon onto their heads, turn it upside down and let the water flow sporadically enough to wet their whole bodies. And they rub it. And they wipe it with the towels. Then they let the water flow sporadically once again and wipe their bodies with the clean side of the towels. Literally, it is not different from wetting their towels and rubbing their bodies with it, but doing this way is easier and more satisfied. Then they come back their squads to have dinner. The darkness begins to fall down.

***

Huy hands over his watch to Vu and returns to his hut. The Big Dipper has emerged from behind the lone keruing tree top – it is about to nine o'clock. The air is cold, a kind of touched and indescribable coldness. The dark blue sky above his head is thick of stars. His first away-from-home New Year eve is passing slowly without knowing it has just brought him so many thoughts and mixed feeling of happiness and sadness, of love and nostalgia.

A moment ago, sitting at the watch position, he has reviewed many images.

The last evening before his departing, Ma stood quiet on the roadside when he jumped quickly onto the bus to return to his unit. When the bus moved, he stuck out his head and saw her wiping her tears. Ma tried to repress her sober and tears to keep him from much sorrow. Yet he also realized then that she was sad so much because of their separation without knowing how long it would be.

He recalled his youngest sister with her round eyes. She was full of four years old when he left home. His classmate Tuong Van once visited his home, seeing him holding his little sister in his arms, she praised: "My God, what cute eyes she has! She'll break lots of hearts when she grows up!"

He recollected the road to school where stood some early blooming flamboyant trees. In the evenings going home from school, he would walk very slowly to watch the falling flamboyant orange-scarlet flowers; and the times he and his friends played truant, came to La San Mai Thon to swim in the river. They swam to the other side, where stood a small isle with many nipa palm trees, to catch the small crabs. They usually went out to drink coffee in the evening then. His friend Ha took the crabs to his home to roast and then took them to the café, then they all sit chatting, eating roasted crab, and drinking tea.

He recollected the New Year eves when the sky turned into a pale blue color and the stars became far off, the incense burner on the ancestor altar was lit and the aloe wood scent was faintly spreading. Ma would arrange a fruit tray to worship the Heavens and Earth in front of the house. The *bánh tét*[9] pot, which was cooked at a corner of the yard, also began to cheerfully yell to inform that the cakes were about to well done. The flickering fire lighted up the moving huge dark shadows. The children gathered around the red firecracker string, chatting gently, and waiting for the time when the firecrackers blew up and splashed about. In the immense night, some warm and holy thing pervaded – a faint and invisible yet enduring thread which connected every soul together. "Is it called the holy spirit of the homeland?" he wondered. One after another, the images followed a stream of imagination rushed into and occupied his whole mind, led him return to the bygone days, though he still gazed at the plain before him.

Huy enters his hut, opens his rucksack and pulls out his diary; he intends to write down some thoughts, which remain in his mind after the watch, yet unknowingly, he puts it back again and walks out toward the platoon's campfire.

Everywhere, the fires have been built already at twilight. The flickering campfires light up a corner of the forest. The sounds of singing and crying and yelling and beating can be vaguely heard, near and far with the winds. The whole platoon is sitting around the campfire, except the men on duty. Truong is holding a half-gone can of liquor to pour it into a bowl; he suddenly looks up and spots Huy.

"Well, Huy, come here and take your seat, you new comrade deputy head of squad three. You come late, so you must take three bowls at a time," he says.

Huy sits down between Phuoc and Chi 'pheo'. He takes the bowl, smiles at everybody and speaks loudly, "Excuse me, please, I never drink liquor, but I will take this entire bowl to share enjoyment with you all."

Then he slowly pours the liquor into his mouth. Its hot and acrid scent almost makes him choked. Yesterday, he was told that he had to hold his breath and take a long swig to avoid being choked. Yet it is almost unavoidable now. Nevertheless, he finishes the bowl successfully. He returns the empty bowl to Truong. He winces and feels a stream of hot air pervading from his stomach up to his throat, his flesh gets hotter and he is nearly sweaty though the air is rather cold. Hoa, Head of Squad 3, is playing the guitar and singing the words which are altered from the song lyric of "Dry Leaves In The Spring" by some soldier in his regiment:

"I come back to Sam Pua, the remote place, and encamp near Cuom Mountain. After the days of building the base, with the nights

coming out to lay ambush, I go on fighting in the K5 Belt campaign.
Sitting on the troop carriers, we reach Sisophon and drinking for three
merry days. While we are drunk, we never know that our mothers are
waiting for their sons in the homeland..."

He looks around at the others. In the flickering firelight, each
one's face has a deeply and secretly sad expression no matter what he
is doing – talking, smiling or quietly sitting. Hoa finishes his song.
Everyone is silent for a moment. There are only the soft crackling
sounds of the damp woods. This song lyric is simple, but it seems to
tell them about the recent time, about their lives and emotions and
truthful thoughts in these days.

The Vietnamese warriors who are sitting here, or at some camp
nearby a forest, a riverside, a stream edge, or on some mountain slope
or some hilltop all over Cambodia are mostly very young. Their dark
sunburnt faces still remain some innocent and childhood lines on the
mischievous curl of lips, yet also so mature and meditative in their
sparkling eyes. Some guys whose soldier-age are not enough one year
full, right before putting on the green uniforms they are still naughty in
teasing their young brothers and sisters, still yell innocently in a
cricket or fish fighting. Yet in the last battle, some of them was gone
for good; when they lay down, their eyes still wide opened amazingly
as if they could not believe that they would have died when their age
were green, their dreams were full, and they still did not ever know
what was a kiss onto a girl's cheek.

Hoa turns to him. "Huy, you sing a song. Everyone here sang
already."

"Give me the guitar," he says.

He holds the guitar whose back is peeled off and whose front
cracked, plays softly a few notes then looks up at the others.

"I'll sing a song by Tran Tien to remember our dead
comrades."

Truong passes the bowl of liquor to him. "Take another bowl to
get your inspiration," he says.

Huy drinks up the liquor in the bowl and begins to sing. For a
moment, the thrilling liquor yeast and the warm and close air of
comradeship and his haunted private feelings mix up and fly up into
his singing voice. He feels as if his heart too were dissolved into the
close and faithful ideas and emotions of the song.

It tells about the innermost feelings of some soldier, in fact, of
many a soldier, before the death of their close comrades; tells about

the first kiss of a young soldier. This kiss is not to give a tender and beautiful young girl. It does not land onto a virgin's sweet lips, which are like fresh grass or roses. It does land onto the half closed eyes of a friend who has just fallen down. This first kiss is not for the sake of man and woman's love; it is for the sake of comradeship. And the soldier sings the song with the "firing words". It is not a loving song to give you, my little sweetheart. It is a marching song I give my friends and lull my friends their last and forever sleep.

In this moment of the eve, the song is rather uncanny. It is not suitable at all to the last minutes of the year – when people are often excited with their hope and belief in a luckier new year, with their promising intentions and desires. Yet it is really touched. When they hear it, the soldiers of this company feel that it seems to say about them. Their eyes glisten in the firelight. Are those things their tears? Or their eyes are just stricken by some grain of dust coming along with a wind?

He comes to the last words of the song:

"Let's sing the firing words by our heart of love.

Let's sing the loving words by our heart of fire.

Let's sing the firing words by our loving heart.

Let's sing the loving words by the fire in us."

His heart too bursts into flames. The flames of love and regret and pain are burning his heart.

Then it is the turn of Minh, a Saigonese, who enlisted at the end of 1984. He holds the guitar in his arms and yells, "Now, don't sing the sad songs anymore, we're near to be heartbroken already. Let's dance, my buddies! Is soul all right? Soul dancing is really easy, you just do as you like!"

The sounds of guitar resound urgently and jubilantly. Some guys pace into the center of the circle to begin the dance. The paces whirl around the flickering firelight. Then all of them stand up and join the dance. Some guys take along with them some water can or a pot, dancing and beating. The night is shaken in the rousing sounds. In the immense and deep sky, the far off glistening stars seem to joint together in a graceful waltz.

It is late now and the midnight will come within some minutes. Truong is busy to insert batteries into his little National radio. This radio is used only about one hour daily, at the hour of poem reciting and night story-telling program. The atmosphere is calm down now. The whole regiment is quiet. Everyone talks in soft tones as if they dare not break up the sacred moments. Huy sits with his arms folding around his knees, his head bends down. He feels as if he were falling down to a non-bottom abyss. He has drunk so much liquor and vomited a few times until he has been only able to vomit some bitter sticker liquid. Chi 'pheo' grabs his shoulder and shakes him lightly.

"Huy, Huy, you try to drink a little tea to neutralize the effect of alcohol."

He shakes his head then lies down onto the ground, curls his body up. He still hears the far off voices but his limbs are exhausted. He lies dreamily, half awaking, in a countless moment. Suddenly he hears sharp peals of shot of AK rifles. Then another. Then the sounds of gunshots and cannons burst out everywhere. He opens his eyes, tries to sit up. In the sky, the immense night curtain is slit into pieces by the red lines knitting across each other like the wings of stars. The gun smoke pervades like fog and covers the air with an acrid smell. On the horizon, the B40 and B41 rocket launchers are fired, bursting out into colorful bundles of light: the fresh orange, dark green turning into dark blue color strips; and at their edges there is a purple color sinking into the darkness. The sounds and the hues seem to sing and dance together. The night is extremely splendid – a wild and innocent beauty. The peals of firecrackers and fireworks to welcome the eve of the year 1985 resound and appear at a jungle corner in the northwest of Cambodia thus.

CHAPTER 2

----, 1984

*T*he last day of my first year in the army... A forest in late
evening... The evening in the forest is not as beautiful and
peaceful as in songs. It hides some enigma that makes the soldier's
heart heavy.

The falling leaves touch each other crackling so softly. Sound of
the vague AK gunshots...

----, 1985

Today should have been the commencement of the campaign to
sweep out the foe's strong base A. Yet our plan is delayed because of
the death of a Cambodian leader. My division will throw out its whole
power, with the co-operation of a Cambodian regiment. And my
regiment is the main force to straightly attack the base.

My warrior life really begins these days. A battle at division
level, in the campaign of the whole front; A battle that is not at all a
chance for every soldier.

Today, all over the world, people take off the first calendar sheet.
And in my home city, everybody is happy and joyful, maybe.

Perhaps my mother is doing some work right now; her sad eyes
maybe screw up missing me. Maybe sometimes, awaking in deep night,
she would weep silently. Ma! Never did I give you any pleasure but the
worries. When can I do what I expect for you: You sit among the
charming grandsons and granddaughters, telling the fairy tales by
which you would bring me into the sweat tender dreams in my
childhood... you smile without worry of debts and rice and clothes for
us...

---, 1985

A poem written in a hurry:

This Spring and My Nostalgia

When does the spring come? – I never know.
My homeland winds can't reach this place.
I wait in my endless sorrow
For the day this war goes away.

Is it true that the spring comes back?
To bring good news there's no sparrow.
And there's no flower in this forest.
How can I forget where I'm now?

In the jungle just all of us,
Who are protecting our homeland.
When can we all come back again?

What do I think in those long nights?
With cold frost drops soaking our clothes,
With the lone moon so far away,
With the stars build their fires of hope.

I recollect my things of love…
My Ma would daily stand sorrowfully at the porch,
Waiting for her poor son somewhere
Please, for me, oh gentle Winds, touches her white hair.

A A Oi,
"Old mothers are as 'ba huong' banana,
As 'nep mot' steamed glutinous rice, as 'mia lao' sugar "[1].
I'm away from home fighting long and hard.
Don't cry so much my dear Mama!
I'll go on in operations,
With whole my belief – your loving heart.

If bad news comes some day, Mama,
Your dear son is alive no more!
Don't fire candles, don't show flowers!
Don't let your tears flow over!
'Cause they'll bring you more sadness.
Your brave and good son's done his best.

I now miss you so much, Mama,
I now love you more than ever,
Mama!

To every where the spring just comes.
But at this place it's not present.
Both the blue sky and gray dull ground,
Bring me great lonesome and deep wound.

Here, every the soldier's in deep nostalgia
Of their homeland in the end of year,
With long softly hairs and nice young faces
Of slender girls in their white dresses,
With nice and fun festival bazaars,
So familiar yet so far ... so far ...

I miss the innocent white of schoolgirl clothes,
And I miss the fall leaves dying yellow the old roads.
I miss the summer rains came to and fro in a hurry,
And I miss long streams of hair made souls rainy

And just sometimes in those long nights,
There come my childhood recollections
The spider makes his web on the branch
For what the mason bee just flaps her wings?
Oh, how many of our memories have been fading?

Oh my dear old friends,
Boys and girls who are so charming
How many of you now still think of
Your long ago good ideals and love?
Who still keeps on his (her) own nice dreams?
And who is swept into life streams?

In the long night my melancholy spreads.
Every old face dimly comes back ...

---, 1985

What's the date today? My notion of the time now is just about the mornings and evenings, just about the days and nights that endlessly continue to each other.

Why am I sad? I can't find the exact answer. Remember? Yes! Sometimes, something reminds me of my family and friends, and every night when I can't sleep a wink, looking through the mosquito net to the starry sky, in the sounds of falling dry leaves, in the sounds of twisting trees in the cold winds of the night, I am listening to the silent sobs of my heart. The future is a dark vague space. And the present is so painful and heartbroken...

Who are the heroes? Only those normal and nameless soldiers are the heroes. Their hands hold arms, their flesh suffer the pain and their blood flow. They come to the life to be alive and desire and love... and then to leave in a moment. They do not think about far and high things. Their dreams and their desires are simple. Those are true men. How can I find a man who just exists in my imagination – an untrue and invisible man, built by so much pieces of image from books? I realize that now. Is it late? – I can't conclude.

Is it right we were born to suffer great misery, to build our dreams, to enjoy our uncompleted happiness, and then to die? The meaning of life is so obscure and metaphysical.

Ampil! This name of place will imprint on the bottom of my heart, with things that I just realize about the faint boundary between the two directions of thought.

A few days more will be Tet. It's so vaguely!

---, 1985

Tet in the jungle

I am writing now the lines of words which overflow from my indescribably restless heart about the days I am living, under the dim light of the lamp. For what I write? I am no longer keen on the task of writing, but there is some innermost feeling just burning in my heart... My blood seems to be blocked in every artery.

The dark and immense space covers upon me like a thick huge net, with the tiny, far off holes – the stars. The night seems to be condensed. Far away, the campfires of the units are flickering. The sounds of singing and shouting and beating are near and far up to the wind directions... Oh! The Tet of the home away young warriors in a desolate jungle!

Last night, the Eve, I was no longer conscious to welcome the holy moment. The old soldiers who joined up before me seemed to be so sad too. They concealed their melancholy by laughing, jumping and dancing, yelling and singing. The warm companionship bowl of liquor was passed to each other... My God! I was deadly drunk before them all. My dear friends! Please give me your sympathy! Ma! Please forgive me! The liquor made me drunk, but it was indeed the deep sorrow knocked me out before I could enjoy the holy moment with my companions and my people.

Tomorrow, I will take my operation to the new combat. Among the young but arid faces around me, which one will remain and which one will leave for good? Laugh loudly, sing and dance!... Let's be merry because we may never be merry again. Do the mothers and lovers know that their dear folks are preparing to go, then come back or go forever – with a keen belief and love and a determination for victory? The blood will overflow, the flesh will be dissolved, but the Vietnamese soldiers will never fear! My mothers, my sisters, let pray God for your sons and your lovers be peaceful!

Ma, I love you and miss you so much, Ma, my eternal loving mother! I don't know that if I can come back to you in the future or not. But I will never be a weak and coward soldier. Please understand me, dear Ma!

The lamp is near to run out of melted fat and dying out. But it will be bright again tomorrow...

Huy just rereads the latest entries he has written in his diary. He folds it up, looks out at the grass plain. A wind is blowing, makes the fire on the lamp near to die out. He takes his rucksack, puts back his diary into it and puts out the lamp. He comes out of the low hut, heads for his hammock, which he has hung already, uncovers the net and lies down on the hammock. Recently, he has often hung his hammock between the keruing trees before the hut to sleep outdoors. He likes to lie and look through the thin mosquito net at the night sky. When he was a child, he already loved the night sky and its far off stars. The books such as Saint Exupéry's *"The Little Prince"* or Alpholse Daudet's *"The Stars"* which he has casually read later made him love them more. The stars were the wonderful dreams that made his childish soul full of so much imaginations and beautiful desires toward the high, far, holy heaven. His childhood is gone now. The innocent, pure images also lose partly some of wonder. For him, the starry sky is just a material sky now, with its material heaven bodies – its cold and inspirited planets. Those thousands of stars are no longer the lively and emotional creatures like human beings. There are no longer the stars of his childhood! However, the night sky with its bright stars still consoles his melancholy and innermost feelings.

He folds his arms behind his head, silently counts the stars scattering on the lone keruing treetop in the plain. One, two, three...

one hundred and one, one hundred and two… Suddenly, a star – the one hundred and fourth – is bigger and bigger… Then it smiles at him, very tenderly. It opens its eyes to look caressingly at him. Oh! It is not a star, but Ma now! Ma is smiling silently. Ma's hair floats along, flying with a rolling motion in the immense and bright night sky, with million, million tiny shining stars…

CHAPTER 3

Since the tenth day of *Tet*, it is raining continuously for days. The sky is low, leaden gray and heavy. In the whole unit, the air is quiet and desolated. The boys only come out if necessary. They huddle in the huts to play *tiến lên*[1] or lie side by side to confide to each other.

Huy huddles himself up, thinking ramblingly and listening to the voices of Phuoc and Danh mixed into the sounds of rain beating onto the thatch roof. Danh is telling some story about his homeland Moc Hoa, Long An province. Huy hears vaguely some details about *Ven* and *Vang* – the wise hunting dogs of which Danh was very fond when he was still home.

In the platoon, Danh is the one who is most respected among the new soldiers. He takes operations or digs entrenchments as enduring as the old ones. At first glance on him, Danh looks not any of a strong man, he is tall and thin. Compared with Minh, Hung, the citizen soldiers who joined the unit at the end of 1984, he looks so much weaker.

As his stories told, Danh worked very hard since he was a child and got little food to eat.

During the days they were attacking Ampil Base, without Danh's support, Huy might have been fainted from exhaustion. During his training time at Quang Trung, he and his mates usually had drills of operation, with heavy equipments. But those are nothing to compare with real operations.

At the army training center, the operations were just like to take a stroll about. You're tired? Just take a rest! At first, the company leader looked so serious but he was easy later, so Huy and his mates took advance to wheedle like children. In fact, it was nothing so heavy then, just only the detachment parts of the 12.7mm machine gun. Yet, recently, the first time Huy has walked in one breath four miles without a rest. On his back was his rucksack, with clothes, personal things, one case of K56 cartridges and the launching doses and defuses of 82mm mortar; a four liters yellow water can hung down loosely on the cover of the rucksack. On his shoulder was a load of six 82mm mortar shells and a rice belt; an AK riffle. In addition, he carried a three-cartridge-magazine belt pouch on his chest and a water bidon on his hip. Averagely, each soldier has to carry about 65 pounds.

When he had walked about two miles, his head was dizzy. His feet had got blisters already, now the skins at those places were peeled of, painfully rubbed again the shoes. In addition, the sandy ground in the dry season was contracted up like concrete, made his heels rebounded after each heavy pace. He looked at Minh who was walking before him; he was nothing better than him, uttering the cries of pain. Nevertheless, Huy tried to go until he got the first rest. He sat flat on the ground, his back against his rucksack. He closed his eyes for a moment. His throat was dry and painful because of thirst. He tremblingly opened the bidon cover. The water gulps were cool with the night air.

Those were no longer the normal water gulps: the water then became the nutrient, became a special sweet wine. From the moments like this one, Huy realizes that human's needs in the most essential times – when you suffer the absolute lack, when you are nearest to the death – are just the little ones: air to breath; water to drink; and something to eat. Then the love of life comes back, and you can peacefully think and dream again. Yes, just so it is enough for you to find in yourself the full and exciting life.

Huy drank slowly and little by little. Chi 'pheo' had told him that he had to drink just a little, as little as possible, because had he drunk so much, he would have been over sweaty and exhausted soon. On the other hand, saving water in one's bidon was the vital matter in this terribly dry tough land.

When the operation restarted, he took some steps and felt dizzy. His feet which have been much less painful in the rest tortured him very worse now. And he walked more and more unsteadily.

"Let me help you to carry the load of mortar shells." Danh who walked behind him said hurriedly.

Huy hesitated and then shook his head. Danh did not carry much less than him. He had no AK because he was a subordinate soldier, but instead, there were two K56 cartridge cases in his rucksack and eight mortar shells on his shoulder. He tried to walk for a little while then fell down. Danh pulled the load of mortar shells out of his shoulders.

"I'm still well; just let me carry for a while. I'll give you back when you're better," he said.

This time, Huy had no strength and will to refuse Danh's faithful help. So, Danh took the load on his other shoulder. Really, without the load, Huy felt easy again. Walked some distance, he looked back. Danh still stepped normally, but his breath was heavier. I feel a little lighter, but Danh get double heavier, Huy thought. Suddenly, he felt a strength coming from nowhere that dispelled all of his weary and pain. He stretched his arm to get back the load.

"Thanks, Danh. I am well now."

Since then, Huy really forgot his misery. He thought about his merry memories and dear and tender images then smiled to himself. The operation in the night passed gently, no longer a terribly long nightmare for him as before.

In the last afternoon right before the gunshots completely ceased in the battlefield, he and three other men had alternately carried the wounded soldiers from the front line to the emergency camp of K23. The hot sunlight radiated straightly on him made him exhausted. The whole group had been continuously going back and forth for two days like a working shuttle without a rest to carry the ammunitions to the battlefield and carry the wounded and dead men back. In the last trip, they carried a dead man who had died the day before but had been left at the battlefield to give priority to the wounded soldiers. Trying to come to a point half a mile from K23 camp, gave back the stretcher to the others, Huy felt that his head terribly ached and his eyes dazzled.

"You go on," he said. "I want to take a short rest."

"Yeah, you go later then," Danh nodded, looked worryingly at him. "I'll go with them and help them if necessary. They looked very tired too."

Huy sat down, half-lying, one of his arms against on the ground. He took the bidon up to his dry and peeled off mouth. Only a few drops of water left in its bottom. Huy drank it bottom up, felt that his thirst unchanged. He tiredly closed his eyes. Some seconds later, he could stand no longer and lie down on the sand, near a stunted bush of high dry grass, letting the little honey bees to swarm freely over his face, letting the slanting sunshine to flow over him.

It was twilight when he opened his eyes again. He tried to stand up and found a short way to return his camp.

Reaching the camp, Huy entered his hut and lay deadly. He was unconsciously until the next midday. He heard Phuoc's voice calling him to have lunch but he felt his body crumble and not hungry. Phuoc entered the hut and shook his shoulders.

"Now, try to get up and eat a little. You will get fever if you continue to lie."

"No, I am not hungry. Leave me alone." Huy shook his head and weakly said, eyes closed.

A moment later, Danh came in with a bowl of smoky gruel. He helped Huy to sit up.

"I make gruel from cooked rice to make it easier to eat for you. Now, try it."

Huy looked at Danh with a touched feeling. He tried to eat up the gruel though his tongue was too bitter to eat. Danh brought in a bowl of hot water and two headache bills. Having eaten the gruel, taking the bills and two hours of rest, Huy woke up and felt really better. He was able to get up and walk, though with a little tremble…

All of a sudden Danh turns to Huy and asks, "Huy, you got any paper left? Give me one sheet. To write to my lover."

"Sure, just a moment," Huy nods.

When he just came here, Huy brought along with him many books and notebooks – three diaries, some notebooks in which he wrote the lessons at the H15 training center, some English exercise books and some novels. Unfortunately, he had to come to the forest where they temporarily encamped in the campaign. He was not able to come to the rear base so he had to carry all of his things in his rucksack for the whole campaign. In the rest time of his first operation, he has threw away some of the books of which he very regrets now. He tears some sheet of papers and gives them to Danh, smiling:

"Well, when you hold your wedding, remember to telegraph me."

"Sure!"

Outside the hut, there are plashing sounds of the steps on the rain-water-flooded ground and the rustling sounds of the nylon raincoat, and then Minh sticks his head in.

"Huy, brother Thai call you to the company house. Bring along all of your things to get your new duties," he says.

Huy is not surprised; he knows that sooner or later he has to be transferred to the new unit. When he just came here, they did not send him to a direct combat unit but the transportation company because they were preparing for a very big battle. Now it is the time for the units to train in cooperation with other arms and branches of service to attack Base 201, he has to come to the firing unit to drill and prepare for the battle. On the other hand, this is as well in order to give supplement to the units who have lost their troop strength.

However, Huy feels a little sad. He has shared with his friends in No. 22 Company the first away-from-home *Tet*, shared with them the warm bowls of liquor and the nights of confidence, how can he not be melancholic now?

He collects his trivial things and puts them into his rucksack, hands over his gun to Phuoc.

"Well, so long my friends. I wish you all well and take well your duties. Send my regards to brother Hoa, brother Truong, brother Chi and the others."

Phuoc and Danh nod their heads, look at him sadly.

"We wish you well and peacefully at your new unit."

Huy carries his rucksack, puts on the raincoat and leaves the hut, walks toward the company hut.

Lieutenant Thai, Head of Company, is sitting on a sedge mat spreading in between the hut; in front of him sits a youngster. Huy realizes that this young man has received him before at the division headquarters. Thai speaks loudly when he enters, "Well, here comes Huy. You take a bowl of tea to get warmer." He points his finger to the other, "This is Phuc, regiment organizing and mobilizing board's assistant. He will lead you to the 3rd Battalion later."

Huy nods hid head at Phuc. "I've come here with him from the division headquarters before the campaign," he says.

"Well, so you're the old friends already, good, very good." Thai leans forward to pour tea into the bowl, and then gives it to Huy.

"The 3rd Battalion is the mobile combat unit of our regiment for many years, brother Huy, fighting so well," Phuc says, "Captain Van, Head of battalion, is a good player, but so serious too. As for his soldiers, they work and fight very well, and play and make waves extremely well too!"

Thai lifts up his tobacco pipe to his mouth, takes a deep drag, spits out a big cloud of smoke then gives it to Huy.

"You take a drag of it, then start. It is about some ten miles from here."

Huy takes the pipe, pinches some tobacco and lights it. He was used to this kind of tobacco since he joined No. 22 Company. Chi 'pheo' was his grand master; he has trained him how to smoke without choking. Huy thinks that huddle-bubble pipe tobacco is better than normal tobacco. It makes you ecstatic in a short moment. You just take a puff of it and feel enough like smoking some cigarettes. Sitting and waiting until the intoxication ceased, Huy stands up, says goodbye to Thai.

"Well, I'll go now, sir."

"Work well at the new unit, and come to regiment headquarters to visit us sometimes."

Huy and Phuc leave the hut. It is still raining a bit. There is some pleasant scent spreading in the air, perhaps it is the smell of a kind of wood burning in a kitchen hut nearby. Phuc looks at Huy, smiles and asks, "You've fought in a great battle recently, did you fear?

"Why not, I was scared to death. When I carried ammunitions to the 2nd Battalion, the bullets just whizzed over my ears and the big shells and cannon balls just boomed and banged around me, not far more than ten yards."

"It'll be harder when you come to the direct combat unit. You have to fight endlessly, not having such an easy life like at the regiment here. Why didn't you apply to stay and work in our country?"

"Well, we're soldier. I have to go where they assign me. It was impossible to stay in the country though I liked or not. In fact, I also wanted to come here to know. And once be here, I'm a little afraid."

Phuc nods his head repeatedly but keeps silence as if he is busy in some thoughts. Huy too speaks no more. The two young soldiers cast down their eyes, step faster under the net of rain.

It has stopped raining when they arrive at the camp of the 3rd Battalion. The hut locates on a low hill. Around it are the bushes. In front of it, at the right-hand side, there is a big keruing tree with a strange shape. From the foot to one third of its trunk, it is inclined at an angle of forty degree with the ground surface. Then from that point up, the trunk returns its natural posture again, goes straight upward the sky.

Huy looks at it and thinks perhaps it was broken by some wild animal when it was young, but it still stood up consistently. A young soldier sits at the foot of that tree, whittling at a two inches diameter branch, perhaps to make a hoe handle. He spots Huy and Phuc, drops the branch and the knife on the ground, stands up and walks toward them. The distance is shorter now so Huy can look clearer at him: a solid face, a sunburnt complexion, a pair of witty and merry eyes, and a well build.

"Good morning, my comrade, brother Van's at home?" Phuc says loudly.

The young soldier nods his head, gazes at Huy as if to assess him, then turns to Phuc, replies with a genuinely Mekong Delta accent.

"Brother 'Yang' sits in the hut. Please come on in."

Captain Van, Head of the 3rd Battalion is sitting and writing something at the table. The four edges of this table are four small trunks fixed in the ground, at the top of each trunk is a fork to bear two horizon bars of bamboo. The little bamboo laths are connected together by the wild green creepers to make its surface. Captain Van looks up to welcome when Huy and Phuc follow the young soldiers entering the hut, and then bend his head down, continues his writing.

The young soldier pulls them to a long, low bench, similar to the shape of the table, but its width is narrower, enough for sitting only. "You brothers sit down here and have your drinking and rest, wait for brother 'Yang' a moment," he says and reaches the table, pours a kind of greenish water from the water can into two bowls, and carry them to the newcomers.

"It's *hà thủ ô*^{2} water, so cool, you two try it."

Huy and Phuc take the bowls, drink up the water with a long swig, and then look around. There is nothing in the hut except the table and some benches. On the walls hang three rucksacks, and at a corner, there is a gun rack with two AKs. Nevertheless, it is neater than Thai's company hut where there is not any table or bench and people just take their seats on the floor.

Huy's eyes turn around a whole circle then come back to the beginning point – Captain Van. He is about some thirty of age, tall, and has thin but broad shoulders. He has a fair complexion, student-like, far different from the image in Huy's mind on the way here. There is some strange funny line on his face, though he is seriously working now. Huy carefully studies him for some more moment and finds out that it is because of his mouth. It is a little twisted, goes upward on the right lip, as if all the time he is about to stretch his lip to smile.

Two minutes later, Captain Van finishes his work. He folds up his notebook, looks up and gazes at Huy, Phuc. His dark, bright eyes squint then he laughs loudly.

"Excuse me. I got to come to report the combat plan at the regiment headquarters tomorrow so I try to finish it. Well, Phuc, if I don't make mistake, they informed me yesterday that you will lead Huy to here, is it Huy, right?"

Phuc nods for confirmation:

"Yeah, he is Huy, finished the non-commissioned officer course at H15 center in the country, and came here last December. He stayed at No. 22 Company recently, worked so well. On the way here before, I told him about the 3rd Battalion already. Especially I introduced so carefully about you, the famous leader. Why, you have something to reward me, sir?"

"Just so! For what you said behind my back, I do not give you my punishment yet, now you want to get reward! Well, come here, I'll give you your reward!" Captain Van says.

"I'm not a fool, sir," Phuc laughs, replies. "I know so well your talent of *varma ati*^{3}! Well, Captain, I register my lunch at your battalion today. Please kill chicken to treat your guests now."

"Not any chicken here, there's just the 'army's *prâhok*^{4}' for you," Captain Van laughs merrily, then turns to Huy, he says, "Well, Huy, come here, let me introduce to you a little about our battalion. I'm Thach Van, born in Cao Bang, you knew it already?"

He tells Huy about the names of the officers of the battalion, companies and platoons, about the overall situation of the battalion, and then he says, "Now you will come to the 12.7mm platoon as your professional training. However, you're temporarily a soldier. You just come here, so they will not respect you if you lead the battery at once. On the other hand, you have too little experience to do well the leader's duty. Just try to work and fight well, then automatically when the men of the platoon make suggestion I'll officially appoint you. OK? Anything else?"

"No, so may I come to the platoon right now, Captain?"

"No need to hurry, just stay here and have lunch, and I'll send Kien to lead you there. Nothing left for you to eat there now." Captain Van turns about to look for Kien, the orderly, but Kien is gone out.

"Kien! You prepare for the meal now!" he calls loudly.

Outside, it is raining again. From the back of the hut comes a good smell of frying dried fish, and then Kien appears, carries a tray of cooked rice and food.

CHAPTER 4

*I*t was raining uninterruptedly for days. The forest rains, as a huge whitish faded mosquito net, blanketed upon the height. The pouring rains, like a bass guitarist in his high inspiration, cascaded down the hut roof.

The rains poured down over nights as if they wanted to spin endless stories, to lament for someone. The whole sky sank into the rains. Chip, U Moi's pet starling, did not hop around and stir everything up as usual. He huddled at a corner of the rucksack and lay quietly. Only his mischievous round eyes turned around, looking questioningly at the men as though he wanted to ask suspiciously, 'Why is it so cold? Why is it so sad? Why can't I see the sun with his warm golden beams?'

The weather was strange enough. In late January, when their battalion just came back to there for camping, the burning sunshine was so intensely hot that made everyone tired to death. It was launching straight down at the soldiers' heads, so blazing as if it wanted to burn red the whitish sand-field stretching out of the forest, to dry out the ragged dry dust-covered leaves on the bushes and the old keruing trees. Then since the first early rain of the season at the beginning of March, it was raining endlessly, dimming all of the heavens. In this first rain, all of them almost burst into tears for happiness, felt inexpressibly delighted. Since the weather would be cool and pleasingly relaxed; there is no longer the sleepless nights with their sweaty slimy bodies; there is no longer the crowded flies and bluebottles coming from nowhere. Since they would no more hard come to Ampil Lake, about six miles away, for bathing and washing and getting water to use at their camp.

Everybody of the platoon flowed out of the huts and yelled joyfully when the sweet water began to fall continuously, began to spin an endless whitish string of big heavy raindrops. Let it rain! Just let it rain! 'We pray God for rain, to get water for us to drink!'[1]

They took off and whirled their clothes over their heads, naked like newly born babies, like innocent and artless angels. Then they all jumped up and down, this one sang, that one cried out no meaning words, the other threw his back down onto the ground, with his face up to the sky, his limbs stretching out, his mouth opening wide to let the overflowing raindrops fall on and console him. Let it rain! Just let it rain! Let it rain to clear out all the dust of this earth, to sweep out all our worries and sorrows, to flow out the nostalgias and thoughts that made our hearts painful and broken. Let us be mixed into, dissolved into the sweet crystal water drops...

But the rains was just generously falling, days and nights, as though to satisfy their wishes, without interruption through the first week of the month, hiding the heaven and earth behind a dim dark curtain. There were no more clothes to change because the hanging clothes were just still damp. The soldiers could also go nowhere to hunt wild animals with the fierce rains like that. It was only rich of water, all the time the tubs made by nylon raincoats covered on the ground holes were full of water. There is always a truth: when there is so much sunshine one'll prays for rain; when there is so much rain one'll misses the sunshine. Nature never provides anything of balance – non-excess and non-lacking – as human's desire...

Quan is absorbed in writing. He is writing a short story for the Army Literature magazine. The cool wet air and the sound of the even endless falling rain seem to excite his inspiration. Maybe this time the editors will not refuse my manuscript, he thinks. It is written from my deep emotion; it is mixed into my faithful lively sensations, and is all of true things. It is not a mediocre story but containing all the smiles and tears and sweat drops soaking our faded uniforms; all the splendid golden sunset splashing upon the woods in late afternoons; all the fragile sacred moments between the life and death of my companions, that is the whole of our lives here, in these days and nights, was condensed, transformed into the words.

After the dry season campaign early this year, Quan's battalion returned to this place to protect the Cambodian conscripted laborers to build the K5 defense line along the Cambodia-Thailand frontier. It is now a relatively leisured and peaceful period of time for his unit – a mobile combat regiment of the division; a regiment has been moving up and down, operating constantly across hundreds of miles along the frontier of Battambang and Siem Reap province; fighting from this battle to that, from the great to the little ones as same as the time before he joined it.

This forest stands about six straight-lined miles from Ampil Lake in the southwest. It is a primitive forest, mainly of keruing and chengal trees scattering on the stretches of white sand, which are like the ones at Cu Chi, homeland of his grandmother. It is indeed leisured here, literally very leisured. The army units of Pol Pot and Son Sann, bobbing somewhere now in Thailand border areas, are stunned and exhausted by the last general offensive. They are in the period of defense to recover and strengthen their vitality, so certainly not be able to creep in to harass. Now, these are the days of peace, the rare and valuable days and nights of rest and returning to the normal life without sounds of gunshot, without hard works, without the moments full of suspense during covering themselves to wait for the firebreak time. Nevertheless, sometimes, Quan and his companions feel bored, and they miss the eager enthusiastic operations, miss the attacks and the smell of burning gunpowder spreading all over the battlefield.

Quan writes stingily, with lines of tiny slim letters. It is very short of paper here. The notebooks, which Quan bought as he stopped by the Sisophon market, are only some double pages left now. At the editorial office, the men would have thrown his former manuscripts away at the first second when they found that the articles written on both sides of the paper sheets. They would have thrown them away testily, without even a glance to know what had been written on them, though Quan had carefully put on the top of the first paper a big note full of eagerness and entreaty: "PLEASE DO SYMPATHIZE, WE HAVE NO PAPER!"

"At the Army Magazine office, certainly the majority used to be from the army, if it is not all of them. They surely know that such a rare thing paper is here, in the theater of war! They certainly understand that how painful I and my fellows feel as we have to tear gradually our letters – the sole lovely vestiges closing to our hearts – from our beloved women who are too far away now, merely to roll shag. It is only because of the comradeship," he thinks.

There are guys who never care about letters and words. Because this one is illiterate, that one is betrayed in love, another one has received no more his family's letters long time ago. But they all need paper, though it is just for rolling cigarettes only. And the papers, either a sheet of blank notebook without any ink dot or a letter contained lines of loving words; either a sheet of soft, thin paper or of big size, tough, breakable one used to write reports – will be along to shag or *hà thủ ô* leaves turning into smoke, blackening the lungs of the home away soldiers.

You can keep your hungry for smoking and waiting for a chance, when you can borrow or steal at the regiment headquarters a newspaper or a magazine. But if you were a "rich man" or a "little owner", who possesses some sheet of papers, no matter whatever, how can you sit and see your friend to tear his hair or his beard because of craving for smoking, especially when the shag is left but there is no paper. And such abnormal cigarettes are very good, better than any famous cigarettes in the world. They are good because of the lack and sharing, because of the close and dear comradeship.

To say about paper without saying about the stamps is an extremely serious mistake. Each guy gets three army stamps per quarter. It is ineffective indeed! Luckily, many guys do not need stamps as mentioned above. So, all of the stamps in the end are used for their sacred and noble missions. They are glued upon the envelopes of letters or the envelopes of the manuscripts to serve for literature.

To say about the envelopes, there is another matter. How can the soldiers have literal envelopes? The envelope here means a piece of paper, sometime with frivolous words and pictures, folded up, and carelessly glued with the cooked rice. However, this is on one hand, on the other hand, once and again, the soldiers are also rich and get plenty of things: paper, notebooks, cigarettes, pipe-tobacco, cakes and candies and children's letters sent from the country to console and encourage them... Such times come at the beginning of campaign seasons or at the great festivals or anniversaries in the homeland. But such lovely chances are so rare and insufficient, and the lack is still the lack.

His manuscripts are already so slovenly in their form, but it is still acceptable if things stopped there. Yet not at all. His manuscripts bear enough hues and colors too. There is fresh green or purple ink in his fountain pen, which is originally the dye that the villager gave him while he was in the rear base. And there are also lines of words written in pencil, because a story here never goes through in one sitting. It is always interrupted at some line or paragraph by a thousand and one reasons: the foe's sudden raids, taking operation, doing the missions or getting a fit of malaria... And those lines of words are sometimes so dirty and faded away because of rainwater that they are quite unreadable. Whenever he has to throw away such a damaged sheet, his heart is painful as if it is rubbed with salt.

Hundred of painfulness, hundred of misery for each gone manuscript – the sole manuscript, without a draft or a copy to save – yet his stories left no trace, or perhaps they were published in some edition but Quan cannot be sure.

There is often nothing to read for months here. And the torn wrinkled up newspapers or magazines from the regiment headquarters are also out of date and found haphazardly one or another edition without any order. Sometimes they get the editions of the January or February of last year while it was October then. Maybe they were published in the editions which I did not read, Quan consoles himself, and continues to give most of his rare paper to literature, for nothing else but a simple truth: for him, writing is an intensive urge.

Quan finishes his story with two words "THE END", and stretches out his body, takes a very relievable long breath. It was started since his unit has been staying in the base, but when it was half done, so much busy-idleness to prepare for the campaign season forced him to temporarily forget it.

"Oh, this deed of writing – of 'litrachoor' career – is so uncanny! It tortures one, causes him to forget both sleeping and eating, makes his head crazily hot with so many questions: how can I continue this half done story? What words can I use to express this too much meaning moment? Does this pen obey me? Does it shake with my shaking heart and flow up on the paper surface as my blood flow excitedly in my arteries? Or, does it determinately resist things I want to say? Writing! It is both so easy and so hard. But it is also very wonderful; bringing a gentle happiness to one's heart. The happiness of writing is so simple but so great that there is nothing else can compare with it, when one get a paragraph or a clause which is fit with his heart, saying out exactly his deep and high emotions or ideas..." Quan thinks, and turns to U Moi.

U Moi is carefully whittling the round small bamboo laths to build a cage for his pet bird. He really loves his starling. The thorny bamboo forest is no way near from here, about some ten miles of forest path. In fact, Chip, his starling, does not like any cage. But during the operations U Moi was forced to put him in the cage, lest this curious, playing-indulged devil should be absorbed in hunting and courting some beautiful female bird in the rest time and could not come back on time when his unit went on.

The old cage was damaged while U Moi had to roll many rounds to shun a pouring salvo of the enemy when they attacked Ampil Base early this year. U Moi was very sorry for that, he cursed all the time the devil enemy who helped to damage his valuable cage frame which was not made of simple bamboo but the shiny polished redwood laths. Anyway, he might have been glad that his Chip was safety. When they was arranging for the operation, Quan told U Moi not to take along his bird, but he still stealthily took it along with him by one way or another, did not want to be parted from his pet for such a long time.

"Hey, U Moi, where're the old man and Thuan going?" Quan asks.

"Them two go looking for something to eat and all," U Moi grumbles, without turning up his face, "I want to go, the old man prevents me, saying I'm unlucky and just bring the unluckiness to them. You see, what a bloody resentfulness! Hm, when we were at Takong Krao, who was the man who hunted monkeys and chopped fish for the platoon? Who was the most skillful hunter except this U Moi?"

"Well, don't be so sad," Quan consoles him, "There is no fish or animal here for you to hunt. And the old man is right with his superstition. You know, he's a man of the religious land of An Giang. Just because the last times, when you went along with them, you all walked so far but got nothing. In fact, there just some sour wild leaves to get for the soup here, no need to go crowded. The old man wanted to let you have spare time to make the cage, not to criticize you at all, you know that."

"If only it is sunny, I'll bring the shovel out and catch some 'sand lizards' to broil in a minute," said U Moi.

It is the nickname his platoon gave him. His full name is very florid indeed: Phan Quang Dung. The reason for his nickname is nature has set his over-marriageable-aged face in a military style, with a very high defensive spirit – means that it is convex and concave and has plenty of big and small pimples and pimple scars just like a best quality termite mound. In the battlefield here, nothing more valuable than a termite mound that appears somewhere during an extremely terrible battle. "*Ụ mối*" (termite mound) is the most firmly and safely natural defense work. So, this nickname is not at all contemptuous but contrastingly an honor for the man who gets it. U Moi knows so well that, so he likes his nickname very much.

His homeland is a mountainous district of Nghe An province, so he is very good in hunting. In the nostalgic nights, U Moi often tells his companions about his interesting hunting trips. When he just joined the platoon, nobody could hear clearly his heavy accent, but gradually, they were accustomed to it. The men of Nghe An-Ha Tinh are often called "*bọ*" – literally meaning father – as a common name. The people in Nghe Tinh have many local words, so there are so many funny anecdotes about them too. Hereunder is one of them (My dear readers, this is a Vietnamese wordplay story, so it is not easy to tell it in English, please pay your attention to the tone marks):

The platoon just received some new "*bọ*" recruits. Having come home, the head of squad said, "Well, you all follow this guy to the well to have a bath then back to have lunch."

Having washed, the new recruits entered the house. The meal was served, a little bit more luxurious than in the other days to welcome the new comrades. But suddenly the old ones who were sitting around the table stared surprisingly at the new ones. They just stood confused.

"Hey, take your seat and have lunch now, why are you so embarrassed?" the head of squad asked.

Some of them timidly took their seats, but one guy still stood there like a fish out of water.

"Sit down and eat, for what else you wait?"

"Y-e-e-s, yes, I'm having no "*đọi*" (the bowl).

"Not hungry, huh? Then take a little bit more for pleasure."

"Ah-h-h-h-h, I'm having no "*đọi*"!"

"Alright, not hungry then just be there, huh. We're soldier, just come and eat when possible, don't wait for invitation. Whenever you're hungry, you can come to the kitchen to eat."

The newcomer looked at his fellow-countrymen, and then at the chewing mouths, swallowed his saliva. He was hungry and angry and fears but could not say a word.

"*Đọi*", after Nghe An local word means a bowl. His B52 bowl was lost somewhere on the way. Yet because of his accent, the " ' " mark turned into the ".." ("*Đói*" = hungry turns into "*Đọi*" = bowl), so the southern land soldiers just thought he said he was not hungry! Then, when one of his fellows finished his meal, gave the bowl to him, he ran out to the water tub in front of the house, hurriedly washed the bowl and ran back, ate greedily as if he would have been starving for a century before the surprised eyes.

"Oh, you say you're not hungry, why do you eat in such a terrible way now?" the head of squad asked.

One guy gave explanation, he pointed to the bowl:

"He says he has no "đọi", that is he has no this one!"

The whole squad was doubled over with laughter. The head of squad laughed hysterically, but tried to speak:

"I think I got to compile a dictionary to explain your bloody strange words!"

Sure enough, this is only an anecdote. Maybe it has appeared since the days of resistance to the U.S. Army or even some time before that. Yet such anecdotes are often repeated to tease the soldiers born in Nghe An-Ha Tinh.

Quan recollects those anecdotes and laughs merrily. U Moi looks at him surprisingly.

"Why do you laugh alone?"

"Nothing, I just remember something."

U Moi bends down his head again, continues to whittle the bamboo laths and sings in his throat some Nghe An folksong.

"If [you] love, love to the end. If [it gets] problem, let it go with problem. Don't [act] like the hare at the end of the moor. To play with his shade as [he is] merry and play with the moonlight as [he is] sad..."

Quan approaches the hut corner, where his rucksack hangs on a fork of the wood pillar – a "camping model" of hook for hanging clothes and rucksack of the soldiers. He takes down his rucksack, pulls out the nylon pack holding his documents and books, carefully puts the manuscript in, folds it up and hangs back the sack on it position. He smacks his lips. "Well, I'm dying for tobacco. It might be like drinking the godly wine of the Jade Emperor in the Heaven Palace to get some bloody drags of shag now!"

His hut has total four hooking forks, that is to say four men staying in it: Quan, U Moi, Gia Huong (Huong the Old man) and Thuan the Lanky. In the platoon, Gia Huong, its deputy head, the eldest, is twenty nine. And Quan is twenty seven. All the others are about nineteen to twenty two. Their platoon gets four huts, that is to say it has sixteen gunmen. The real number is twenty five gunmen, but seven men are absent: three guys got heavy malaria, staying at the rear base. The fourth is Trung the Daring – head of the K53 machinegun battery, who died in the last battle, and two wounded men lying now at the division hospital at Chup and the last one is Phuong, head of platoon, who deserted after the Ampil Battle.

Quan temporarily takes the leader position of the 12.7mm platoon. In fact, he is the acting head of platoon since 1982, but in early of 1983, Phuong came from the division's training center and replaced him to lead the platoon. A man of chances, Phuong had so many maneuvers and wanted to get higher rapidly on the ladder of position, not by his ability but by his ruses.

To say fairly, Phuong was skillful in plans of training or fighting, or in distribution of duties. Yet he was a man of talking than of doing, and he had just a little experience in fighting, he applied for studying the primary officer course when he had just come to Cambodia and joined a few trivia battles, and then as he returned, he faced the most intense campaign during the last four years. Perhaps his desert was a good thing. A coward leader can cause bleeding or death uselessly and groundlessly, Quan always thinks so.

He had a blood and bone experience on this matter. It was a battle at the end of 1980 at the east of Svay Chek district. He was a B40 gunner of No. 12 Company then.

His company was returning to its base after a ten-day operation then. There was no rice and water left, but the unit was only three miles away from its base, not more than one hour of walking. In the dry season in Cambodia, the most vital thing was drinking water, because sometimes they walked about twenty miles, crossing the immense fields of Battambang. Above their heads lay the red hot sun and under their heels lay the concrete-like ground, with the remaining half-burned feet of rice clusters. The streams or ditches of water just flowed in one season – the rainy season – and in the dry season they became low curving drains, with only a lay of dry mud. Throughout that long distance, there was now and then some lone tree or a low withered bush, not enough to cover a head. In their operations each soldier had to bear a rather heavy load and sweated so much, therefore they needed water to make up for their bodies. The older and careful soldiers always kept a bidon of water in their rucksack, and only took it out at extremely necessary moments.

Yet that time, the company came near its base already, and at the last rest before, everyone, including the most careful man, had drunk all of water. Someone who had not drunk so much had also given their water to the younger soldiers who hadn't got any water left. When the company came near a one-seasoned big stream at the center of the plain, it fell into the enemy's ambush. More than eighty enemy gunmen had hidden themselves under the stream, at a dangerous arc. The company scattered rapidly to counterattack. Yet they were tired and hungry and worst of all dying of thirsty and the battle just pulled about. The enemy had prepared well of its spirit and material to destroy them with the tactic of opposing the leisured with the tired. It determined to keep them in its pincer jaws.

Head of company then was Lieutenant Vu, a man born in Thanh Hoa who was very gay yet very excellent in fighting. He was calm enough to make a retreat plan then he sent his orderly to creep to each part to tell about it. The company would drag on the fighting to the evening when it was really dark. They would took advance the dark to slowly retreat then. The firepower including the 60mm mortar and the K53 machinegun would draw out, with the formation of three-man groups, to a safe position and fire to support for the rest. Platoon 4 would be the last to retreat.

His plan would have been successful if Dung, Head of Platoon 5, hadn't been such a coward. When the orderly has just told the plan to the direct quads and Platoon 4, due to his fear of dying of thirsty, Dung ordered his soldiers to run westward, to the direction of the base of the 2nd Battalion without Vu's order, instead of waiting to cooperate to retreat safety. The soldiers of Platoon 5 who opened the blood way to escape only survived one third. The other two third of them died right there or was seriously wounded and lost so much of blood that they died later when the 2nd Battalion sent a troop to reinforce. That besieged time imprinted deeply into Quan's memory, because among the dead there were Khoa and Dat, his very close friends.

Outside the hut, more than a hundred yards away, there comes suddenly the loud voice of Thuan.

"Brother Quan, U Moi, come to the kitchen... We get something to eat already."

U Moi looks out around and then he says, "I see Thuan carrying something like a duck, brother Quan!"

"Well, perhaps they shoot a wild duck at the lake."

"This hell lake was really useless, I never see a bird and all, and the fish was tiny like an ear-finger, much of bone, and few as well." U Moi grunts.

"Well, you only have no chance yet. How can the old man and Thuan shoot well like you? Do you know why this lake has no fish and bird? The 8th Regiment has stayed here and just continuously fired explosive, how can the big fish left. And when we attacked Ampil lately, the sound of cannons made the birds feared and escaped all. This wild duck is maybe a heavy wounded soldier so it stays here to wait for its death." Quan replies.

He and U Moi enter the kitchen. Everybody is seated around near the bowls of smoky hot water. Binh and Phai the Crazy are cooking the duck. Thuan turns to Quan, says seriously, "Brother Quan, a moment ago, when I went by the battalion house, I met Kien the orderly. He told me a thing. Know what?" he pauses.

"Just say out! You always take important to thing as small as a mustard seed." Tien the Toad shouts at him.

"Our platoon will have one gunman more," Thuan says, "I heard that he just came from the training center in the country. Perhaps he comes here to replace brother Trung."

"Really?" Quan says calmly. He is serene, rarely showing his emotions. In fact, this news is as exciting to him as to the others. At the battlefield, it is very good to get one more man, because the number always gets reduction with the wounded or sick men. "Having one more man is a partly reduction of the weight in working, fighting and a joy for everyone. But I hope that he would not be a second Phuong." Quan thinks hopefully and looks at the duck.

"You or Thuan shot him?" he asks Gia Huong. "This duck looks about eighty of age! We'll chew it at our will!"

"I did it. It was funny. We went on and on and found nothing. I was so bored and wanted to return. Thuan begged me to go to the lake, thought that we maybe got something there. Then we came there, seeing this duck was staggering on the lake edge. He got a broken wing and could not fly. Maybe he was shot or got a piece of mortar shell during the battle." Gia Huong replies.

"I told him to try to catch it alive to get its blood to make blood curds and all but he refused. He was afraid that the duck would escape so he shot him. Wow! I feel hungry with my recollection of the blood curds. If only we get ginger, the duck soup and fish sauce mixed with ginger, and eating it in this rain weather is really wonderful!" Thuan says.

Everybody keeps silence. Outside, the rain falls again. Thuan's desire suddenly evokes a nameless nostalgia of their homeland. The nostalgia which has the odor of green rice flakes in the arising water season; has the smell of field mice fried with pepper and citronella; has the scent of the field-firing smoke in the golden evenings.

CHAPTER 5

Chip is very naughty. It just pecks at Huy lips repeatedly so that he cannot get a sound sleep. Huy seizes it then curls his finger to take some light flips on its stubborn head. When it is released, the bird flies up to a branch before the hut, purses its peaks to curse him: "*Get the hell off me! Get the hell off me!*"

U Moi always teaches his disciple nonsense words, and this starling just rashly applies them without any suitability. Sometimes, while everyone is sitting to talk together merrily, suddenly it screams out, with U Moi's heavily and unintelligibly local accent: "*Night, go to 'eep! Night, go to 'eep!*" Sometimes, at quiet noon, it would fell sad and cry continuously: "*'est for kool! 'est for kool! 'est for kool!...*" Once, when Captain Van visited the platoon, it loudly shouted at him: "*Hund'ed of widows, hund'ed of widows, p'ay fo'etin' your house, p'ay fo'etin' your house!*"

Huy often searches for the grasshoppers in the grass to feed it, so it is very fond of him. Except U Moi, he is the only one who can call it to land down onto his arm or whistle to entice it to follow him to the forest.

There is some consolation and joyful in having this bird, but sometimes they are crazily tetchy with it. It carries the spoons that someone forgets to put away to the plain and drops them there. It pecks at the can of shag, drags along the shag out to drop it scattering on the ground, then it jumps onto the can edge, rocking and dancing, until the can turns aside down, splashes up the shag and rolling paper. Then, the guy flies up to the tree; throws out its check and twitters a long victorious song, as if it has finished a great feat.

Yet the funniest thing is that it also knows well to retaliate upon someone. In the platoon, it hates Phai the Crazy so much, since he often threatens it with a small branch whenever it disturbs everyone. Once, when Phai was sleeping, it sneakily flied up over him, dropped onto his face a lump of shit with the exactitude of a combat pilot at master level. That time Phai actually went cuckoo and almost killed it if U Moi did not prevent him. Since then, Phai ignored Chip, tried to cover his eyes and his ears, left it alone to play at its will. It is really a pity for Phai, because he has to swallow the leek of being defeated by a little but very insolent bird!

Huy stretches his body then sits up. The sunshine is scintillating through the leaves outside, scattering onto the ground many small and big light flowers. After the day he joined the platoon, the rains have stopped. Up to now, things brought about by a rainy week have disappeared without any trace. The water tubs just remain a part of the water carried from the lake. The sandy surface is dry and hot again. The air is sultry again. Only the trees retain some green and cool appearance of the rains with their small greenish buds.

U Moi, who is sleepless all the time, sits up too. "Huy, let's go out to dig "*giông*"[1] holes," he says.

Huy nods, heads to the corner of the hut where placed the shovels and hoes and picks up two among them and lifts them on his shoulder.

From outside the hut, Chip flies in. It circles around U Moi and cries noisily.

"You always bother our sleeps. Some day I'll get crazy and kill you to cook with bamboo shoots." U Moi points his finger to threaten it.

"Hurt the 'tork kids! Hurt the 'tork kids!"[2] The bird screams loudly. U Moi glares at it, wonders, "My God! From where the hell this little imp learns that? It seems to understand human language!"

Huy laughs at U Moi's bewildered face. "He doesn't know anything of your words. Yesterday, when I fed it, I recited the verses: 'The stork went out to find food in the night...' Now it hears your saying cook with bamboo shoots so it remembers the next verse and speaks out for you!"

Having realized the truth, U Moi nods and chuckles then goes to the tub, takes a little of water into his towel, wipes his firm fortification-like face.

The two young men go eastward where they did not exploit so much; maybe the "food-resource" is still rich. The stretch of sand lies behind a clearing without big trees save some low bushes, and in some places the full-of-thorn big cacti scatter. It stretches about five or six hundred yards then crossing a low pebble hill toward the huge old trees, where is the beginning of the ancient jungle.

The '*giông*' hole bottoms are about a half of yard to one yard deep, up to the size of "the host", and often go sloping down a short distance and then turn upward to go parallel with the earth surface with a L shape.

It is not so difficult to dig these holes to catch the lizards. You only need to look carefully at the footprints on the mouth of the hole to avoid flogging a dead horse. Previously, without any experience, Huy just tried to dig when he found a hole, eventually it turned out an empty hole, or was occupied by another creature; sometimes a big old toad; sometimes a huge red scorpion holding high his claws to defend.

"You must look carefully for the little scratches on the sand of the hole-mouth," U Moi explains. "Those are their footprints. Then you can dig it. The hole with its smooth mouths gets nothing to catch."

Sometimes, they dig to the bottom of the hole but fail to catch the creature, it jumps out and runs to another hole to hide, and they have to start from the beginning again. Huy has learnt his lessons from his last experiences so he keeps along a fresh branch with many small twigs. He hits right away any lizard appearing in an effective way.

They go around for a short time and get six big ones, each about two inches long, not counting the long tail.

"All right, it is enough for today," U Moi says. "We must save them for later days."

Huy drags U Moi to the shadow of a grove to take a rest. He digs out from his pocket a pack of shag, rolls a cigarette and hands U Moi the pack.

They have asked the men of transportation platoon to buy the shag and tea when they followed the regiment trucks returning to the rear base a few days ago. Their platoon gets a chance to smoke and drink tea as much as they like, making up for the hungry days.

Huy happily takes a long drag on his cigarette then slowly blows out small circles of smoke. He looks at the hill. Under the sunshine, the black and white and gray pebbles at all sizes and hues are glistening like the precious gems. The whole hill is shining brightly.

"Dung, brother Quan joined in seventy nine, why doesn't he return home yet?" He asks U Moi.

"You don't know really? He gets no relatives now to want to return. Before he joined the army, he'd lived in a pagoda." U Moi stretches out his legs, tells Huy about Quan's life.

Quan was the only child of a couple who were dealers. On a trip from Hue back to Saigon, the bus plunged into a chasm and they died right away. That year, Quan was four years old, being looked after by a rented nanny. After the accident, his grandmother brought him to her house. Yet four years later she got heavy illness and was dead too. His parents' properties were disputed and shared and spent all by his distant relatives; yet nobody thought of the duty to foster and teach the miserable eight-year-old child. To say more exactly, they were very interested in that matter, yet anybody also believed faithfully that it was other's responsibility, not his or hers. They tried to pass the buck to each other, blamed each other and cursed at each other day after day about the duty of taking care and teaching the child but ignored his need of food and an active love and caring.

Quan slowly returned to the city, wandered and lived by begging for a while. One day, he was soaking wet in a heavy rain and took a cold, lying unconsciously in front of a small pagoda. There were an old monk and a young novice who stayed in that pagoda. They found him lying curled up and carried him in the pagoda to take care. Afterward, the old monk let him stay at the pagoda and brought him up. He had been sent to school and then passed his baccalaureate when Saigon was liberated in 1975. Then he entered the college, but during his sophomore year, the old monk died. He was very sad. He loved the old monk as much as he loved his father. Moreover, the war was breaking out at the frontier, so he volunteered to join the army and since then he considered his unit like his own family.

Huy sits still, listens to U Moi's narration.

Out there, the sunlight is milder slowly, fades out on the yellow-brown withered blades of straw grass on the right side. The evening shadow in the forest curtains down so fast. Usually, the sunlight is just blazing, yet a little later, the trees grow dim and sink into a hazy yellow light; and in the deeper end, just a gloomy dark space is in sight. The flying squirrels and flying foxes begin to come out to hunt preys.

"I never know that brother Quan's life is so sad like that," Huy thinks.

During the days living here, Huy has only figured out that Quan is reticent, yet sometimes he is also playful, often telling jokes in a humorous way. He never appears to be difficult or serious, yet he is respected by all the men in the platoon, even Gia Huong, the eldest. All the soldiers are attached closely to him; there was almost no distance between them and him. Huy has found out in Quan some thing which is so close to him, so like his nature. He could not pointed out clearly what it is, but he feels it, though for half a month staying here, he has never got a really conversation with Quan, except the normal exchange words.

"That time, I got a letter informed that my mom was dead from a heavy illness. I lay and wept all the time, got no food, no water. Brother Quan consoled me, and he told me about his childhood..." U Moi adds. "We come back now, Huy, it's late."

The whole platoon has gathered already into groups outside the kitchen hut when they reach the camp.

Right before the hut is a six-man group: Phai the Crazy, Trung the Bear, Thien, Tien the Toad, Binh and Hung. On the left side is the other with Moi the Tetter. Ly, Thai, Phu, Trong, Cuong. The third group includes Quan, Thuan the Lanky, Gia Huong. Each group is sitting before a ration of rice and food.

"Just a moment, my dear comrades," U Moi says, "each group will get two 'earth chickens'". He enters the hut to broil the lizards. Just a moment later, the good smell of broiled meat is spreading over. Then U Moi reappears, on his hands are the broiled and skinned lizards, showing a white flesh just like the broiled fish. He gives each group two of them then sits down with his group.

The evening meal includes a basin of sour wild tree leaves soup, a plate of salt mixed with powdered red pepper, a plate of canned meat, just like the lunch and the previous days' meals. Everybody eats delectably though there is nothing to say of deliciousness, except the broiled meat. Yet two lizards for a group are so little, each of them can only take a bit of it.

The time they just defeated Ampil Base, they could find some amaranth, cabbages, gourd or green papaw fruits, which planted by the refugees living in the base, to cook soup. The fruit and greens were limited, yet so many units went there to pick, so only a few days later there was nothing left. Trong had an idea to take the papaw treetops, sliced them, washed carefully, then soaked them in the salted water to dissolve the sap, and then cooked soup. However, after they ate this kind of soup, everyone got a sound stomach ache; no one dared retry that soup again.

For a week, the soups were only the boiled water mixed with a little salt and seasoning powder to help them to eat cooked rice easier. Yet without fibrous food, they all were heavily constipated. Luckily, Gia Huong found by chance a kind of wild tree leaves which were like apricot leaves, but thinner and having a sour taste. He cooked a little and ate alone to try it, and then found that it was safety. He had the boys to search for this "gift-of-God" vegetable for soup since then. More luckily, there was full of this kind of tree in the forest, so they were worried no more about the soup. Yet this kind of soup was quite good at first, but after several weeks, they felt bored to death with such a sour and acrid soup.

It is twilight when they finish the meal. Quan gathers the whole platoon for meeting. Having finished the task, he says, smiling.

"My friends, it is full moon tonight. We will make tea to enjoy the moonlight. I suggest that Moi'll prepare some new attractive 'films' to 'project' for all of us to enjoy. Well, dismiss!"

Everybody stands up and returns to his huts. At the east, the fourteenth night full moon, like a bid golden plate, is rising up.

***

In the army, the "film presenter actors" are been very fond of and pampered. He just sits cross-legged imposingly and opens his mouth to narrate things which he has read or watched in a deliberate way.

Cigarettes? You friends have already rolled for you some very big ones, just call out and someone will light it up, place it right at your lips, so you just puff as much as you like.

Tea? Someone will pour from the inox mug into a bowl the best first turn of tea, the greenish, strong and smoky one, and hand it to you.

And if you still feel dissatisfied, still want to wheedle this and that by the way of bending you spine sideway and stretching your body, saying that you is uneasy at your neck or your shoulders, there will be all at once two massagers at the "international level skill" to massage you alternately with full of tricks. The young men who have master skill in narration often get the honor to be the special guests in the parties or feasts of the nearby platoons, or even of the nearby companies as well.

However, "the trade of love takes care and pain". It is not easy to get the position of a king without throne with only one step.

Firstly, you need to be a learned man who knows thoroughly many famous works of the past and the present. Secondly, you need to have such a good memory that it can work continuously and enduringly in a "marathon story", sometimes for a few nights. Thirdly, you need to have an innate skill in narration art. That is to say you have to know the way to make the story become more interesting, more attractive; have to add and invent with a talent inspiration the small and big yet quite various details; and, have to know the way of pausing on time when the story comes to a climax, to make the listeners want to listen more, though the subjective situation requires that it should be stopped there.

Because of those harsh requirements, the number of the masterful storytellers becomes limited while their values become higher.

The extreme bliss of the platoon is that it gets such a man who brings its general renown and helps other guys to be honored through him. That man is Moi *lac* (Moi the Tetter).

Moi enlisted in 1983, stayed at District 1, Cau Ong Lanh market. Once you are a soldier, you can not avoid tetter; therefore, people have a ground to form a very impressive Vietnamese compound noun: *"linh lác"*[2].

A soldier must have tetter like rivers and lakes must have fish, or forests must have animals; this is a law! Huy himself got tetter when he was training at Quang Trung though he always kept himself clean: sometimes he got three baths a day! The whole company got it too. Perhaps some guy who has got the source of micro fungus on his body jumped into the water pool and spread the skin disease to the community.

So, back then, every evening after the meal, the whole company had to do the "general offensive to destroy the tetter"! Yet the medicine was only Iodine or 90 degree alcohol. This disease's particularity is that it often gathers right at the "centric organ" or "the headquarters" of the guys. Therefore, the spectacle then was very turbulent and funny. Everyone was together rubbing their bodies engrossingly, together shouted the cries of assault, and together danced disco or rocked soul to get cooler from the hot feeling.

Nevertheless, tetter is not an irremediable disease, sooner or later it is also destroyed, except the extremely special and rare exceptions, for instance in the case of Moi. The ringworm spots on him spread all over the surface that has the pores! And, it seems to be much attached to him, so if he cured it at this place, it would move to a nearby area. In the long run, Moi the Tetter is exhausted and has to surrender in this unequal war: he shakes hand with his ringworm and "lives at peace" with it. He is only suffered a single matter then: to be careful to avoid making them bored and want to takes an adventure to other bodies...

Night. The whole platoon sits around outdoor on the mats.

The moon rises up to the zenith, casting down a mild, haft clear light. The sand bank under the moonlight was smooth with a strange mysterious white milk color. It is no longer a dry coarse material that makes one's eyes painful as it is in the daytime. It is soft and thin now, like a silk scarf waving up and down through the mounds and valleys and hills. The lone old trees, the low bushes and the lines of far-off trees under the moonlight looked vague and unreal, like in a watercolor picture. On the trunks of nearer trees, the places where the moss or lichen grows are gleaming, and the leaves seem to be covered by a thin layer of silver. The hidden places where the moonlight cannot reach are darker but also illuminated by a weak reflected light.

Whenever he sits under the moonlight, Huy always fells peaceful and calm down though he is in some worriment. The moonlight seems to be a source of uncanny strength. It consoles, soothes and lifts one's soul up to a far and high space, where it dissolves into the general soul of heaven and creatures.

The clear moonlight helps the watching soldiers to have a wider vision and be able to find out the happenings more easily. It makes the away from home nights shorter and merrier and more comfortable. The young soldiers sit around, chatting or listening to some narrator or dancing together the soft and slow *ramvong*[3], tango, bebop, slow or the exciting and thrill cha-cha-cha, waltz... Because of those things, perhaps the moonlit nights for the soldiers are the wonderful nights.

Moi is telling an interesting point at the first part of *Wuthering Heights*. Everyone sits quietly and listens to him.

Once in a while, some wind passes by and moves the leaves. Moi's exciting voice causes them all to forget the time. Suddenly, a flashlight comes from the south, about three hundred yards away, moving up to the platoon place.

Trong, who is sitting at the gun emplacement, shouts loudly:
"Who's that?"

"It's me, Tam of the mortar platoon!" The moving shadow shouts back to reply and puts up the light.

Tam comes nearer, enough for them to identify him under the moonlight.

"Well, the 12.7 platoon is enjoying the moon too. We're playing at our camp. Brother Dat misses Moi and sends me to invite him there to tell some story. I knew already he has a show here; yet Dat doesn't hear me, just tells me to go here. All right, now let me sit with you a little while."

Phai the Crazy and Trung the Bear make room for him. The three of them are hometown men in Tan Binh district, and came here at the same time. Tam is very fond of story narration and admires Moi event more than his own lover. Once, when Moi came to the mortar platoon to tell story, there was no paper left, Tam tore his lover's letter to roll cigarettes for Moi.

A short time later, Trung the Bear suddenly stands up. His face is strangely anxious. He walks quietly out of the circle. Moi stops, stares at him. Usually, Trung likes to listen to stories so much. He never misses any story. He walks slowly to the gun emplacement, but when he is some ten yards from it, he stops and sits down on the ground. His posture under the moonlight is so sad and lonely.

"He misses brother Trung the Daring and thinks again!" Phai the Crazy grunts.

Everybody keeps silence for a long while.

Phai leans forward to Quan, continues, "He looked so strange recently, brother Quan, as if he is mad."

Quan frowns. He looks thoughtful at Trung for a moment then says:

"Everybody should pay attention to Trung, console and encourage him. Especially Phai, you know?"

They all fall into silence again. Some seconds later, Moi breaks it.

"Well, we'll continue..."

The night flows quickly. The moon is at the west horizon now. The stars are gone away, just remain the brightest one. The wild cocks' crows echo from somewhere so far.

The story is more and more interesting with Moi's melodious voice. A moment later, when Moi takes the bowl of tea to drink, Quan says:

"Well, let Moi finish this section, then we stop. We need to take a rest 'cause we'll begin to drill with the companies the tactics of fighting in accompany with the tanks tomorrow."

CHAPTER 6

The next morning, Trung's mental state gets worse. His illness begins to show itself. Everybody comes out for training then. Only two guys stay in the hut. Phai is arranging for the meal, and Trung sits nearby to help him. Trung suddenly bursts into sobbing while he is sorting out the bad rice grains. Phai stares at him, sad and worried.

Previously, the platoon had two guys named Trung: Trung the Daring, head of battery, and Trung the Bear, gunner no. 2 of the K.53 machinegun. Trung the Daring died in the last battle; left behind him a great loss for everybody, especially for Trung the Bear.

Right after receiving the greenhorns, Trung the Daring paid close attention to the short, sturdy, broad shouldered guy, who has an awkward gait like a bear, but his face is gentle and naive; his sad brown eyes are not any suitable to his big, square face. Naturally, he felt that he loved the latter like his younger brother who had died from a disease at his ten years old. Once, when they lay talking, Trung the Daring told Trung the Bear about his sad and hard childhood. Within a few days, the two guys with the same name attached together more than the siblings did. The older Trung looked after the younger Trung, taught him, gave him advices and even soothed him.

Trung the Bear's shape is bold and redoubtable, yet his face and nature is very gentle and timid. When he was home, Trung worked at a garage. He was born in town of Phan Thiet, Binh Thuan province, and his family was so poor. He failed the entrance exam when he was fifteen. His parents did not know how to do just when his single aunt who lived in Saigon visited his family. She told his parents to allow him to come to Saigon. She adopted him and brought him to the city. Later, she helped him to apply for an apprentice position at the garage until he took his military service.

His aunt was a vegetarian. She did not make him to eat after her way, but Trung was already accustomed to a hard life, and he did not want to bother her, so he too took vegetarian meals. In his military training time, he had the vegetarian comestibles that she sent him so he kept on this habit. Yet after coming here he gradually have to eat meat like the others. He hates guns and wars. When he just came, he often said that he would only shoot aimlessly; and that he did not get the heart to kill just the lizards, in fact, he had only got the sins of killing mosquitoes, bed bugs and cockroaches.

The day Trung the Daring died, the platoon accompanied No. 12 Company to get the first thrust into the foe's base. After crossing the first open space at the first defense line, they continued moving to take the vital positions to cross the second one.

Ampil Base was the headquarters of Sonsann. Its power as the scout's reports was about ten thousand gunmen, with all kind of arms from the 130mm cannons down to the personal guns. Besides the soldiers, in the base there were the Khmer refugees and the wives and children of the soldiers and officers. Among them, there were also the Vietnamese. After they occupied the base, the platoon's soldiers picked up a few notebooks in which there were some notes in English and Vietnamese too.

Ampil Base had altogether three defense lines which were three concentric arcs, far away from each other about eight hundred yards. Each defense line was a wide high earth bank; behind it was a four feet deep trench. Along the lines, per fifty yards, there was a big shelter, with many log layers upon it; the diameter of each log was at least two feet. In addition, there were the open gun emplacements for the personal and machine gunners. Between these lines were the minefields. When No. 11 Company was attacking the first line, they fell into a minefield and got four men wounded and killed. Eventually, they had to retreat and moved to other direction.

The battle outside the second defense line was at the peak of tense when one of the two tanks that No. 12 Company accompanied ran over an anti-tank mine and got heavy damage, not be able to move on. The soldiers deployed in a transversal line, moved up ahead the tank to protect the rear to carry back the wounded men. The K.53 machinegun of Trung the Daring's battery moved up along with platoon 6, and the 12.7 battery was led by Quan was moving at the left-hand side then, in the formation of platoon 5. Trung the Daring led his battery; his AK fired short peals of gunshots. The bullets then just whizzed over their heads, so they did not know how to dodge. They only stopped and lay down when a mortar shell or a cannon ball broke out nearby.

Trung the Daring was running when a B40 rocket shell broke out about four yards in front of him. Trung the Bear and Tien the Toad were ten yards away at his back then. Trung the Daring died at once.

Tien and Trung the Bear dropped the gun, darted onto him, just to see his pale gray face, his half closed eyes, with the bloodshot in white part of the eyes, and his bloody mouth corner. His body was fraught with big and small wounds.

Trung the Daring died at about five o'clock, January 7, 1985. The sunset was like a red flame from the front of the soldiers, the west, throwing down onto the sandy bank a yellow red dreary light. In the battlefield, the soldiers were slowly creeping toward their foes like a flock of giant ants. Here and there, there were many holes made by the broken shells and balls; and on lot of them were the dark red dry spots of blood. Since then forward, Trung the Bear became another man. He darted on, pushed Tien the Toad, gunner no. 1, down aside onto the ground, snatched at the triggers. The first time in his life, he knew pain and resentment. He did not bend down to avoid the burst of gunfire from behind the second defense line of the enemy, but turned the gun mouth to the flashing fire buds, fired continuously. Those gun emplacements shut up right away after his salvos. He fired like a mad man. His head was empty, just remained the words: "Brother Trung is dead!"

The battle dragged on from the dawn of the seventh until late evening of the ninth of January. Trung did not cry in that painful day. During the next two days, when the battle was continuing, he did not cry too. Except from the moments of fighting, at which he jammed his mouth but still be lively a little bit, in all his other activities he was half-witted. In the victory night, the platoon's soldiers caught by chance a pig and killed it for a party. He did not take part in the party. He went away to a desert place, sat plunk on the ground and sobbed for a long while.

His heart was very heavy and spleenful in the later days. Sometimes during the nights, waking up suddenly, he could not sleep again. He lay awake there, listened to the blowing forest winds, the sounds when someone was turning his body aside or the snores of his companions, and imagined that he was hearing the calm and familiar footsteps of Trung the Daring, who just entered the hut after a watch; imagined that his vague shadow was approaching him. Then he realized that it was only the sound of the winds passing over the thatch roof, only the shadows of the branches outside flickering on the ground and the hut's wattle walls. He recalled the image of Trung the Daring lying there, with his eyes wide shut, with his bloody body, and felt as if he just waked up from some nightmare. In a moment, he lied himself that all of this was just a bad dream; that Trung the Daring was still alive; and that if he sat up and wiped his face with his hands, brother Trung would have stepped toward him, smiling and gave him his half smoked cigarette.

"*Does the death come so easily?*" Over and over again, the question like a drill just whirled in his head. It whizzed up while he was eating or walking, talking or doing anything. Trung knew that man had to die. He had seen how his grandmother passing away in her low seashore house. He had also seen the deaths of other people who were familiar or unfamiliar with him. Yet he never knew such a sudden death in a flash moment. Within just a wink, a strong and healthy and kind man who had loved him as same as had been loved by him just remained a slimy motionless unfeeling heap of flesh and bone now.

And Trung was startled when he recalled of himself then. He had fired, not aimlessly, but straightly to the human bodies. He knew that there were bodies collapsed after his volleys. They were the barbarous bloodthirsty men who had killed brother Trung – he knew so well that. Yet he still got a feeling of horribleness toward himself when he looked down at his hands. These hands bathed in blood already! Due to these very hands, there were the wives losing their husbands, the children losing their fathers, the soldiers losing their companions…

His head terribly aches now. His thoughts are going twirling. In his ears resounded the sharp gunshots of the machine gun. He bursts into short painful groans.

Suddenly, Phai hears Trung groans and mumbles: "Aunt! …I fired… fired at them… I killed them! Brother Trung… I fired and killed them!" His non-timbre, gibberish, mixed into his crying voice, and especially their unsuitable meaning makes the words so strange and horrible that Phai was startled. He turns his face up, stares at Trung astonishingly. Somebody's shadow hides the light at the doorway, makes inside the hut darken in a moment, and then that man enters. It is Quan. He has already stood outside the hut for a long time now.

Quan looks at Trung, feels so unhappy and sorry for him. For a long time living closely to each other, he has understood every joy or sorrow, every strange nature of each person in his platoon, not only with the sympathy and love of a big brother, but with the generous heart of a gentle mother, especially for Trung. When Trung joined the platoon, he just followed him, asked and worried on everything. His questions were naive like a child's.

Quan has realized that inside the rough appearance, Trung's heart was of an old gentle *sœur* who does good deeds in her whole life. He was not the kind of man who gets a strong spirit to adapt and cope with the adversities and difficulties of life. After the first days of being homesick, Trung felt that the soldier life was so warm and close. At some certain point of time, he wished that their life would be like that forever; he and his dear companions in the platoon would be able to live together until they were old, like people in a family.

"I am no longer homesick now. I feel that to live like that is very joyful and interesting. I wish all of us in the platoon will live together until we are old, brother Quan." Once he told Quan.

His very simple mind has unconsciously forgotten the reality. He has lived in a daytime sweet dream, full of joy and love of the away from home warriors. Then the dream was broken. The reality was like the sharp blades cutting into pieces his happy and peaceful days. The reality was a fierce storm blowing by, left behind it a collapsed world of spirit.

"Everything is temporary and illusory and ephemeral, my dear Trung! Including our life, including our joys and sorrows and suffers. Especially here, in this very life!" Quan blurts out a lament. But it is choked in his throat. His very pain now is illusory too, he knows, and believes so. Yet his consciousness, his will and his heart seems to have no relation with each other.

He senses – with all his beliefs and notions which has been founded and become a firm personality of a man who has been living under a pagoda roof for his whole childhood – about the inconstancy and phantasm of everything, yet still feels a substantial pain, with the sensations of a living man.

Quans reaches Trung, slightly squeezes his shoulder. "From tomorrow on, you will replace Phai to be the platoon's cook, and he'll back to the machine gun battery. Don't torture yourself again, Trung," he says and turns to Phai. "Phai, you hand over your task to Trung, and help him for a few days, instruct him your cooking tricks."

Phai nods and looks at Trung. He still sits headed down, shrinks back his big short neck in between his trembling shoulders like a bear trying to get his winter sleep.

During the next few days, Trung is increasingly abnormal. He often stands stupefied, stares at some invisible point ahead, mumbling desultory, no-meaning words. At nights, the watching often soldiers spot him lurching from this house to that in the dark like a ghost.

Three days later they will attack Base 201, so the whole unit drills keenly. Everybody is very excited in waiting for the battle. That morning, the platoon is practicing manipulations in moving combat at the sand bank, about five hundred yards from their camp.

"Battery dismount – move!" Quan just shouts the order when Moi runs to him in a great panic. His face is as pale as a ghost's.

"Brother Quan, Trung's mad!" he tells Quan, panting heavily. "I was helping him to fry the salted shredded fish then I turned about but didn't saw him. I ran looking for him and found that he was holding the AK rifle that Gia Huong left in the hut, pointing the barrel into his chin, laughing in a strange way with a terrible face. I crept sneakily to him and kicked out the gun, and then I hugged him and soothed him. He didn't resist me, just at time laughed and at time wept. I held him for a moment and found that he was calm down, so I left him there, hid the gun and knifes and ran out here. What can we do with him now?"

"You let them drill a little more then come back to rest. I'll go and see him," Quan tells Gia Huong.

He and Moi the Tetter reach the camp. Trung the Bear is kneeling down by the kitchen hut, his mouth is full of soil and sand. Quan darts toward him and pulls him by his shoulders to help him to stand up. Trung laughs foolishly:

"Brother Trung…you go to the moon with me to pick plum fruit. I just back from there… Them fruit good, very good… So big a shark in the lake, it bites me and cut my hands off, brother Trung!" he bursts into crying.

Quan frowns. Trung is ill indeed. "Moi, you call Tien and Huy come back quickly, go along with me to bring Trung to the regiment for cure. It's very dangerous now!" he says to Moi.

They escort Trung the Bear to K.23 at about three o'clock. If Trung does not act up for a long moment by sitting motionless, they would come earlier.

Quan tries hard to convince Captain Son, K.23's head doctor to transfer Trung to the higher level army hospital where has the conditions to bring Trung back to the country. Son just shakes his head to show his determination, ignoring Quan's entreatment.

"It's just because he's so excited. He will be normal again in a few days. Don't be too provident," he says. "Maybe he fears to fight so he pretends to be mad like that. Need to wait to determine that if he's really insane or not. I meet such kind of guys so often!"

Quan is a very calm man, yet he cannot stand losing his temper with Son's rigidity. He tries to control his angry, "He's my soldier, sir," he stresses his voice, "I understand him much more than you do. He's ill and he needs to be cured at a suitable place. If you hesitate because you're afraid to lose your cheap prestige, the result will be very worse. You'll get a bad reputation as well as regret for all your life then, just think it over again…"

Son waves his hands, turns his back to go. Quan's face is as red as a drunk's. Hot blood suddenly flows up his head and pervades all through of his body. "He was almost to commit suicide, don't you know!" he shouts. "Whenever he still remains in this place of guns, it's still dangerous for him and the others…" He lowers his tone, "Doc! You must make a lucid decision right away. You're a good doctor. You love the soldiers too. I still remember how good and how devoted you were when you treated my own wound. But this isn't your specialty. Please listen to me. We need to bring him back home as soon as possible. And please send a kind-hearted guy to escort him too. I beg you, faithfully beg you, sir."

At last, Doctor Son is touched and agrees to do as the latter's suggestion. Quan still insists on reminding Son to send a man to take care of Trung regularly during the time him staying K.23 until the doctor goes bananas. "You think me a fool and conscienceless, don't you? To bother me all the bloody time like that. Go back now! I will do what I think necessary," he shouts.

On the way back, the three men walk quickly in quiet. Occasionally, Huy turns aside to look at Quan, feels loving him so much. His face is gloomy. His normally peaceful and calm appearance is lost. He looks like a heart broken mother looking down to her dead little child on her arms. They arrive at the camp when the late quarter crescent moon rises up to the top of sky.

CHAPTER 7

The forest is once again in the air of the commencement days of campaign. The different regiment and battalion troops move up and down everywhere. Every soldier in faded clothes, with his gun and military equipment and supplies weighted on his body is taking long strong paces. Between them – from the old ones who have been parted from home for years to the new ones who just came there at the end of last year – there is no difference now. They are used to the long operations under the hot sunlight and clouds of dust in the daytime or under the flickering stars of the dry seasoned in equator region in the night. They are used to the smell of dirty uniforms a weeklong operation without a wash. They are used to the overnight sleepless operations and the tense moments waiting for the order to start the battle.

The wings of troop, like the turtles with their heavy shell, creep slowly and determinately toward their fixed aim ahead. This one goes back to the west, continues to fight. That one goes straight to the north to set up position to protect the conscripted workers who have to build the K5 belt defense line along the frontier corridor.

On the way, the soldiers from different units just expect to see again some of their fellow-countrymen in the other units. The soldiers' voices of greeting and laughing and teasing to each other are echoed along the long distance, gone with the late spring breeze blowing through the deep pensive forest and breaking out its millions years of silence:

"Hey Thang, fight well! Get a lot of 'antiques'[1] and drop by my camp for a merry drink!"

"Hey, Van, send my regards to my little sister when you write to her. I'm too bloody lazy to write now. Go luckily."

"My friends, what a pity for you to go there encamping for all the year. Try to keep loyal to your old wives at your home if you find some nice female monkeys there!"

"Good health and good victory, my friends!"

"So do you, my friends! Good health and take well your duties!"

Huy looks up and down for Xuan, his school mate at H15. In the delegation coming here, only he and Xuan joined this division. Without knowing Xuan's regiment and battalion, Huy just walks and looks and yells, "Xuan! It's me, Huy! Xuan H15! It's Huy, where are you?"

All of a sudden, a soldier runs down from the front end of the formation at the opposite direction and yells back, "Who is Huy H15?"

"It's me!" Huy replies hastily.

The soldier heads for Huy with a smile, "Xuan's not here. He went to the regiment headquarters for mission. He told me about you."

"Wow, what's his duty to go there? What's your unit? Is he all right?" Huy shoots out a salvo of questions.

"Xuan is the battalion's orderly now," the soldier bursts into laughing, says merrily. "We are of the 7th Battalion. We will encamp here for a long time, can't go back now. Be sure, Xuan is well and gaily. Well, I have to go now. I'll tell him that I see you. Take care, my friend!" Not having finished his words yet, he turns his back and runs away.

"Good health, my friend!" Huy yells at his back, reproaches himself for forgetting to ask the guy's name.

At noon, they stop for a long rest nearby a tank battalion. The clusters of trees scatter on the withered plain, and the T54 tanks stand under their shadows. Each group of five tank soldiers is sitting around to have lunch by the tank, seeing Huy and his companion pass by, they invite them merrily and friendly.

"Come to eat, countrymen! Have lunch, comrades."

Huy feels a little happy and touched, though he knows that they just invite for form's sake. The sentiment between the different army units and services in these days is absolutely close, showing by such simple things. He nods his head, thanks them and asks, "We are looking for water to cook rice. Is there any water hole here, men?"

"Yes, yes, my comrades. Just go straight along this path some hundred yards, there is a big water pool," a man replies.

Following the instruction of the tank soldier, they go about five hundred yards more, cross a thick forest, and find the pool. That is an oval sunken plot, about five yards in diameter, lying on a grassplot. It has water due to the heavy rains last month, but so shallow now. The fallen leaves and the skins of dark green moss float on the surface of the stagnant water. On its edge, there are plots where the grass is crushed on and the animal footprints scatter on the fresh mud surface.

The water's color is distastefully opaque yellow and muddy. Yet it is also lucky to have such kind of water here. Huy spreads the nylon raincoat, double folds it up, and pulls from his pocket the hammock strings, ties the ends of the raincoat to the ends of a big stick to make a temporary water container. Then they put off their cardboard hats, go down into the pool and fill the hammock with water. Although they get some reserve water cans, Quan always encourages them to look for water and save their available water for the necessary moments.

They come back the camp. Phai has built a fire already. He quickly pours rice and water into the pot and lays it on the stove which is dug into the ground, ignores the rice washing procedure. "It's more bloody nutritious to eat it like that." Phai explains though nobody says a word.

Having finished the meal, everybody looks for a place to hang his hammock or spread the mat on the grass to take a deep rest. Huy is looking around for the place when Quan calls him.

"Huy, come here, there's a place to hang your hammock here."

Quan hangs his hammock between two small trunks. On his right-hand side is a big branch lowing down from a nearby tree. Huy hangs an end of his hammock to that branch and the other end to the trunk at the end of Quan's hammock. Then he lies down on the hammock with a feeling of relaxation.

He closes his eyes and tries to sleep. He is so tired with the operation, but he feels that his mind too wide awaked to get a sleep, as if he has just drunk a cup of strong coffee. He raises himself up and looks at Quan. Quan does not sleep too; he folds his arms under his head, looks at the vault of green leaves above.

Huy hesitates for a moment and then says, "I feel so pity for Trung, brother Quan! I don't know how he is now!"

"Hope that he would be well again. He's a good guy... and so rare one..." Quan sighs.

Huy is astonished. He does not know what Quan means. He thinks silently for a while then asks, "What do you mean rare?"

"In fact, this matter is too difficult to explain," Quan says. "Moreover, it is just my way of thinking, Huy. You know, people often see the men who are to be mad after a shock, a mental injure, as the weak and piteous ones. They feel pity for but disregard those men too. In fact, those men are much more noble and respectable than too many sorts of people. They are loyal to things that are truth and rightfulness for them, and when these things are violated, they can't stand it. They are much more humane than many people."

Huy listens to him with confusion. His explanation is even more unintelligible than his remark. However, Quan's sad low-toned words come deep into his memory. He remembers almost each word. "I will understand them some day!" He promises himself. He thinks of another matter. "U Moi told me about you. Why don't you want to return home, brother Quan?" he asks.

"No, I miss the city, but I have no relative and no place to consider as my family or my home. I can't live apart from the companions here as well. Our platoon is my home now, Huy."

All of a sudden, Quan smiles and looks at Huy with his bright eyes. He is not handsome. He is tall and slim and little stoop shouldered. His face is a normal person's, not so ugly, and not so good-looking too. It can be forgotten easily a short moment later by some passerby. However, his eyes are abnormal. They get a tender and wonderful shine. That shine makes anyone feel himself kinder, more confident when he looks into those eyes. And when he is silent, his face is strangely placid; placid but not frigid and difficult to come closely. From him radiates an inward beauty that is difficult to express. Since the first time he met Quan, Huy can not resist a natural trust and love toward him.

"That day when you came to the lake to get water, U Moi pulled from your rucksack the notebook and read out loudly. You are too bloody romantic, Huy! Your poems get emotions and inner strength, but are still loose. They are your monologues, not the sort of poetry for anybody but yourself. I see that through those poems and diary pages, you are so sensitive and have so many illusions. That is no good for you at all. Due to it you will suffer so much."

Huy stares at Quan. Once again, he is very surprised as he realizes that with those simple words, Quan says exactly things of which he felt vaguely himself. "Damn it! Brother Quan knows me than I understand myself!" he cries to himself.

"Don't trouble yourself about those untrue illusory questions, Huy," Quan continues. "You had better reject your discriminating notions about human nature. Human is just simply human. Human is both of good and bad, kind and unkind, heroic and coward. Good or bad, kind or unkind, heroic or coward in other's opinion is just an outside cover, a phenomenon and a momentary manifestation. If it is on time and suitable to the chance, it is good. Otherwise, it is bad. That's all, Huy. Certainly, the level of those natures was different up to each person. But it is useless to assess and praise or despite the others and to put your trust in the others. You need only to turn back to consider yourself and to trust human in general, not in any certain person..."

Quan pauses suddenly. He feels an inexpressible writhe arising in his soul. He has experienced and felt of what he just tells Huy by his own losses and failures. He feels himself now in a divided-mind mood. Huy is so young, so innocent and frank as a child. Huy is as same as him in his childhood: full of thirst for knowledge, full of innocent dreams, full of beliefs and hopes.

"Do I need to tell him these things? Is it really necessary?" he thinks; the bygone day images come back to his mind: Quan a little boy, who was dazed when his aunts and uncles said, *"Your Pa and Ma are dead!"* – *"What's dead, uncle?"* – *"That is you will never meet them again."* – *"Where they go?"* – *"They go so far."* – *"How far, aunt?"* – *"So far, even I say you still can't know, so stop asking."* – *"When my Pa and Ma back then?"* – *"They'll never come back, they go away for good!"* He hid his face in his hands, sobbed. It was the first time he sensed the death as a separation, sudden and not understandable. Then Quan a hungry boy, wandering on the streets, getting blows from the bigger urchins, getting bites from the dogs, getting curses from the adults when he took risk to enter a house to beg for a little meal. Then Quan a boy in a monk' s robe, his back kept straight, sat solemnly listening to the old monk who was explaining about the reasons of having and loss, about the being and non being...

Once, he taught Quan, "Don't believe in what people say, even that is the most respectable man you ever know, even the Buddha, if He appears in front of you; don't believe in the books, even a canon that was highly praised and revered, when you not ever verify and experience it yourself. Once you have verified and experienced it yourself, once your heart is in harmony with the grounds, once your heart eventually tell that it is the right, the common sense – we call it our conscience – then you obey what your conscience urges you."

Quan has felt and experienced and proved himself the righteousness of that lesson after so many years of meditation. He has understood one thing: the common sense, or as called by the old monk, the conscience, is indeed not in morals or ethics or laws. All of them can be changed along with history. This common sense is a much higher thing. It is permanent; belong to each community and to each person as well. It has been transmitted for thousands of generations, formed and existed in the struggle for existence. It is personal because it lies hidden in each separated person's consciousness and subconscious. It is also common because it is the string to link each individual with the common life. When one individual has a deed that is unsuitable to that common sense, he can hide and lie other people, but not himself. He might feel ceaselessly insecure and tormented and painful, though occasionally or for his whole life.

He turns to Huy who is opening widely his eyes now waiting for his words. Maybe in his mind I am a perfect man, an example for him to follow, Quan thinks and continues:

"Don't put all your beliefs in anybody, Huy... even me or the others, otherwise, when your beliefs fall down, you can't stand it. And the important thing that you need to remember is the real good and the truth is always relatively. You have good nature and belief, so you just believe things that make no damage or pain to anyone around you are the good ones and need to be done, and that is enough. To live just like that, you have to struggle very hard with yourself already, Huy."

Quan stops. He signs and keeps silent for a long time.

Huy is still bewildered with his words. They are like the lightning flashing in a blink and illuminating the deepest, darkest spots of his sense. However, he does not understand all of them, only tries to remember them. Suddenly, he figures out a strange thing: Quan says as if he were a monk, yet he still acts like the normal people, still holds arms to fight bravely, heroically too. There is some uncanny paradox in this man! He thinks like a philosopher, but he lives like a man full of enthusiasm, full of passion for live.

"Why do we fight here, brother Quan," he asks. "Why don't we let the Cambodian soldiers take care of their own affairs? I've heard the explanation of Mr. Ngo, regiment political commissar, about this matter, but I feel it is unconvincingly. Some days ago, I listened to the radio at No. 13 Company. Brother Vu turned on the Pol Pot radio station to listen to what they said. Damn it! They cursed Vietnamese volunteer soldiers us as the invaders, just as we cursed the US army long ago. Do the Cambodians regard us as the foreign invaders, brother?"

"Our soldiers' nature is different from the US soldiers'. I say different here not about the good or bad. The different is in conception, in culture, in ideology, in national tradition. The US soldiers did not understand Vietnamese people, therefore, they were afraid our people or treated us with contempt. For us, we are not so much different from Cambodians; they and we have the same basic culture identity. We understand and love them, and these simple-hearted people understand

and love us. As for the reason why we have to fight like that is a matter too complicated to tell. It is true that we had better withdraw off Cambodia earlier, but the situation now is so confused. You'd better not worry and wonder. After all, we are just the grains of sand that were swept into the revolution of our age and history."

"Why do we have to avoid the truth, brother? I think if we can't define the meaning and purpose of our struggle, how can we have enough belief and will to fight. Since I was a child, I already liked the knight stories and the grand poems and old proclamations. I think that for men the noblest work to do is fighting, is to 'wrap one's body with horse leather.'[2]"

"This saying from Ma Yuan is one of your illusions too, Huy!" Quan seems sorrowful. He stops and falls into silence for a long while, then continues.

"And it is also an illusion of many people. After all, the wars only serve the machination and hunger for glory of the rulers. This is clearly in the invading wars, no need to argue any more. Yet even the wars to protect one's country against the invaders or the civil wars are just the same. History shows that once the country was free from the foreigners' ruling yoke, or once they have overthrown some formerly corruptive regime and got the power in their hands, the rulers often forgot thing that was beneficial to their country and people. They or their successors only wanted to strengthen their power or enjoy luxurious pleasures. Just the grassroots and subordinate soldiers have lost so much yet gained so little or nothing. Except for national independence's sake, a war does not bring them any good thing. All they need is simply a little house and a harmonious family, a small field or plot of land and a peaceful life... So many men have died; their names have been buried deeply into the forgotten dust just for a few become the heroes remaining in the historical books. Since the original notion of hero of the ancient time became a doctrine – heroism – it has been transfigured and degenerated into a terrible charm and deceit, and has been used as a mask to cover the evil things...

"You know, each person's capable to become a hero or a talent to devote to his or her society; originally, they have this potentiality in them. Yet it is very difficult and so rarely for a man to be a real hero... I used to think over of this question, but then I felt that is was so complex. There are things we can feel them partly but we can't describe them clearly in words, Huy. Well, we should not say about it any more. Maybe the more you think things in a simple way the more you will feel easy and seldom meet trouble. Sometimes, I wish that I've known nothing. After all, that is really better."

Quan reviews in his mind the kings and heroes' names, the political chess games for power that were full of terrible evil and deceit, full of tear and blood of so many innocent victims. These have been written clearly in the historical books. In any age, in any place all over this small Earth, such things still occur. They still occur, though in various forms. When does man really abandon all of the discriminatory concepts that are in name only to lead a content and peaceful life; to live not for hate and resentment and jealousness sake but for love and creation sake; so that each man would become a star or a little sun that shines with its own light? Does such a day come to the world?" he wonders.

Huy looks at Quan, startled. Not until today does he get a real conversation with Quan. He says many new things. Although Huy does not understand all of them, and disagrees with him at some points, his heart is filled with a love and esteem toward him. Unknowingly, he suddenly has a vehement wish to take and squeeze Quan's hand strongly for a long while.

After being thoughtful for a while, Huy blurts out, "You like to write like that, maybe your major at the college was literature, is it right, brother Quan?"

"I've studied philosophy. I like it since I was a little boy. Back then, every night, after reciting the Buddhist scriptures, my master often explained to me many things. When I was a little older, I read the dry philosophic books more passionately than the novels. However, philosophy can't settle personal questions, Huy. It is only an opening door for us to see the light outside. As for where is the source of light, each one has to look for it. You see, I write because I'm happy while I do it. I never think what I've written is good or has any value to others. However, I still send them to the others. I think them are my concern to the others, my will to share with the others and my love of life. I do every thing I can do then I feel peaceful in my heart."

"Perhaps you write poetry too? Let me read them some day, please."

"I have no talent in poetry like you. My poems were so bad. Literally, they weren't poems but only my thought being set in verses. I will give them to you. All right, get your sleep now. Tonight we'll walk to conceal troops at the foe's base. Tomorrow will be a hard day."

Huy turns aside and closes his eyes. He falls asleep immediately.

CHAPTER 8

After long months of moving in operations and fighting at the frontier, the battalion returns to its rear base at last. On the way back, everyone is indescribably happy when they begins to see the blue and thin clouds of smoke over the *thnot*[1] trees and the thatch roofs appear vaguely behind the clouds of dust made by the troop carriers ahead.

Good-bye the solitary jungles!

Good-bye the impoverished barren frontier land!

Dear *phums*[2]! Dear Khmer mothers and sisters! We come back to you now!

Along the way, Huy stands clinging to the bars on the truck-bed, looking longingly at the little ragged stilt houses on the roadsides. The Khmer old people and youngsters and children are excitedly and joyfully waving their hands to welcome the Vietnamese *koongtops*[3] who just return from the battlefields. They yell merrily as the trucks come near.

"Vietnam Cambodia samaki!"[4]

"Sok sbai ch'roen boong p'on koongtop na!"[5]

The soldiers yell in chorus to reply them:

"Vietnam Cambodia samaki, si prâhok, sok sbai, tau sngai, nuk prâhok!"[6]

"P'on srei oi! Srolanh boong te? Boong srolanh on ch'roen na!"[7]

The clear peals of laughter of the country girls still vaguely follow the Zil trucks for a long distance, in the noisy booms of the running truck engines.

More than anybody, Huy sinks into a gently moving feeling. So far, he has been living his whole life in the city. He has been used to the crowd and turbulence and so many familiar and unfamiliar people around him. Then suddenly he has spent a half of year in a new strange life, without anybody else save his companions; without anything else save the immense, solitary valleys and hills and forests. He did not expect that he will be so moved like that as he sees again the villages and villagers. As if this is not a strange place with the strange people but a very familiar and intimate one. As if this were his own old village and his homeland that he has been long time separated.

It takes two days to return to his base. In the first evening, as the Zil trucks were running across the town of Battambang, the sunset light was almost given in the dark. Huy still tried to look back when the truck on which he stood was already a long distance from the town. He gazed at the coronas of white and yellow electric lights reflecting upon the horizon, felt a deep nostalgia of homeland filling his heart.

At last, after two days of travel, during which the rucksacks, the guns and the soldiers were hustled in the trucks' bodies as the shads stuffed in a fish-can, they arrive at the base.

It is early April now – the month of fruit harvesting season. The land on which the base has been built was originally a big mango garden nearby a phum; therefore, around the houses are the old mango trees with their crowded ripe fruits.

The platoon has three houses and a little outbuilding for the kitchen. The head of platoon's house is in the middle, ten yards from it is the kitchen, and the two other houses stands at two sides, about fifty yards from the middle one. The other direct platoons of the battalion – DKZ82, 82mm mortal, communication, scout, transportation – stand near to each other in the same way, forming a whole circle. The house of battalion command board is in the center of this circle.

Huy stays in the middle house with Quan and other 12.7 machinegun gunners. The K53 battery gunners stay in the wing houses. On their arrival day, their houses are devastated. Spider webs cover everywhere, termite mounds scattered inside, together with tufts of nut grass. The posts and house's ribs are also heavy damaged by the termites. The young men were assigned to stay at the base to protect it just wander in the phum all day long; sometimes they had their meals with the villagers until dark. The houses are damaged quickly due to short of care and the invasion of the insects and wild grass. It takes a week for the platoon to cut wood and bamboo trees and knit thatch to rebuild the houses and the trenches.

Daily, having finished their duties, Moi and Gia Huong lead Huy out to phum Chandai to visit the familiar people. The battalion built their base near phum Chandai since early 1983, more than two years before. Therefore, the old soldiers have had so many friends. They call the old people mother and father and the young men and women sister or brother in a natural intimate way, and are treated the same way.

Huy is very surprised and admires his friends as he sees Gia Huong and Moi the Tetter talking to the people merrily and easily. He guesses that he has to try to learn Khmer language quickly so that he can speak and hear like them.

In these northwest districts, wandering on the immense fields, once in a while a walking traveler would find some clusters of tree or bushes make a greenish line on the horizon. Those are the wild trees growing around a phum edge. Crossing those clusters of tree and bushes for some hundred yards more, the stilt houses would appear before the stranger.

Supposedly, somebody could stand hovering on the sky at some hundred-yard height to look down, he would see the greenish ovals, the zigzagging gray-whitish lines, the blue streaks, and, in the northwest, a long big dark green streak that are rising up over the withered yellow grass flat of the immense northwest fields in the dry season. Those are the phums and streams and water canals and lakes and mountains with dense forests approaching the frontier area.

Chandai is a relatively crowded village, with about two hundred big and small stilt houses that stand circled in an egg shape. A six-yard-wide road cuts into two pieces the Chandai egg, running from the Ang Trapaing Thmor at the East, across two rows of houses in the phum, across the immense rice field, and reaches the district center of Phnom Srok after its ten-mile run.

Within the phum there are many narrower paths, about three yards width, for the ox-carts. The house-yards here are as same as those of Vietnamese villages. In the front yard and around the houses are the mulberry trees and fruit trees, such as mango, tamarind, guava and jackfruit... Usually, in front of every house, near the wooden ladder, stands a four-feet-high wooden frame, filled with the black, spongy, moist soil. In this frame are the verdant clusters of onion and other kind of greens, or the peppers full of red little fruit. At a corner under the floor located the cattle stable. Outside the sparse wooden fence, people often build a smoky fire to drive away mosquitoes at night. Whenever he passes these houses, Huy often feels a strange smell mixed up from the smell of cattle droppings, the particular smell of *prâhok*, the good odor of lemon flowers or the sweet scent of newly picked corns hung loosely under the floor. At first, this smell makes him very uneasy, but later it becomes familiar, even a nostalgia for him.

In the phum, the inhabitants are divided into two groups at two ends of it. The group at the north, smaller, is the rich ones who had plenty of cattle and property. The group at the south is the poor and just married couples who set their families apart from their parent's. The soldiers more often visit and make friends with the latter group.

The evening of the second day since their return, Quan summons the platoon to discuss about the works of next weeks: to clear the battalion house, to cut wood and bamboo and thatch to rebuild the houses, to grow vegetable... Then he informs that the battalion has promoted him as sub lieutenant and head of platoon, and promoted a certain series of platoon's soldiers too, and he suggests everybody to vote Huy for head of battery.

"You know," Quan sighs, saying in a low voice, "I applied for continuing my service, but I never want to accept the officer post, never want to consider the army as my long life career. It is because I know so well that I cannot find from somewhere else the love and attachment of a small unit at the squad or platoon level. That distance is longer when one gets higher post. Yet I have no choice now, I either accept officer post or must leave the army. Once I received this post, sooner or later I will be apart from you. The soldiers life just like the clouds and water ferns, gather and then disperse, without any firmness... I hope you all understand me."

He bends his head down in the sorrowful and silent air. A moment later, he says, "Now, we take an openly vote. Anyone agrees to vote Huy as head of battery please hand up!"

The whole platoon hands up, except Moi the Tetter. He states, "I have nothing to criticize Huy. In the last battles, Huy proved himself a good soldier. But he is a newcomer, if the '82 and '83 soldiers are his subordinates, I'm afraid that he would not be obeyed in difficult cases. I suppose there is so much time for him to learn and prove himself more. So, I suggest Thien instead."

"I thought of this already," Quan says. "But he is voted by all of you, there is nothing to worry. However, I too see that he needs to learn a little more the experience of the older comrades. What do you think, Huy?"

"I agree with Moi's and Quan's opinion," Huy leans forward, saying slowly. "I would like to continue the post of gunner No.2 some more time. To be head of battery is really over my ability now."

Thien applies for stating, "You comrades know," he says loudly. "We '82 soldiers will demobilize at the end of this year or early of next year. I am willingly to accept it if you all vote me. And I hope Huy and the young guys will learn actively to replace us early, accomplishing the common duty, so that our platoon will always get honor."

Quan nods and asks again, "So all of you agree to vote Thien the battery head? Is there anything else? Dismiss!"

Huy leaps to his feet, heads for Moi the Tetter, pulls him by the arm. "Brother Moi! You teach me Khmer, please. About twenty words per day."

"Dear me! Twenty bloody words per days! You think it is so easy like that?" Moi laughs and begins to invent. "Years ago, I took brother Lam, '78 soldier, as my master, and massaged him four times a day, yet he teach me how many word, don't you know, Huy? Five, only five! So, you see, learning is not just learning matter and all! All right, find something to make a little ceremony for having master tomorrow then I'll teach you. You will talk with the villagers plenty of stuffs and all with only three days of learning. Hehehe, and only three days then I left nothing to teach you! You ought to take Ly as your master if you want to say well. He flirted and got Sa Pien, the nicest girl of this phum, you see. I cannot compare with him."

"Well, then I will learn from both of you, of course."

"Hey, Huy, I'll lead you to the phum for dancing tonight, so joyfully. I dropped in the head of phum house this evening and saw him arranging the batteries and electric bulb lights and all."

"How can we go out to the phum at night? It was forbidden."

"You're so naive. Forbiddance is just forbiddance affair, we go is our affair. We're best soldiers at that. Soldiers can't be like the monks!"

"Let me apply for permission of brother Quan."

"You don't say anything," Moi makes a gesture with his hand. "Just go. He doesn't forbid us, but cannot openly agree this matter too. He just gets worry for us if you say. So, just sneak away. You do what you have to do now, and be ready to go as I whistle."

About seven, there is a piercing whistle imitating an inspiration song of some nightingale. Lying on the hammock to wait for it, Huy sits up, casts a furtive glance at Quan. He is still buried in work, takes no heed to the whistle. Huy was so eager already since the afternoon when he heard the animatedly amplified music echoing in from the phum. The melodies were so strange but so bustling. Huy walks out of the house. In the dark shadow, Gia Huong, Moi the Tetter and Ly are standing; each one holds a Chinese flashlight in their hands.

"Need to take along the gun, brothers?" He murmurs.

"No, nothing happens in this phum, Huy. However, you can pocket a 'guava fruit'[8] to be sure."

"Then wait for me, just a moment."

He comes back inside the house, digs out from his rucksack a mini lemon color grenade which he has got in Ampil Battle and puts it in his trousers pocket. Suddenly, Quan asks him when he just turns his back, "Huy, you go out to the phum?"

"Y-e-e-s," He stammers.

"Remind them to come back early. Go."

He lets out a sigh of relief, stepped out quickly.

They takes the short way across the residence of communication platoon, entice some more fellows there, and cross the trenches. About five hundreds yards more, through a bush, the nearest houses appear in sight. The sound of music is already close to their ears. It comes from the big yard in front of the pagoda where the villagers would gather to dance or watch the "*l'khol*"[9] shows. The electric lights reflect a dim corona in the dark night sky.

Huy feels as if the leaves in the vaults above his head are whispering loving words. The sound of a breeze sinks into the turbulent music just like the sound of trembling breaths and sweet confidential words of a pair of lovers. The night scent condenses charmingly. There is something in the space just moving restlessly as little waves. Spring seems to linger at somewhere nearby. Love seems to be inviting ardently, entreating persistently the hearts to open widely to embrace the life.

"Is it Love who's calling me?" He asks an old tamarind tree just left behind his back.

They elbow their way through the youths. Here and there, the uniform coats appear vaguely in the crowd standing around the dancing floor. Huy looks at the dancers, about ten couples are pacing after the melody, their arms and bodies moving softly and harmoniously. The girls wear brightly colorful Thai *sarong* and at their hips are glistering metal belts. Each of them almost has a soft, charming and full of femininity body. "Or it is thanks to the sarongs?" he considers. Tonight, he suddenly realizes the silent seduction of this kind of skirt. It honors the beautiful curves of the young girl's body. It elevates the most soaring verses to praise gently and silently the lines of youth.

Suddenly, Moi taps slightly on his shoulder. "Do you see that girl in green shirt and purple sarong with yellow hem? The third one from the right side up...That's Sa Pien! Beautiful?"

Huy searches for her, and gazes at her for a long while. He finds that it is difficult to stop looking at her. She is indeed a very pretty girl. Her delicate body looks so slender at the wasp waist, yet so attractive at the breasts and buttock that plump out under the thin cloth. Her face is fresh and charming like a wild flower in the early season, and a stream of black, soft silk-like hair flowing down onto her round shoulders. Sa Pien is not dark like many other Khmer girls. She gets a fair smooth complexion of a noble Miss Saigon. Huy clicks his tongue, "Yeah, pretty indeed, brother Moi!" and he turns to Ly, "Brother Ly, is she really your lover?"

Ly nods and smirks.

In the platoon, even in the whole regiment, Ly is possibly the most handsome and seductive fellow. He is tall and brawny like an athletic. His face is determined with the long and delicate eyebrows like the swords. But what makes the women heed to him most maybe his mouth. It is indescribable fresh and charming, with his reasonable thick, scarlet lips – like a virgin's – bringing about a soft and warm feeling. His hair is bobbing naturally, and a curl of shiny black hair dropped down onto the high and wide forehead. Anybody who meets Ly the first time cannot help admiring that bright beauty.

However, inside the excellent appearance, Ly is only a mediocre, superficial and empty-headed fellow. He is not bad, but has no distinguished virtue too, and just the same in fighting – not so daring and brave, yet not so coward. Through his days living in the platoon, Huy knows that most of them do not like Ly. He is somewhat selfish, just concerned about himself, and just like a peacock – all the time stretching out its feathers – to seduce the beautiful girls falling into his sight, as if that is the nicest and most deserved thing to do in his life. Huy partly agrees with Ly at this point, he always think, in life, if there is anything higher and nicer, more deserved for us to take willingly our life to swap than love. Yet something in Ly seeming to make he believe that the former does not really love, never really love anyone.

The dancing music is over. The dancers, who have just finished their turn step back, make room for the others. Ly heads to Sa Pien. They look at each other fondly. The fellow leans his body forward, saying something into the girl's ear. Then the two of them sneak back off the crowd and disappear.

Huy still stands near Moi and Gia Huong, looks eagerly at the dancing people. This turn, the communication soldiers take part too. They take stiff, clumsy paces in the peal of laughter and yells of the local youths. Gia Huong tells Huy and Moi, "If you two like it, just come in to dance. I' m old, I'd prefer watching."

"I stand watching too. I do not know how to dance. It would be much ridiculous if I take it."

"Don't worry," Moi encourages him. "It's not difficult at all. You see, there's not any soldier fellow dance well, but they just take it. The main thing is we'll be merry with it. Just take it, Huy, very merry!"

Moi pulls him coming to the center of the circle of people when that dance is over. He is bewildered and blushes with shyness. But the village girls come out already to make dancing couple. The girl who stands face to face with him smiles at him and shoots a long volley of words. He understands nothing, just feels that her twitter voice is as gentle as a nightingale's song. He looks at the girl, does nothing but smiles.

The music bursts out eagerly. He adventures to take the clumsy paces, and mimics the girl to wave his hands up and down. His shyness and embarrassment disappear when the melody is half over. His heart thumps no more in his chest, and his legs are confidentially flexible again. He begins to fall in line with the dancing. His legs and arms move about naturally and unconsciously after the music. The dance passes so quickly in his longingly regret.

CHAPTER 9

The platoon has renewed the roofs and walls of their houses with thatch and wattles made of *thnot* leaves. With the good smell and greenish color of fresh leaves, the houses become brand new, full of fresh, cool air now.

Moreover, the houses are cozier and more beautiful with the "vases of flower". Phai picks up some kind of flowers at the fields and arranges them in the vases made from the water cans. Dark blue Madonna lilies and scarlet flamboyant and coral flowers and dreamingly purple daisies; the flowers are arranged so simply but uniquely. Phai the Crazy looks slow-witted yet he has a fine taste.

In the evening, after finishing their meal, Thien says, "Tonight, I will treat you all to a specialty. I'm sure that there is not any restaurant has it." He gathers all basins and vessels then places them on the table and the floor. Then he fills them with water. Huy, Phai and Tien watch him with great curiosity. They try to guess yet can not figure out what he intend to do.

Having finished his arrangement, Thien rubs hid hands together, smiles enigmatically. Huy can control himself no more; he asks "What the hell are you doing? Why do you said to treat us something yet we see nothing, and find that you arrange to cook nothing too. These basins and vessels are placed there for what?"

"Don't be so eager. Soldier means that you have to learn to be patient," Thien keeps secret persistently.

Perhaps the old ones such as Gia Huong, Quan or U Moi have known it already, yet they just smile without saying a word so that the young soldiers are crazy with curiosity.

The night is falling down. Thien says, "You guys run to the kitchen and bring here all of the lamps now."

He lights the lamps and puts them near the basins and then asks, "Phai, is there any cooking oil left?"

"Yes."

"All right, half an hour later you all will have a special food."

Just a short moment later, the forest termites appear crowdedly. They fly around the firelights then fell down, struggle to creep out of the water. The termites here are so big, with the plump bodies.

Huy opens wide his eyes, asks Thien, "You mean that you'll cook these insects really?"

"Yeah, what the hell else you think! Why are you so wise yet now too slow-witted like that, Huy?" says Moi the Tetter.

"Dear me!" Huy exclaims.

"The termites, grasshoppers, or crickets... are the most elegant dessert for the most elegant people, you know," Thien folds up his arms in front of his chest, begins to explain, "It is an extremely original 'drinking and eating culture and civilization' of the highland ethnic people! You can't just want and then you'll get it. It must be timely, at right place and right season. For example, you guys live in the city, how can you get this kind of big fat termites?"

When the flying termites reduce to an inconsiderable number, Thien puts out the lamps, just leaves one of them. He gathers all of the "dessert" in a basin then says to Phai, "Follow me to the kitchen." Less than five minutes later, they come back. On their hands are the plates filled with the fat, greasy fried termites. A tasty smell pervades to seduce the gluttonous mouths.

"Well, we enjoy it now," Thien says. "What a pity there is no more tea. Otherwise, it is really splendid to drink tea after this stuff was eaten."

The young soldiers open wide their eyes to watch the others eating slowly and delectably the fried termites. Quan laughs loudly and says, "Don't be afraid. These termites are so clean. You just try a little."

Phai hesitantly pinches a termite and smells it, then clicks his tongue, "Smells so good, so attractive! Alright, alright, I'll take a risk."

He closes his eyes, opens widely his mouth and puts the termite in. His face is deformed as if he just swallows a quinine bill without cover; it shrinks and then slackens immediately. He chews in an extremely delectable way. He yells loudly, "Excessive! Wonderful! Hey, eat it, Huy, Tien, so delicious!"

His hand pinches some mote termites to put into his mouth while he is saying.

Huy comes near, pinches one of the fried termites. He chews slowly. A greasy taste like fried peanut dissolves on his tongue. But it is much more delicious than fried peanut! Once one has tried the first, he just wants to continue the second. And then one more. Then one more. Just so, Huy takes part actively in the discovery of "the highland ethnic people's eating and drinking culture". Four full plates of fried termites are gone soon.

After eating the original fried forest termite, everybody seems to be excited. All of a sudden, Phai suggests, "Tonight, I suddenly feel my heart so anxious! I'll tell you all a story – my first and sole love story!"

Everyone cheers and encourages his abrupt devoting spirit. Huy laughs and yells with them, wondering that by what tortuous way, by what extremely subtle imagination link, the love feelings in Phai's soul can emerge from the greasy fried termites. He thinks over and over, and at last gives it up, he can only guess that the case of Phai is a lively example of human's rich and various and complex imagination capacity.

They bring the mats out to spread in the front yard to sit on. The half full moon casts down a dusky and dreamy light. The summer breeze is lulling gently on the mango branches. There is no tea, but Phai has picked up *hà thủ ô* leaves to make drinking water. When all the soldiers already settle their seat, Phai begins his story.

"It was exactly ten months and five days before I joined the army when I met her the first time. I was following my uncle to work as a mason apprentice then. He and I were working at a house on Dien Bien Phu Street, near Nga Bay roundabout, in front of Long Van theatre. I was responsible to paint the doors and windows.

"Once, when I was painting a window frame on the first floor, I suddenly saw a young girl walking by on the alley below. She was about fourteen or fifteen of age. Surely, she did not pass the secondary high school yet, because she still wore a red tie. And I then was full of eighteen years old some months ago. Just seeing her, I knew that a *'coup de foudre'* love had just hit me with its deathblow! I stood numbed, looked down at her until she entered a nearby house. My soul either flew up to the heaven, or sank to the sea bed, a very strange feeling that I never knew before…"

Phai stops and pours into the bowl a little water and drinks it up with a long swig. Then he is silent for a moment. Suddenly, his face is radiant, strangely, and beautifully too! A short moment later, he continues.

"I don't know if she is beautiful or not for an outsider. But form then on, I could never imagine her face and her figure clearly. I just knew that for me, she was wonderful like a little princess in a fairy tale. In my imagination, she was all of most beautiful and sacred things. In fact, she was just a very young girl…!"

Huy is once again very surprised. Phai speaks in such a florid and attractive way. A daily silent Phai suddenly casts his skin, becomes a poet to praise a girl. "Love makes miracle!" he thinks.

Phai continues his story, "The following days, I came to the working place very early, stood at the top of the alley to see her going to school. At midday, I wait by the window to see her coming home from school. I just met her some couple of short times daily, but those were the happiest days I ever knew.

"I figured out she had a little young brother, about nine or ten years old. I began to make a plan to win his heart. He would be a love-bridge between her and me. I managed to strike up a conversation and make friend with him. I invented a series of exciting adventure stories to tell him. And I bought him ice creams, cakes, and candies and so on, within two days, I became his best friend.

"He told me about his older sister; that her name was Thu and that she was learning ninth grade and that she was very fierce! She never showed herself as a gentle sister toward him. Nevertheless, it was his opinion! No matter how she was in fact, in my heart, in my eyes, in my dreams, she was still the best princess of my life.

"My work at the house was about to over. Just a few days later, I had to follow my uncle to work at other place, or became a jobless guy again. I decided to meet her before being apart from her without knowing the day I could meet her again. I thought it over. I foraged for the psychological and romantic novels of my older sister to find a best solution. Yet, those novels had nothing but the strained dates according to the authors' intentions. I was so helpless and didn't know what to do next.

"There came the last working day. I tidied up the tools, cleaned the paint drops on the floor, and finished my work within an hour. Having nothing to do then, I sat and thought to find a way to meet her. Suddenly, an idea occurred to me. I looked for the little boy.

"Fortunately, it was Thursday then, and the kid was free from school. I had stood near his house for a long moment already when I saw him strolling out the door. I waved him. He ran to me, smiled broadly, 'Brother Son!'[1] (I worked as a painter then, so he just called me after my job.)

'Hey, kid, you come to your house and bring me a double sheet of paper and a pen. Quickly!'

'What for?' he asked doubly, then answered to himself at once, (I have to admit that my future brother in law is very smart. Is she smarter than he is? I pray God for no!) 'Well, you want to write letter for my sister Thu, don't you?'

"He brought me a paper sheet. 'Where's the pen?' I asked.

"'My pen just fell and damaged.'

'My God! How can you be so foolish like that? Find another!'

'I have just one pen. I dare not take the pen of Thu. Her pinches are too painful!'

"I scratched my head and looked at the boy hopelessly. 'Then do you get any pencil?' I asked.

'Sure.'

'Well, bring me a pencil. Go now!'

"There was such little trouble, yet I still completed my first love letter of my life. It was extremely uncanny. Perhaps it was the unique love letter since the ancient time to our time, and even to some hundreds of years in the future! A love letter written with a pencil! And just with four lines of verse and a scrawling drawing showed a smiling mouth with a set of decayed teeth!

"The poem was not my creation but I had read it by chance in some autograph book of one of my girl classmates. It was as follows:

> *Do your legs allow my legs to follow?*
>
> *Does your hair agree to give me just one of it?*
>
> *Do your eyes agree to look aside to wait?*
>
> *And does your heart agree to keep my love?*

"As for the smiling mouth, it was indeed 'my work'! I didn't know why I drew like that. Perhaps, it was because the verse was so little in a double sheet of paper.

"Anyway, I was so pleased with my unique letter. I folded up the paper, gave it to the kid, instructed him carefully, 'This noon, when Thu comes home from school, you give it to her! Wait until it has been read, listen to what she will say, watch for her attitude. And then you come out to report me immediately.'

"Not be actually sure, I encouraged him a little more, 'Try to do it. When it is done, I will drive you to the zoo to watch the gorillas. And treat you a round of extremely delicious three-color ice cream!'

"From then on, I waited palpitating for the news. I bought a loaf of bread, sat and ate it right at the window of love, gazing at her door.

"Ten to twelve, she went home from school and passed under me.

"Five to twelve, her door suddenly bang opened!"

"A middle age woman appeared. In her hand was the kid's "future brother in law of Mr. Son?" She roared, "Show me who is the fellow Son! Blast it! My little niece still wets behind the ears yet he already want to seduce her!"

"Perhaps she cursed much more, but I had no time to listen to them. I jumped down the stairs, ran to the door, and jumped onto my bicycle; my face was pale like a ghost. My uncle who was sitting near the door asked surprisingly, 'Where do you go? Just a moment, I get the money then come along with you.'

'I go first, I have something to do urgently,' I shook my head.

"I was some hundred of yards from the house yet I could not regain my calm yet; my heart still danced lambada in my chest.

"The next day, I came there. I dared not came near her house but stood a short distance from the alley, hopelessly waited for my "brother in law manqué".

"I seized him at last. I glowered, asking, 'How the hell did you do to get that result, the little imp!'

"He winced, 'Not my fault! I waited and gave her you letter right after she came home. But my aunt caught me when I just pulled the letter from my pocket. She asked me what it is. Then she took it, opened and read it. Then she cursed. I get some terrible lasts onto my butt too!'

"I was almost to faint. So, my dear Thu did not read the letter yet. I tried to calm down and asked him, 'Afterward, did Thu ask you anything?'

'She just teased at me, saying that I deserved to get lasts!' he said.

'My God!' I could only yell out the words."

Phai turns up his face, looks at the moon and concludes, "That was my first love story. I got a terrible failure right at the qualifying round, and there was just a little detail of it, yet I could not forget it. Don't know how she is now, my little princess!"

Everybody falls into silence. They are moved due to the simplicity and innocence of the story. An actually strange love story, and, without a literal end! Yet it is still an actual love story and very charming too.

Phai adds after a long thoughtful moment, "Afterward, I never come back to that place. I want to keep in my heart the image of an innocent girl for good."

His story reminds the soldiers of their own memories. They sit side by side under the moonlight which is dying the whole space with a milky color. The moonlight brings them back to their far childhood place where flew the blue river, with the smooth grassplots on both sides, with the floating white clouds and the melodious sounds of flutes.

***

Next morning, having finished some little works, Huy sits writing letter. He will send it home whenever there is a chance. It is beautiful today; and his heart is filled with a strange joy.

Last night, he had nice dreams. The uncompleted dreams were fraught with wonderful colors and images. All familiar people in his life were pretty and happy in his dreams. He remembers vaguely now that he met a charming girl who got brown eyes and a long cloudy hair. The dream told him that she was Thu. And a red sail ship of which he suddenly became the captain. And a strange desert had many dark blue sandy bands, with numerous purple cornflowers. Then there was some merry party, with many splendid bulb strings and long firecracker strings. He suddenly woke up when he was looking at the bursting firecracker strings. He opened his eyes and saw that Tien was beating slightly on the head of his bed to turn the watch.

He writes continuously without a rest two big size pages. When he finishes it, he rereads slowly, nods his head, then puts it away and walks out of the house.

The sun rises high. The yellow sunlight is immense and warm. The green trees and plants are waving eagerly. The spring seems still to stay here and there. Suddenly, He remembers what U Moi told him yesterday. Only four days more will be the fifteenth of April, the *Chaul Chnam Thmei* – the traditional New Year Festival of Cambodian people. U Moi has experienced it one time. Huy is eager and wants to go to Chandai to watch the villagers arranging to receive the festival. "There will be lot of interesting things," he thinks.

A crow perches on the far treetop suddenly screams loudly, and it flies toward the north, perhaps someone is killing cattle there. He looks at the crow with its slowly flaps, and thinks of Quan's poems. They show a searching for the absoluteness. That absoluteness seems so near yet actually so far away. And they rouse a hunger for living – a full, completed, satisfied living. And because it is after all only a hunger, it rouses a great and immense melancholy that goes up over the humble worriment, suffering and grief in the everyday life, comes to place so high and immense and bathed in sunlight. Just as right now, when he looks at the crow spreading widely its wings in the blue sky, his heart is also filled with an immense hunger and nostalgia.

Quan wrote not many poems. The notebook he gave Huy is half size of a pupil's notebook, about one hundred pages, but was tore off almost a half. It contains total about ten poems. Some are dozen-line long, and some were only four-line long. Yet all of them are really masterpieces, if Huy considers himself as a man who knows something about poetry. In them, there is an uncanny strength. In them the form and content combined and mingled with each other to make the beauty, to say the great things yet there is not anything of pompous, mannered or affected. The single words are the simple and familiar ones. Yet when they stand side by side in his poems, are settled on some strange order, they seem to be absolutely changed by a miracle. As in the story of Cinderella, when a good fair brandished her magic wand to turn the mice and a pumpkin into a splendid carriage and four, the words suddenly live up and move about and contain new meaning and rouse hundred and hundred strange sounds and colors and images. Huy was stunned when he read them the first time, and just stunned like that, maybe more, when he read them the second and third… time. Through them, love and desire and hunger – in one word, the whole life, with the unexpectedly simple and pure truths – bring back the breaths into the stiff dead words. He feels ashamed to think of his own poems, "Those are actually real poems! And what about yours? Not poem at all. So from now on you must stop doing that bullshit!"

He still stands there and thinking ramblingly when a hand presses slightly on his shoulder. He turns back. That's Quan.

"Do you want to attend a wedding, Huy?" he asks.

"What? A wedding?" He is surprised, "Who'll hold wedding, brother Quan?"

"A friend of mine. They invited Gia Huong and me, but he's getting fever. Go with me, Huy."

"Sure I'll go. I juts want to go to the phum. Is their New Year festival joyful, brother Quan?"

"Rather. Just like in our country. They also cook *bánh tét* and *bánh ít*[2] and dance and play handkerchief throwing, sing 'azei', watch cock fighting…"

"What's to sing 'azei'?"

"That's a kind of repartees sing between boys and girls, like the $hò^3$ in our southern countryside."

"Wow, it sounds fantastic! Can we play with them in the festival?"

"Sure. Let's go. It's time they make ceremony now."

The music band is playing a joyful melodious tune when the two reach the house. The young girls in fluttering colorful sarongs are scattering in the big yard around the house. The breeze is so gentle and sweet smelling. The honey sunlight floods over the trees and plants and covers the faded white thatch roofs with a viscid yellow.

A man spots them and comes near to salute. He says something to Quan then smiles and leans his head down to salute them again, and then paced quickly to the back yard. Huy asks, "Brother Quan, what did he say?"

"He requested us to wait for a moment."

Huy nods. He pulls Quan by his arm and they walk toward the crowd who is standing around the house. Quan says, "They are to do 'chon dai' ceremony, that is literally tying hands. People tie the bride's and the groom's hands together with a thin ribbon. Afterward, the couple hand in hand comes up the house to bow their parents and older relatives. This action means to be as a tie of marriage for good, just like the pink thread in old Chinese tale."

Huy listens interestingly to Quan's explanation. Suddenly, the crowd spreads out, the bride and groom comes.

Their wrists are slightly tied together by a yellow gold thread embroidered silk ribbon. The groom wears simply a pair of trousers and shirt. The bride, contrastingly, is very splendid in a charming Thai sarong. On her upper body is a strange short blouse, like the image of the dancer on Apsara cigarette box, with plenty of lace and gold thread glistering pleats. On her shoulders is a thin pink silk $krama^4$. And on the chest of each one of the two is a red big cloth flower with hundreds of five color fringes. Both of them are young and beautiful.

They climb the wooden ladder and enter the house. Huy sees nothing more because many people have already surrounded the doorway. He looks around. In the yard, the sets of table and chair are placed already under the tree shadows. Generally, everything looks like a Vietnamese countryside wedding, except some particular customs and ceremonies. Suddenly, he feels his neck tickled in the back as if someone is looking sneakily at him. He turns around: a pair of brilliant black eyes gazing at him with curiosity and friendliness – a young, rather, a little charming girl. Her white shirt makes her dark smooth complexion more distinguished, but she looks really pretty. He smiles at her. She replies him diffidently with a smile. Then she bends her head down, shyly. Huy still gazes at her. A short moment later, she turns up her face, shoots a quick glance at him, but as she catches his eyes, she is embarrassed again, turns aside and walks quickly out of the yard.

Huy watches her walking away, feels strange and joyful. Then he turns toward the youths who are laughing and talking in the yard. The dark girls, with their thick powdered faces and red lips, are mincing in front of the flirtatious young guys. Their faces are glowing with happiness, as if it was their own wedding. The sounds of laughing and talking are at times lowered down, at times bursting out noisily. The air seems to be full of invisible molecules moving and hitting each other ceaselessly. Huy's eyes suddenly stop at a greenish sarong: Sa Pien. She is standing at the ladder foot, looking up the house, her soft hair floating about in the breeze. She looks very pretty indeed. Huy pulls Quan's arm, "Brother Quan! That's Ly's lover!" Quan does not answer. His face is pensive as if he is thinking some important thing. His eyes are lost at some far distance. Huy stops disturbing him, he turns back to look admiringly at Sa Pien.

Any beauty always brings him an admiration and amazement: the beauty of a lonely and desolately dry tree, of a bunch of daisy lying quietly on a riverside grassplot; of a thunderstorm evening with gray, heavy clouds and terrible thunders and bolts; of the imposing mountains and forests purpled and dimmed slowly in a late afternoon. Each one always makes him thrilled or breathless in respect. Yet the noble and pure and mysterious beauty of women is much more powerful. In a very short moment, it makes his heart clenched and flooded with some immense uncertain melancholy. In this moment, the melancholy that seems to exist since the ancient time – it must have been pressing upon the hearts of so many savage ancestors – resounds worryingly as the wailing, gloomy tolling bell in a late winter evening. In Sa Pien, there is such a mysterious beauty. Huy gazes at her without a blink. A moment later, Sa Pien walks away and disappears somewhere in the back yard.

About half an hour later, the ceremony is over, everyone sits down at the tables to eat and drink. Quan laughs and talks merrily with the guesses while Huy just sits stupefied. Being not able to speak anything, he just shows his enthusiasm by drinking. He clinks bowls with them, smiles and uses his hands and his face to express his joy.

Drinking a few rounds, Huy feels more excited, he asks Quan, "The villagers are so kind and plain, aren't they?"

"Most of them are like that."

"Yet in our unit there are some guys don't like them. They say that the villagers just pretend, because they all are enemy people; that any house also has children and relatives followed Pol Pot, how can they like us soldiers. For instance our friend Thien, he treats the villagers as his enemy, doubtful and with antipathy all the time."

"They are the plain peasants. If we are good and sincere with them, they will be kind with us. As for our soldiers, there is this kind or that of people too. Some love the Cambodians sincerely, some just make friend to take advance, and some consider Cambodian as the fools and inferiors. The minds of such men are full of prejudge and discrimination on complexions and races and all, although Khmer people and we are the same race of dark complexions and pug noses. However, that is the point of view, the nature of each one. They have their personal reasons, Huy."

"I think that for anybody of any nation or race, if other people are kind and sympathetic with him, he certainly has to treat them the same. Isn't it better to be good and sincere to all the people, brother Quan?"

"It's so simple to say that! Yet it's not so easy to do in fact, Huy. It's so good of you to think like that, but sometimes we do the good and get all of misunderstanding and antipathy..."

A young fellow walks near, grins to salute Quan and Huy. He waves his hand at Huy and asks him, "*Smuo ei?*"

Huy knows these words. They mean "what's your name?" He smiles and replies, "Huy!"

The fellow points to his chest, "Su Smak!"

Huy stretches his arm to shake hand with Smak. Quan says, "Smak are very jolly. He taught me the way to throw the casting net and all. He is the best casting net thrower in this phum."

Smak looks at Huy and shoots a long volley of words. Quan has to explain again, "He said that you follow me to visit his house someday. He will let you see his fighting cock. It is the champion fighting cock in Ponley commune. If you like to play fighting cock, he will give you a couple of chicken to breed."

Huy nods repeatedly, he can himself say something in Khmer language now, "*Okul ch'roen, Smak!*"[5]

Suddenly, Smak pulls Huy's shoulder, and turns him around with a strong jerk. The youths are gathering, forming a big circle at the yard center. The music turns into a new melody, quickly and bustlingly. Smak holds one of his arms in front of his chest and wriggles his body, "*Ramvong!*" and pulls Huy to stand up.

The heady bouquet of spirits rises up, Huy walks to the dancing circle without hesitancy. He looks through the girls who are covering their mouths with their hands and giggling. His eyes stops at a familiar hair and figure: the young girl at whom he just smiled is leaning forward her body, laughing and saying something with a girl nearby. Huy paces quickly to her. Just turning her face around, the girl is startled as she sees Huy standing right in front of her. She steps back in a panic, her round eyes stares at Huy. Huy smiles broadly, points to the dancing circle center, "*Ramvong?*.. with me!"

She shakes her head. Her older friend taps slightly on her shoulder to encourage. She looks very quickly into Huy's eyes, and then runs away. Behind her, a peal of giggling is dropped back, just like the clear clatters of tiny silver bells. Huy yells after her, "Don't run, little sister. Please stop…"

He starts to run following her, but his shoulder is pulled back slightly. That is Quan. He laughs gently, says into Huy's ear, "You speak in Vietnamese so how she can understand it. Well, we return there and sit drinking a little more and then come back."

The two companions return to the table, drinking some more bowls of liquor and then say good-bye to everybody. Huy steps toddling as if he is walking on a soft cotton mattress and some uncertain feeling just stirring up in him. Is it a sweet emotion due to a young girl? Or is it a joy to be in touch with others and get friends at a remote place in another country?

CHAPTER 10

Around the platoon's houses, the vegetable draws a green fresh picture.

The water spinach and radish buds raise themselves up to welcome the sunshine. At the house-sides, the gourds and fiber melons on the trellises are blossoming with many tiny yellow and white flowers. In the early sunlight, the butterflies and bees are hovering around the trellises to gather honey. The paths that link the houses together and run toward the battalion headquarters have been cleaned and banked up. From a far distance, they look like the sinuous light yellow treads knitted over the thick green grass cover.

Quan stands nearby a trellis, study carefully each leaf to search for the worms. He touches slightly on the young leaves. A joy appears on his face.

Huy sits nearby him, rooting out the grass among the vegetable beds. He looks up and says to Quan, "I'll come to the phum to ask for some muck loads this afternoon. They grow so quickly, don't they?"

He has experienced the gentle pleasure of watching the greens growing up daily. And he is overjoyed as the gourds and fiber melons just have their first tiny flower buds. He croons a children song, *"My dad goes to plough in early morning. My mom goes to plough in early morning. My dad is a peasant. My mom is a peasant..."* and sticks his nose to the flowers to smell them.

He has kept watching with great curiosity those flowers daily, since the time they are only some tiny greenish buds to the time the petals are withered and the peduncles slowly swelling up, becoming the little gourds or fiber melons.

He has kept watching with great happy when the vegetable beds are taller and denser evidently day after day with the summer rains.

The daily watering, the loads of muck and green manure, the sweat drops falling down to the beds, all of them have turned into green leaves and sweet fruits. Those greens and plans have been looked after with love and now are ready to repay the hard works of

Huy and his companions. The real joy and happiness turns out so simply!

Huy thinks of the happiness of the mothers in giving births. He imagines the joy of the artists in their creation. And he thinks that sowing and planting, though just a little gourd plant or some vegetable, and helping them to grow up, is in essence not different from the tasks of those mothers and artists. That is the happiness of being a little God, being a man who creates and maintains life and beauty.

Quan breaks the silence, "Yesterday, Mae[1] Sa Rinh brought me some Chinese pea seeds. We'll hoe up a few beds to sow them this afternoon."

"Mae Sa Rinh is Sa Pien's mother, isn't it?" Huy blurts out.

"Yes," Quan replies shortly.

"Sa Pien is so beautiful," Huy says, full of admiration, "The first time, when I've met her at night, she looked so pretty. But the day we came to the phum for the wedding, she looked so much prettier at near distance and in the daylight. She and Ly are actually well matched!"

"Yes, they're well matched," Quan says. His tone is somewhat strangely, but Huy does not recognize it.

"Why do you visit the phum so rarely, brother Quan?"

"I'm too lazy to go, I'm very busy as well, you see."

"But it would be better to hang around at the phum sometimes. It's so bored to be at home all the time. Brother Quan, I've learnt a lot of Khmer, but they're all for flirting, so I can't talk to the old people and children. You teach me some more, will you?"

"Well, I'll give you the book 'Self-taught Khmer language'."

"Wow, just there is that kind of book! It's so fantastic!" Huy is overjoyed.

"A friend of mine at the regiment gave it to me long ago. But I seldom read it. I've mainly learnt from the people. You need only to talk often with the people and you'll speak it well. You need to know a few basic words, of course. This book is rather easy to understand."

U Moi is strolling nearby; on his shoulder is Chip who is singing in high inspiration. Huy whistles a few notes. The bird flies toward him and perches on his stretching arm. It rubs its peaks to his arm and twitters softly as if to greet him. Huy says, "U Moi, I bet you that this guy Chip knows how to flirt the girl in Cambodian."

"I didn't teach him. Never heard a Khmer word from him too, what did you teach him?"

"He won't speak now. He only speaks when he meets the real object. You'll see when the girls come to our well to get water this afternoon."

They have dug a deep well near the kitchen. The well is full of clear and good taste water. So the villagers who live near the base often come here to get water, because it is much farer than going to the pool in the phum, and the water there is not as good as here.

Huy was so glad when he saw again the young girl at the wedding among them. He has taught fellow Chip some words to tease the girl. He trained the bird by saying the words and luring it with a fat grasshopper and pointing to the girl. She saw his doubtful manners, but she dared not look straightly at him, just sneakily shot a glance sometimes, and then bent down her head shyly, looked even prettier. So far, he has known that girl for a rather long time, yet he dares not say a word to her, except the risk in his drunk that day. It turns out that he is just a shrinking violet! Just coming near a girl, his heart already beats drum and his face is as red as a beetroot.

Suddenly, Quan gazes at him for a long while. "A moment later, you should ask some guy to cut your hair. Your hair is too long now."

Huy pulls a face and sticks out his tongue at U Moi. Unknowingly, he was afraid of haircut since he was a little boy, so he never wants to have his hair cut if there is no forcing, though he really does not like to keep long hair. He was so freely in hair matter since the day he came to the frontier because the warriors get too much freedom here. If some guy does not want to get his hair cut, he just finds an excuse to shirk away at those chances. Huy has shirked many times of haircut. Therefore, his hair is so terrible that Moi has to complain, "Your hair is as red as corn silk, why do you keep it so long? Get your hair cut now! Your hair makes my eyes irritated!" Now, it is Quan who says about it. "It's so tense now!" He thinks and pretends to call Chip to sneak away. He tells to himself, "Never mind! Just let it goes at my will."

That afternoon, he cannot shirk the very thing of which he is so afraid. About two o'clock, when Captain Van comes back from No. 13 Company and drops by the platoon, he meets Huy standing in front of his house to train Chip the tricks of flirting. He opens wide his eyes, "This is Huy, our comrade, isn't he? Or some bandit who've lost his way here! Come here, Huy, come here! Go to the battalion house with me. I will cut your hair. I just got the clippers."

Huy groans to himself. He is most afraid of this matter, now he meets an amateur haircutter who will use his head for experiment. It is indeed out of the frying pan into the fire!

Captain Van and Huy stroll to the battalion house. En route, he tells Huy some humorous stories about the soldiers. Reaching the place, he enters the house and takes a chair out and places it under a mango tree, then comes in again to takes a mug of water and his "tool box". When the things are ready, he says, trying to make it stately yet it is just so funny, "Well, sit down please, my client. Be ready!"

Huy sits on the chair, pulls a wry face as a monkey who is eating red pepper. Captain Van pushes the clippers, laughs joyously and says, "Do you hear the clippers' groan, Huy? Your hair is sunburnt and so tough like bamboo roots, why do you keep it too long like that! Your face looks more handsome with a short hair. Come on, it'll be over with some more strokes. You try to endure a little more, this slippers is rather blunt and out of oil. I'll sharpen it later."

Huy sits stiff, half smile and half twist his face, waiting for this torture over. At last, Captain Van digs out from his coat pocket a razor blade, wets Huy's hair and shaves the hair foots. Finished his work, he rubs his hands, steps back and looks at his "art work" with pleasure.

"Well, Huy, I'll take my new duty at the regiment headquarters next month. Mr. Bao will lead the battalion," he says.

"Really, sir?" Huy cries.

"Yes."

"Our battalion will be so sad if you go, Captain Van. Mr. Bao is so serious and difficult."

"He's good, yet his family in the country gets trouble, so he isn't happy. Well, try to understand him."

"He often hits the soldiers. I heard that he hit a man with the big rice pot cover until the cover was deformed. Why is he so fierce, Captain?"

"It is a matter of inborn character, Huy. I have also advised him to restrain himself many times. Yet if you do nothing wrong, nobody can hurt you. All right, you can come back now."

Huy thanks him and turns around to come back his platoon. He is moved by the close and simple treatment of Captain Van. He feels sad to think of the day Captain Van will leave the battalion. Stepping some ten yards more, he turns back. Under the scattered yellow sunset spots passing through the thick leaves, Captain Van is leaning down to sweep the hair on the ground.

Huy is washing his body after his "hair accident" when a group of women and young girls come toward the well. They stop and sit down on the ground under a mango tree shadow as they spot him there. Huy quickly finishes his bath then gasps the towel and clothes hanging on a nearby branch, runs into the house. He dares not shoot a glance to see if there is the pretty girl among the group.

Dressed tidily, Huy tiptoes to the door and looks out. There she is! She is waiting for the older women to fill their buckets with water. He flips joyously and goes out of the door to look for fellow Chip. He looks around but cannot find it. Suddenly, he hears its strident voice rising up from a bush nearby the well, "*Ao sa! Ao sa! Boong nouk p'on, dek min ban! Ao sa! Ao sa!*"[2]

Huy opens wide his mouth, laughs softly, trying to make it soundless, and feels very pleasure. In fact, he pays no special attention to this little girl. She looks pretty so he just wants to tease her a little bit. He looks at her to find her reaction. She looks surprisingly at the startling, shy but with pleasure. The other women and girls giggle. They too tease at her in their own language. The bird flies up around the girl, continues to scream out, "*Ao sa... dek min ban!*"

He is overjoyed and can control himself no more. He bursts into loud laughing. Then he is startled, lifts his hands to his mouth to keep the laughter. But the girl hears it already. She turns his head back, shoots a glance at him then bends her head down, blushes with embarrassment. Huy feels pity for the girl who is so shy now, he whistles to call Chip. It flies toward him, perches on his shoulder, turns its head sideway, looks at him mischievously with one of its round eyes. Huy fondles its back and says, "Well done, Chip! I'll give you two big fat grasshoppers."

Out there, the girl is still bewildered, stands stupefied near the well. A woman tells her something; perhaps she tells her to get water then come back together. Huy enters the house to avoid making her shy more, yet his curiosity rises up, so he tears a little hole on the wattle wall to look out there. The girl is quickly filling the buckets with water. Then she lifts up the carry pole to her shoulder, walks away lithely. On her dark pretty face still remains a blush.

CHAPTER 11

Time passes quickly. They have come back their rear base for two months now. During this time, the battalion has taken many operations to search for and destroy the enemy in the adjacent areas. Each operation often takes from five to ten days.

Sometimes, they went southeastward across the rice fields which spread to Tonle Sap. Sometimes, they went toward the north-northwest where the mountains stood silently and solemnly, putting on their coats of dense tropical jungles with huge trees and big creepers. Sometimes, the whole battalion headed for a single point and made a circle of operation; also, sometimes the three companies were divided into there troop-points toward three different directions, and the battalion's firepower platoons laid an ambush at some place in the middle. These operations happened when the early season rains were pouring down. The soldiers often walked in a spacious sea of rainwater, sinking to their hips in the water, and above their heads were the downfalls. The troop, like a long line of boats, cut a path through the green waves of long rice plants.

Many a night, the troop passed closely the stilt houses of some unfamiliar phum under the dim starlight. Once in a while, a few dogs were startled and howled for a while then everything was quiet again. Sometimes, walking close to the wattle wall of some house, Huy could almost hear the stammering words of some child who spoke in his sound sleep, the even snores and someone's turning body sounds on the wooden floor. His heart was filled with a strange and deep feeling. Through those overnight operations, he and his companions have protected the sleeps and a peaceful life for the local people. From those operations, from those jubilant ramvong dances, from those moonlit nights helping the peasants to pound ripe rice, from those sowing-season days helping them to pull up and transplant young plants of rice… the love and attachment between the Vietnamese soldiers and the Khmer people have budded.

The troop of soldiers walked very quietly. Only someone who paid much attention could hear the cloth rustles when two legs of the trousers rubbing to each other and the tramps of marching soldiers that sank into the desolate night. The night was filled with good smells. The tramped dew-wetted grass pervaded a smell as sweet as new born baby's breath. The gentlest odors of wild flowers hovered in the air. Those fragrances were floating over the soldiers' faces, touched their hairs, and absorbed down into their heart beds. Sometimes, they went across larger plots full of coriander and basil clusters. Their smells reminded the soldiers of their homeland, evoked a hunger as they imagined of the big bowls of smoky, delicious *phở*[1].

Sometimes, the troop walked under the dim moonlight of an early quarter night. The man walking behind clangs to the rucksack of the one in front of him, eyes closed, stepped drowsy by his inertia. Occasionally, the "walking sleep" was so deep, the man going ahead had turned already to other direction, the man after him still kept the old direction until he was startled and opened panicky his eyes by a sudden bump to a trunk or a bush.

The battles in those operations were not so tense. They often encountered small groups, about a dozen of gunmen. So the soldiers just surrounded the enemy and fired for a short moment, the latter would have dropped arms to surrender or escape into the larger forests.

During the two months, the battle near phum Don was quite interesting. The battalion's scouts found out a company of Pol Pot's army who just encamped at a deserted phum near phum Don. This phum stood at the east, about twenty miles from the base. That night, two companies were ordered to go into battle. No. 12 Company was the main attacker, reinforced by the 12.7 machinegun platoon. No. 11 Company laid ambush at the northwest to prevent the enemy to retreat into the forest. It was a late quarter night, about the twenty-ninth or thirtieth of a lunar month, so it was dark like hell. About 4 a.m., they reached the desert phum's edge. The troop groped its way as it began to cross the dense bushes around the phum. Walking ahead was the troop's two scouts, next – the Platoon 4 – then next – the 12.7 machinegun platoon.

Thang, one of the scouts who led the way, suddenly heard a raucous cough from not more than ten yards ahead of him. He stopped at once, thanked God inwardly. The company would have stepped on the enemy's hammocks if that Pol Pot's soldier hadn't gotten his cough. Fortunately, the enemy did not find out that our soldiers were very close to them. They might have smoked so much *Cannabis Sativa* that anyone had slept like a log. Even the guards dozed too. Hadn't they been so, our dears soldiers might have gotten big troubles!

Thang waved his hand back, stuck his mouth to the ear of Phu, head of company and whispered, "Enemy!" Phu and a few men went ahead already heard the cough too. Immediately, the company carefully drew back some distance to deploy combat formation. Phu crept toward Quan, said in very low tone, "We'll fire at twilight. You fire first, then my B40s. They would think that thunders break out upon their heads!"

Quan ordered his soldiers to join the gun.

Usually, the soldiers manipulated so quickly. In the course of training, when Quan had forced them to cover their eyes to disassemble and join the gun, preparing for the situation of fighting in the dark, it had taken just four minutes to join. Yet that night the gunners did the task so long, everyone was all of sweat. They palpitated due to being so close to the enemy. Had the latter been able to hear the clatters and fired a B40 shell, the whole battery would have come to the heaven together!

When the cartridge belt had been loaded, Huy crept toward Quan to report. Quan whispered, "Let me fire. You and Thuan back to the sides and lie down."

Everyone was ready for the battle now. Quan released the direction lock, slightly turned it from one side to another to check. After that, he took the height level about at man's hip height, namely the average height of the enemy's hammocks, and locked it again. Then they lay quiet and waited.

In such moments, the soldiers would think and miss so much. They missed their parents, their wives, their children, or their lovers; or even some puppy that they had bred long ago; or even an old guava tree that they had sat on its branch in the childhood summer days. After all, no matter whom and what they missed, they missed them with a deep love. Maybe a moment later, someone among them would never be able to think and miss again.

The jungle fowls crowed repeatedly. It was near to dawn. The night had been fading away. When the twilight of the dawn let them see the shapes of the low bushes, they discovered many hammocks hanging scattered ahead. On the right-hand side, about fifteen yards from Quan, a Pot's soldier sat nodding, his head bended down aside onto his shoulder. Quan placed his left hand's fingers onto the double triggers; his right hand pulled strongly the puller handle to cock. The puller handle just went all of its way, making a dry clang; immediately, his fingers on the left hand pulled the triggers. Then he placed his right hand to the triggers too. Quan fired a long volley about a half of cartridge belt, turning the gun barrel an arc of 120 degree. The tracer bullets knitted many firelight lines over the morning fog. Right after the roar of the machinegun, the B40s were fired, and then all of other guns.

The enemy fired no shot against right then. They were scared to death, just found ways to escape. When they have run out of firing range and regained partly their calm, they strengthened formation and began to counterattack. Yet about half an hour later, they saw their bad situation and slowly retreated into the forest. The battlefield was quiet again soon. Phu yelled, "Everybody comes to clean up the battlefield!"

The dew-wetted low bushes and grass on a larger spot were broken into pieces. Here and there, in a fifty-yard-diameter area scattered the tattered and bloodstained hammocks. Except five dead bodies left, the wounded had managed to escape. The soldiers quickly gathered the enemy's rucksacks and hammocks and guns at the place of action and started to return their base.

That battle, they gained eight brand new foldable-butt AKs, a B40 with its barrel penetrated by a 12.7mm cartridge, a B41, a machinegun and many rucksacks. The soldiers had a chance of floating on air. On the way back, they walked flying, bragging about the latest feat of arms.

Another time, they went to the east of district. After a day and night of walk without finding any soul of the enemy, Captain Van decided to come back their base. They just came near a small phum when the men going ahead discovered about twenty gunmen retreating out of the phum and running to the south. Captain Van ordered the 12.7mm battery to move on to fire, blocking enemy's way to capture them. Huy, Thuan and Tien, the main gunners, just carried the whole gun on their shoulders in moving. The path crossing the phum was muddy and so slippery that they almost fell many times. In addition, anybody was very hungry then, since all last night they had had just only a wisp of compressed rice which was all digested. They found no enemy when they tried to find it, yet it suddenly appeared as they were exhaust and had to stop to eat and drink and have a rest. That was the awkwardness of fighting situations!

After a short clash, they captured ten enemy soldiers. The others escaped into the forest. The Vietnamese soldiers took away the guns of the Pot's soldiers, and used their kramas to tie them instead of ropes. It would be an easy and completely victory if three men of them did not get slight wounds.

Captain Van decided to continue the operation back, without stopping to cook rice right there as it was intended before. He wanted to reach the district capital, so that the wounded could be taken care better at the district medical station. On the way back, the soldiers chewed their dry cooked rice to relieve their hunger.

The 12.7 machinegun platoon was responsible to escort two enemy soldiers. Quan let them walked at the front of his platoon, right behind him. Huy managed to walk near them to talk with them. He was curious to know what they thought. He observed the two captures. The younger fellow was about his age, and the other about thirty, looked taciturn and sullen. Huy came close to the younger one and tapped his shoulder. The foe soldier turned his head aside, shot a glance at him with frighten and reserved eyes. Huy asked, "How long did you follow Pol Pot?"

"Two years."

"Where're you from?"

"Pursat."

"Are you married? And got kids?"

"I'm married, but no children."

"Why did you follow the enemy instead of staying at your home to work and take care of you wife?"

"I was forced to follow them. If I did not, they must have killed me."

Huy looked straight into his eyes, "Really?"

"I dare not tell lie."

Huy nodded. After a moment of silence, he continued to ask, "Then, do you miss your house and your wife?"

"So much. I often wept in the nights, when I was in watch."

"Why didn't you run away?"

"I'm afraid of the revenge of Mr. Heng Sam Rin's soldiers."

"Nonsense! You don't know that if you surrender, you will get tolerance and no punishment, do you?"

"I don't. *Angkar* said that if we surrender, we would be killed or sent to jail."

Huy looked thoughtfully at the young enemy soldier. His face was rustic and nothing of fierceness or cruelty. "Yet how can I know what he has done," Huy thought, and asked again, "Did you kill or rape any civilian?"

"No-o-o, nope! I never do that!" He shook his head repeatedly, his face pale away.

When they reached the district capital, Captain Van sent the wounded to the medical station. The men scattered along the roadsides to cook rice.

Meanwhile, the captures were released one arm to eat. The other arm was still tied firmly at their back to prevent them to run away. They were treated as the Vietnamese soldiers in eating. Having finished the meal, the volunteer soldiers tied up their captures as before. After the meeting between Captain Van and the local army commanders, they would be turned over to Cambodian army.

Huy rolled a cigarette. He sat flat on the ground with his back leaning against a tamarind tree, puffing at his cigarette. The younger fellow looked him smoking with appetite. The other still bent his head down, kept his taciturnity. On the way, Huy had tried to start a conversation with him, but he had just nodded or shook his head, saying no word. Huy asked the young guy, "Smoke?"

"Yes."

Huy rolled for each one a cigarette then placed it on their lips. The older man looked at him, nodded his head to thank. Huy smiled and asked him, "This time you can return home, will you run follow the enemy again, old guy?"

"No, I've just wanted to go home for a long time now," he said, his eyes looked sad. Perhaps he remembered a far away house where his wife and his children were waiting for him.

Huy looked thoughtfully at the two. They look nothing of cruelty or awesomeness, he thought.

"Just looking at their appearance and attitudes, you can never understand why there were barbarous, bloodthirsty Khmer Rouge soldiers who killed millions of their own people without a blink. Perhaps when they have been swept into the game, those fiendish deeds have slowly become familiar; become a natural reflex. In common, the soldiers are originally unquestioning. They are just like the robots; just do things after their leaders' commands. How can't they be mad and fiendish if their leaders are such kind of mad and fiendish ones?

"Is there anything else? Is there anything righter to explain for all things have happened? To explain for the heaps of human bones and skulls have been showing in the glasshouses in every big town and city of Cambodia. To explain for millions people who were shot; who were hit on their heads by the hoes and shovels; who were cut on their throats with the *thnot* leaf edge full of sharp thorns; and whose corpses were thrown into the community graves scattering all over the forest edges and deserted fields?..."

CHAPTER 12

Huy has made friend with many people in phum Chandai. He is very attached to Sa Pien's family, since he often follows Ly and Moi to visit the house. Mae Sa Rinh loves him as if he were her own son. During their conversations, she often holds his hands and asks him about his parents, brothers and sisters, his joy or melancholy at the time. Once in a while, she rubs his head lovingly again. Even his own mother has seldom showed her sentiment with him like that, al though he knows that she loved him so much. So, he has a deep love and is very close to Mae Sa Rinh.

Mae has two daughters. Sa Pien's older sister was married and followed her husband to stay at the district market. And Sa Pien is twenty years old now. In this area, girls at twenty are too old for marriage. Usually, the girls about sixteen or seventeen here have already got children.

Sa Pien's late marriage is due to her awareness about her beauty. She finds that no one among the youths in her village can get her respect; they always show themselves as inferiors before her. For a young girl, non-respect means non-love. For Sa Pien, this has a much more meaning. She has secret dreams and desires about the man who will live together with her for her whole life. He has to be an ideal man, handsome and noble and heroic. The boorish and fool village youngsters who speak all the curt words, under her eyes are just the big babies. She holds them in contempt, listens to their rude flirtatious words with a queen's cold, haughty smile.

Mae Sa Rinh often asks Huy about Quan. She is sad as she talks of him. Sometimes, Mae comes to the base and brings to him, this time a pack of salted shrimp, another time some fruit. The two just sit silent all the time without saying a word except the greetings and good-bye. Once Huy saw her eyes dewed with tears as she looked at Quan. She held his hands and tapped them slightly as if to console him of something. Since the time they returned the base, Huy never saw Quan visiting her house. Whenever he had to come to the phum for some business, Quan managed to return the base early and avoided the paths passing by Sa Pien's house. It seems that Quan has had some special relation with Sa Pien's family. Huy feels it vaguely. He cannot figure it out, yet he dares not ask Quan or Mae Sa Rinh straightly. He is afraid that he can make her more upset.

This afternoon, Huy visits her house alone. He sees only Mae Sa Rinh who is feeding the silk-worms when he climbs the wooden ladder. "Where're the others, Mae?" he asks.

"Puk[1] Ho goes to the mountain field and Sa Pien goes to the market to buy some stuff. Why do you come here alone, Huy?"

"They have things to do and can't come with me, Mae."

Mae Sa Rinh carries the baskets of mulberry leaves to the bamboo bench. She is over fifty, older than his own mother a few years, yet looks so old. Her face is full of wrinkles – the trace of hard years worrying about her husband and children. Mae looks older than Puk Ho because of five times of giving birth. Her sons were killed under the Pol Pot's regime. With so many nights of sweeping and missing her children, how can't she be older than her age? Many times, Huy gazes at her, tries to figure out her young age face. In her young age, she must have been as beautiful as Sa Pien is. Her frame of face and her line of chin still remain some delicateness of a pretty woman. And, there is still some nobleness in her talking and walking gestures.

She told him once about her young age. She was the most beautiful girl in a town of a distant southern province. All the youngsters in the near villages fell in love with her in secret. Her father was an emigrant from Guangdong Province, China. She inherited her father's fair complexion and her mother's nice round eyes. The mixed blood of two nations brought her a wonderful beauty. Yet she was not only pretty but also having finished her ninth grade at the town. Back then, in that area, this was very seldom, even to the boys. Beautiful and well educated, she was a dream, a goddess in the heart of every young fellow in the town. Many young men from rich families who were her classmates at the town wooed her, and when they were refused, they still loved her in silence.

Sa Rinh refused them not because she despised them. She had loved a young man who was very close to her since their childhood. He was Ho, her primary school classmate. Ho's family was very poor, having not a cow for property. Therefore, although he was the best pupil in the school, he had to leave school to help his parents to earn their living.

Contrastingly, Sa Rinh's family was so rich with five pairs of huge oxen and dozens acres of first class rice fields. There were about fifty people working for her parents in the transplant and harvest seasons.

The little girl Sa Rinh and the little boy Ho had liked each other since the days of the primary school. When Sa Rinh had to come to the town to continue her education, she only came home in the festival days or in the summer. The two friends just met each other in those seldom chances. Yet it seemed that the more they were apart and the more it was hindered, the more they loved each other. The innocent friendship turned slowly into love. But their family conditions were as different as chalk and cheese, so they had to restrain their passion.

They loved each other in helplessness, did not know how to do. Sa Rinh dared not let her parents know it. She knew that they would never allow her to marry such a penniless fellow. She had an only way: to find reasons to refuse and delay when someone wooed her. She prayed for some miracle would happen, so that she could live with her lover.

When Sa Rinh was nineteen there was a happening. That happening helped her to reach her dream.

That spring, a man came there from Phnom Penh to invest in estate and rubber tree plantation. His name was Pu Ven. He was enormously wealthy. Sa Rinh's family property in comparison with his was like a little frog in comparison with an ox. He had had two wives and more than a dozen of children who had grown up. His youngest child was older than Sa Rinh too. Soon after he came there, he heard rumors about Sa Rinh's beauty and pride. It was occurred to him that she would be positively his woman. Pu Ven was a rich and successful turkey cock. He believed in his power.

He managed to make acquaintance with Sa Rinh's parents on behalf of a remote businessman who wanted to have intimate friendship. He often found reasons to give everyone in her family rare expensive gifts. And he won their hearts soon, except Sa Rinh's.

Right at the first time when she was face to face with Pu Ven, his strange eyes made her worried and frightened already. He stared at her as a tomcat stared at his captured mouse, hungry, satisfied and delighted. And, just like a cat played with a mouse, Pu Ven was not in a hurry. He tightened his invisible net slowly and carefully, without a slit.

In the autumn, Pu Ven proposed marriage to her. Sa Rinh's parents were even glad with his wooing. The wedding was decided to happen right in that October.

Sa Rinh was almost crazy at the time. She dared not oppose his parents. But she absolutely hated Pu Ven. She thought over and over, and at last determined that after the wedding ceremony, she would commit suicide when she reached his house. She would rather be dead than let him get her.

There was only five days left before the wedding. That night, Ho crept sneakily into her room. He asked her to escape with him. They would go very far, left everything behind their backs to make a new life from their bare hands.

And Sa Rinh followed him. They ran over night, through the villages, through the desolate forests, ignoring the fears of fierce wild animals. Early that morning, they begged a lift to Battambang, and made their living in Chandai from then on.

The old married couple has had plenty of difficulties in their love, so they love each other so much. Now they are old, yet sometimes, Huy still sees that they look after each other in a very moving way.

Puk Ho is a serious and taciturn man. When he met him the first times, Huy was rather reserved before his coldness. He has just really known about him recently. The old man likes the soldiers, but he shows his sentiment only through actions. Once in a while, he takes from his room a bottle of alcohol and asks Mae Sa Rinh to cook a sour soup pot, or to broil some salted fish, and sit drinking with them. Even in the course of drinking, he still says few words, but there is warmness and intimateness in his eyes as he looks at them. Sometimes before, when Huy and his companions visited the house and Puk had just got a few fish by throwing casting net, they would be sure to have a string of fish to bring home. But Huy quickly realizes that Puk Ho does not like Ly. He never looks at the latter's face. He only sits drinking alcohol with Huy, Moi and Gia Huong, that is to say whenever Ly is not present. Huy finds something very unintelligible in his attitude.

Mae Sa Rinh enters her room, looking for something for a little while then appears again. In her hand is a little cloth pack. She slowly sits down on the floor and tells Huy, "Come here, son."

He comes and sits down beside her. Mae unfolds the cloth pack with her trembling hands. Inside of the pack is a jade bracelet. He gazed at her questioningly. He wonders what she wants to do. "Does she want to give it to me?" he thinks.

She looks at the bracelet for a long time. From her eye corners – perhaps many fellows have drowned in them long ago – two lines of tears flowed down silently. Huy is very surprised. She looks up at him when he just wants to open his mouth to ask.

"This is my son Quan's bracelet."

"Yes?"

"He gave it to Sa Pien long time ago. Two years ago."

"-----------?"

"You bring it home, give him back. Tell him to keep it and give it to his future wife."

Huy scratches his head. So there has been really some relation between Quan and Sa Pien!

"Brother Quan gave it to Sa Pien, why do you give it back?" he asks her.

"She's not deserved. She's so bad!" Mae Sa Rinh speaks with intervals, and holds tightly her chest with her hands in a long cough; she winces in pain.

"Are you all right?" Huy stretches his arms to hold her slim shoulders, asks worryingly.

"Don't mind, son. Just a little cough recently," she said.

Huy takes the bracelet. The jade pervades a cool air in his hand. He looks at it for a while and then puts it back in the cloth, folds up and puts the pack in his pocket coat.

"All right, I'll give it to brother Quan," he says and looks thoughtfully at her. The tears, like two little threads, still flow down on her cheeks. A long time later, he says, "Then how did the story happen, Mae?"

"It's all right to let you know, but don't talk it to anybody else. My son Quan doesn't want to let many people know it, you know, Huy?" Mae says and then tells him the story with a strangled voice.

When the battalion just came to build its base near Chandai, Quan often visited the people, talked to them and helped them if he could do it. Everywhere he came, he won the people's hearts due to his kind and sincere treatments. All things he was provided, from clothes to the necessaries such as sugar, milk... he gave them to the old and weak people, just kept the stuffs that he had to save to used together with his companions. He often visited her house. And she soon learned that he had a special affection with Sa Pien. Sa Pien appeared to like him then too. They usually met each other to chat in the house, under the silent permission of her parents. Quan reminded them of their young age love. Everything seemed to be good.

Yet in the matter of love, Quan was too plain to have appropriate behaviors. He loved Sa Pien so much, but he respected her so much too. Just met her and talked to her frequently, he also felt very happy. Even though they have been dating for more than a year, he never touched her hands.

Mae Sa Rinh smiles sadly, "The two made friends so long and long, yet when I asked Sa Pien, 'Did my son Quan touch your hands?' she shook her head, looked unhappy, 'Nothing. He's so polite.'..."

According to the custom of this area, the girls who let a man touch her hands is a virgin no more, and touching one girl's hands without her consent is considered as raping. However, this is only an outdated tradition. It has lost its inviolable solemnity in the old time. How can a young couple keep themselves from touching hands of each other? They get even some much more intimateness!

Nevertheless, Quan was adhered properly to the custom. Once he talked to Mae Sa Rinh and Puk Ho, saying that he would stay here and marry Sa Pien when he would be demobilized. He did not want to accept the officer position because of this too. And that time, he handed the bracelet to Mae Sa Rinh as an engagement offering. He had brought this bracelet with his saving money plus some more borrowed from his companions by a chance dropping by Sisophon Market. Mae and Puk agreed, and they treated him as their son. Quan believed that Sa Pien would be his wife, and he wanted to keep safe for both of them.

He did not learn that a young girl in her flooding vitality was not pleased with plain conversations. She longed for her lover to fondle her, to cuddle her as if she were a little cat or a newborn baby. Therefore, although Sa Pien loved Quan, she was discontented with him too. Yet she dared not say or show anything to reveal her desire.

In the January of the following year, Ly and Moi who were soldiers of No. 18 Company of the regiment were transferred to the platoon. Quan had often visited Mae Ra Rinh's house with some of his soldiers, and since then he led Ly and Moi came to the house just as he did with the others.

Right at the first time he met Sa Pien, Ly liked her passionately. In fact, Ly or Moi or anybody else in the battalion did not know the relation between Quan and Sa Pien. Quan did not conceal his love, but he did not want to expose it to everyone too, just because he was not such a kind of man. He treated Sa Pien well and friendly yet nothing of intimateness, either before his companions or not. It was the reason for later trouble.

Then soon later Ly tried to flirt her, sometimes even with Moi's innocent support. Quan knew it, but he did not wan to interfere it. He believed in Sa Pien. And he did not want to make an unnecessary break between the comrades too. He did not expected that Ly was a modern Don Juan with his quickly ways of winning women heart. Furthermore, he did not expect that even Sa Pien had changed her mind when she had met Ly. She was absolutely attracted by his handsome. But it was indeed by his worldly wise and audacity that Ly won her heart more quickly. He was shameless to embrace her and kiss her, ignored her scorn and revilement. Yet Ly's rude manners only made her fearful and angry at first. Slowly, she found out that she often thought of them, remembered and craved for them. She tried to resist her instinct weakly, more and more weakly. Her reason fell at last. Sa Pien plunged passionately and recklessly into her love drunkenness. She was regardless of anything else; even Mae Sa Rinh's dissuasion and painful tears; even Puk Ho's fierce fury; and, certainly, even Quan's misery or his thoughts of her. Although she sometimes felt sorry for Quan, he had already become an alien.

In fact, she had her own sufferings. For her, Quan was the embodiment of an ideal man, as good as her imagination of a man to whom she would attach for her whole life. Yet she never really loved him. She just respected him, loved him as an elder brother. Had only he loved her simply and intimately like Ly, her sentiment would have turned into a real love. Yet it did not go further in fact. And so, Sa Pien just recognized her real love when she met Ly.

According to the custom, Khmer girls had their own room in the house. Not any man, even the father of the girl, could enter that boudoir. Yet Ly many times entered Sa Pien's boudoir.

Sa Pien voluntarily gave her body to Ly, under the protection of Mae Sa Rinh. After countless times of dissuasion and reproach, she had to reach a compromise with her daughter. She knew what they did in her daughter's virgin room. She felt wretched and sorry for Quan. Yet she still protected Sa Pien, concealed the happenings from Puk Ho, so that her daughter could be happy in her love. Mae Sa Rinh was indeed a good and virtuous and weak mother, who loved her daughter with a blind but infinite love. In this changed-direction love, perhaps she was the most suffered and wretched. Moreover, Quan was no longer close and friendly as before. He avoided her family. Reluctantly, she had to come to the base to meet him, but he just quietly bowed her and kept silent.

Mae Sa Rinh sighs, "I love my son Quan so much, even more than Sa Pien. My sons were killed all, so I consider him just as my own son. Yet he was angry with Sa Pien and then with me too."

Huy sits listening to her, looking at her kind wrinkled face, on which remained lines of tears, and feels that he almost sheds tears with her. He thinks Quan surely laid no blame on her. Perhaps he tried to pretend like that so that she would come to meet him no more. Perhaps he was afraid to meet her again, afraid to recall the warm old days. Can't Mae Sa Rinh figure out this? That is the only reason to explain for Quan's coldness and alien. Huy is surprised as he thinks Quan, like anyone else, after all, cannot avoid the weakness of human. A man like him would have had a better manner. Huy is accustomed to his way of thinking about Quan as an extraordinary man. He is disappointed in him now. "It turns out that brother Quan is also wrong in his behaviors sometimes!" he thinks.

Then he thinks of Sa Pien, and feels pity for her. She is so innocent and silly to devote herself to a man who does not really love her. Obviously, Ly has a passion for her, but he just considers her as a valuable toy. And you will be tired of a toy some day. Until what time Ly still stays here, she is still able to keep him, just because there is no one in the phum who can compare with her, yet he will forget her at once when he is apart from her. He appears to give her no respect, although it is their most intimate time now. He has told the others about personal intimate things between him and her with boast, satisfaction and innocence, as if he talked about some third person.

However, Huy feels that he cannot hate Ly. His nature and characters is inborn. And in this trouble, Ly does not know that he has broken one of his companion's happiness. He just lives after his limited nature and thought. Moreover, many people will be ready to forgive him when they look at his handsome face and attractive smile or hear his inoffensive jests though they might get angry or hate him. You cannot say that one's appearance is nothing! From ancient time on, the human beauty has caused so much misunderstanding and wrong illusion and brought so much trouble. The tendency in human nature is that they always admire and venerate the beauty. And the beauty of human appearance is maybe the most seductive and dangerous one.

He turns back, puts his arm around Mae Sa Rinh's shoulders, consoles her, "Well, don't be so sad, Mae. I'll talk to brother Quan and ask him to visit you." He falls into silence for a long while and then blurts out suddenly, "I love you so much! I love you as much as I love my own mother."

Mae Sa Rinh looks at Huy and sends him a toothless smile. Her eyes are glistering with a joy and moving feeling. Huy holds and crushes slightly her thin, bony hands, looks at her white cloudy hair, and suddenly misses his mother so much.

He sits with Mae for a short while more then stands up. The sun is coming down, and he has to return. "I have to go now. Remember don't be so sad, Mae!" he says.

Mae Sa Rinh nods. She leans her hands against the floor, stands up and says, "Wait a minute. I'll pack a little silkworm for you to fry to eat with rice." She walks to the kitchen for a moment and then returns, carries a pack of silkworm and a big jackfruit.

Huy says goodbye to her and returns to his home. En route, his mind full of disturbing thoughts. He wonders that if he were in Quan's shoes, what he would do. Certainly, it is not his way. He will say straightly to Ly, let him know clearly everything. But what if Ly is insensible? All right! It will be up to Sa Pien then, up to her choice. Yet, at least, things have to be made clear to everyone!

He suddenly thinks of his own case. He has made friend with the young girl. Her name is Soun. His character is still boyish. He likes to see Soun in her embarrass manners, likes to tease her to make her face flushed and then laughs with over joy. That's all! He begins to realize that he has somehow played selfishly with the sincere sentiment of a young girl. So, he is nothing different from Ly after all! He is just like him; just wants to be playful in a superficial way, giving no concern to the results that might be made by him!

He knows that Soun has had a special affection with him. In this remote countryside, a fifteen-year-old girl has already known about love. The youth age of a mature girl here is so short, just existed for four or five years. Under thirteen, she is still an innocent little girl. From thirteen on, she begins her young unmarried woman life. And she will marry at about sixteen or seventeen. A few years later, the glistening eyes and scarlet lips girl once becomes an untidy slovenly young married woman, with lots of small children. She then reminds nothing of the beautiful young girl of the olden time – an olden time just existed not so long ago.

"What will I do to keep Soun just consider me as her brother and understands that I just consider her as my little sister?" Huy winces and asks himself. In fact, he cannot measure his sentiment. He likes Soun, but he dares not let this sentiment grow up. He fears! Yet he cannot define what he fears of. It is not because of military regulations.

Military regulations do not allow Vietnamese soldiers to have illicit sexual relationship with Khmer women. Yet as for the sentiment, how can any regulation prevent the vehement feelings in the young soldiers' hearts? From like to love, the distance is so small. And love means devote oneself to each other. Many soldiers have fallen in love, and have been willingly to receive all stern punishments. Many among them will return home when they are demobilized, will say farewell to the love in the war, left behind their backs their moping lovers, and sometimes, left behind their back even their own abandoned children, because of so much obstacles. But many others will stay here too. They will consider this land here as their second motherland. They are courageous to live and die with love. They will have children; will give this land their sweat, and, even their blood; will become a cell of the Khmer national community, attach to them and endure with them the droughts and the downfalls, the goods and the miseries; will have the same fate with the people who are not their compatriot or their own race, yet have become their compatriot and their own race once they have determinately chosen a way to walk. Huy never thinks that he will love a girl and stay here. His motherland! In that land, his Pa and Ma who begin to reach their old ages are waiting for him. In that land, his younger brothers and sisters are enduring the poor and lacks and difficulties. Sure enough, he has to return home!

Huy is passing the head of village's house some dozens of yards when he spots a woman coming near, with two little boys at both sides of her. She is Ca Puon, an acquaintance. Ca Puon is as thin as a lath. She is about twenty-five, yet looks older than her age. Her dark withered face from lack of eating makes distinguished with her white eyes. The two kids are her sons. The older boy is Kan, six years old, and the younger boy is Lum, four years old. They are so alike – a slim body, a little, black face, the helpless eyes, a white protruding teeth and a yellow-brown sunburned hair. They smile broadly and call loudly when they spot him, "*Mia* Huy, *Mia* Huy[2]!"

He has visited Ca Puon's house many times. Her house is near to Soun's, and she often comes to the base to fetch water. Whenever he gets *Riel* subsidy, he always comes to the little shop of the phum to buy some packet of candy or cake for the kids so that he can later look interestingly at their joyful faces as they receive the little gifts. A few days before, when he was provided two cans of milk, he gave them a can, and Mae Sa Rinh the other. The kids love him. They often dart at him and hug his legs for a long time whenever they meet him. And he loves them too. Ca Puon's family situation is pitiful. Her husband was killed under the Pol Pot's regime, more than a year after their wedding, which was hold by Angkar. Of these two kids, even she too is not sure who their father is. A few years ago, when she was still a little comely, not as ugly as she is now, many villager men courted her. Ca Puon had sexual relations with too many men – she is the only one who can know why – yet when she was pregnant and got children, nobody helped her or took care of her. Being poor, having neither man nor land nor cattle, Ca Puon works for the having families to foster her children. When she is not employed, she comes to the lake to catch fish and little shrimp, but she can only make so little for living.

Ca Puon greets him with her toothless smile; just a few decayed teeth remain in her mouth. "Where you back from, koongtop Huy?" she asks.

"From Ma Sa Rinh's house. Where do you bring the kids?"

"I come to *khang choeng*[3] to pick mulberry leaves for them. The kids want to go with me."

"All right, you go and let me take care of them. I'll bring them to my base to give them a bath. Look at them, their heads just all of scabies. A moment later, I'll give Kan a soap to bring home. You wash them with it to cure the scabies... Well, no! Every afternoon, you bring them to my place then I'll take care of them myself."

"Thanks koongtop Huy so much," Ca Puon says and turns toward the kids. "You two kids follow Mia Huy to have a bath."

With his one arm holds the jackfruit and the pack of silkworm and his other holds the little hand of Lum, he walking and telling the kids a few funny stories. All of a sudden, he hears the soft calling voice of a girl when he reaches the fork of roads where leads to his base.

"*Boong*[4] Huy! *Boong* Huy!"

He turns back. There stands Soun, some paces from him. One of her arm hides behind her back with something, and she looks shy and confused. Her black, bright eyes shoot a glance at him then cast down. The long, trembling eyelashes lower down to hide her embarrass eyes.

"What's up, Soun?" he asks.

"My mother told me to bring this one to give boong Huy," she still stands there, showing off the thing. It is a big pack covered by a dry banana leaf.

Huy comes nearer, takes the pack and uncovers the leaf layer. Those are wild purple guava fruits. He laughs, "Why don't you save to eat but give me, Soun?"

"Mae and Soun picked a lot of them," says Soun. "We can't eat them all alone! Boong Huy bring them home, let other brothers eat them together too. This fruit is very good, picked so far at Tha Lia Krao."

"Boong Huy won't eat them; other brothers won't eat them too. Soun just bring them home and eat them little by little. Soun and Mae were very hard to go so far to get them, we don't take them," he teases at her.

Soun looks up at Huy, her cheeks blushes with angry. "Boong Huy won't take them, so don't visit my house again, Soun will come no more to fetch water at boong Huy's place. We two are aliens now!" she says.

"I won't take them! But I still visit Soun's house. Soun closes the door, boong Huy will sit at the ladder, sitting until I become a big rock! Sitting until Soun allows boong Huy to come in her house, until she comes in to fetch water again!" he laughs again.

Soun rubs strongly her hands to each other. She knows that he is teasing her, and then becomes more embarrassed. After a long moment of silence, knowing that she cannot retort, she says, "Boong Huy say so much, tell lie words. Soun don't hear them no more! Soun come back home now!"

She turns around and run away. Her sarong's flap is rolled up a little, showing a part of her smooth plump calf of legs. Huy calls after her, "Hey, Soun! Don't be angry with me! I'm just kidding! Tell yours Mae I'm very grateful!"

He stands and looks at her until she disappears behind a bush, then leads the kids to his base.

CHAPTER 13

Quan enters his house, his face is thoughtfully, and in his hand is a pack of letters. He has just attended a meeting at the battalion headquarters. The meeting was presided over by Bao, Deputy Head of battalion. Captain Van was presented in the meeting room for a few minutes to announce to the companies and platoons' officers about his new position at the regiment then withdrew to prepare to go.

He recalls his days at No. 12 Company, when Van was its Deputy Head. Van is brave and daring, and loves his subordinates like his brothers by birth. It is indeed from him, Quan has learnt how to love and treat his soldiers at the platoon. And this way of treatment seems to generate not only from Van, but also from an old tradition of the whole unit.

From the old soldiers who have by their own blood colored the victory flags – of their battalions, regiments and divisions – as soon as the units were founded in the Southeast of Vietnam, the young soldiers have learnt so many things which have never been written in any military teaching canon. Those are the lessons in the everyday life, and, in each battle that they have experienced too. Those are the lessons about unlimited endurance, about the close and warm comradeship, about the love of homeland and the craving for freedom and independence; and, most important, about humanity: to know of resentment and to be determined to fight, yet to be so tolerant and clement as well. From generation to generation, those lessons have little by little become blood; have rooted into the soul and heart-bed of every soldier. Such most sacred and wonderful source of power of the whole nation has been accumulated through over a thousand year of history of interminable wars and deaths and grieves. In a battle, all the soldiers become one entity, least of all in their situation. They are all the poor with their pure hearts that haven't been blinded by power and wealth yet. They have common thoughts and common sentiments beside their personal point of views and characters. Therefore, they are easily to love each other and to share with each other.

Quan realizes that some paradox exists apparently: "War is ugly and horrible, yet it is war that lifts man up to some nobleness. It gives man a vehement vitality and deep love of life. And it devotes to the human beings the brightest paragons of nobleness and honor and love". Sometimes, Quan cannot understand himself. He hates war. He does not want to have his hands soaked in blood. He is mostly influenced by the religious and philosophic theories – the lights that illuminate us from the high away places and blot out the borderlines of right and wrong behaviors.

"There is no question of skin colors and nations and races and countries. There is even no question of to be human or non-human. There is only the question of life and peace and salvation. The world will be peaceful and contented if those discriminations exist no more. But perhaps it is forever a world of dream, a world of never-coming-true ideals? The soldiers – though standing on this side or the other of the front line – are all human, and are all similarly in their fear and pain and misery. Yet because of the discriminations and separations, they have to kill the opponents. It is really absurd! Maybe war is one of the most absurd activities of human beings. The wild animals kill because of their instinct of struggle for survival. They have to kill and eat the weaker to live, and then, at their turn, they will be killed and eaten by the bigger and stronger ones. But man kills just either because of the ideas and illusions of his self or imposed by the others. Oh, it is absurd indeed…!"

Those thoughts exist in Quan's consciousness and in his heart as well. But there is another thing existing at the same time: his nation pride, his deep love of his own homeland and people; and a rather simple thing: the close comradeship between the soldiers. The rolled cigarettes sharing with each other; the swig of water left in the bidon bottom that they give up to their companions in their dying thirsty – the compassion and responsibility to their comrades have been more and more deeply through each day. A common humanity and charity cannot be alive because it has no root. The spirits of the ancestors are still awake, flowing silently in each of his blood veins, lingering in his heart and sub-consciousness. His spirit and consciousness come to conflict with themselves. And there is no answer. So many times Quan sits asking himself; so many nights he sits in the silence, try to deposit his mind and thought – as if it were a transparent and quiet river which deposits all of its chaotic alluvium and mineral to its bed – to find a clear answer. But at some point right in the middle of his mediation, all things seem to fade away and vaguely confuse with each other. Thus, Quan is both a normal soldier with an iron will and a philosopher who is always pondering over the truth.

Sitting to mend his clothes, U Moi looks up at Quan, and when he spots the pack of letters he jumps to his feet and says merrily:

"Well, it's so cool! Do I have any letter, brother Quan?"

"You get one," Quan smiles, "It was from Hien."

He recollects the time U Moi just joined the platoon. Once when his unit had to go fighting around their area for five days, they went long and hard works yet they found no enemy. Captain Van let the unit have a rest when they reached the Thmor Bridge, about two miles and a half away from their base. Everybody was tired out then. They had crossed the dense jungle in the west which was fraught of creepers and rattans and thorns bushes and there was no trace to go; the men who led the way had to use their machete to cut the boughs and thorns to open a narrow path. U Moi was a fellow of strong build, and a mountain native too, so he was assigned to carry the "cow-head".

Literally, it is the pedestal of the machinegun. In comparison with the other detached parts of the 12.7 machinegun, the "cow head" is among the heaviest ones, and it is too unwieldy to carry. It is much more comfortable when you carried it on the bare fields, yet when you have to cross through the forest, you was really the most miserable.

Back then, for almost two miles of walking, U Moi could not put the cow-head on his shoulder, but he had to carry it with his arms to creep through the newly low and narrow path. And that was also his first operation. So, when they arrive at the bridge, U Moi was as flabby as a piece of rotten meat, his uniforms were soaked as if he has just jumped into a pond. After the rest, the unit began to continue its march to home. U Moi just sat motionless. Quan walked to him and asked, "Are you very tired? Well, come on, it's near to our base now. You take the AK, let me help you to carry the 'cow-head'."

U Moi shook his head again and again, "Nay, you just let me sit here for a little while, I'll be back later."

Quan frowned, "It's impossible. It's unsafe here. Come on!"

He put his gun into the latter's lap, and took the "cow-head" onto his shoulder. His other hand grasped U Moi's shoulder and pulled it violently. U Moi stood up staggeringly. The platoon joined their troop to depart.

When they arrived at home, U Moi threw right away his rucksack and himself down upon the floor, shut his eyes closely like a drift corpse. Just a minute later, Gia Huong shouted from the other house – that time, he stayed at the base to protect it.

"U Moi, you have a letter from your lover. It was delivered us three or four days ago."

U Moi sprang up to his feet, ran out of the house like a streak of lightning, and then he came back again in a flash, swinging a letter in his hand, he jumped up and down and roared with laughter: "It's my letter. It's my letter, brother Quan!"

"Yeah, it's your letter!" Quan said and winked at him. "Not until now do I know what the power of love is. It can turn an asthmatic cat which is moribund into a dotty who is as strong as a bull!"

It is just the same this time! U Moi stands up hastily, jumps to his feet, darts toward Quan and snatches the pack of letters, searches it, and then picks out one of them. Quan looks at U Moi's merriness, feels something like anxiousness rising in his heart. He never gets a letter from the homeland. Not ever. He can only enjoy the happiness of sharing with his comrades. Once in a while, this one or that reads loudly a letter from his mother or lover, and then asks Quan to help him in writing a reply. Each such time, Quan is extremely elated and enthusiastic as if that letter is his own one.

U Moi carefully tears at the top of the envelope, then sits down on the floor and reads the letter attentively. He reads it again and again and again. Then he carefully folds the letter, puts it into the envelope, and sits thoughtfully for a while. All of a sudden, he smiles broadly to himself, looks up at Quan and says, "Well, brother Quan, Hien said that she had saved up two tenth of a tael of gold, and that she had fed a sow that is about to give its first birth too. When I come home, I'll have my wedding in the next month."

"It's right. You need to marry her soon, she has been waiting for you for many years," says Quan. "Now you go to gather them all here for a meeting. Where's Huy?"

"Perhaps he comes to the other house." U Moi replies and runs out of sight without finishing his words.

A moment later, everybody hastily gather there. They are all eagerly because they have been told about the letters from their homes.

"Is there anything so important that you want to take a platoon meeting, Quan?" Gia Huong asks Quan.

Quan smiles and holds up the pack of letters. Everyone jumps and shouts happily.

Lately, the soldiers who get letters tremblingly tear the envelopes and the ones who get nothing lean their heads close to their comrades' to read eagerly the lines of words.

When the soldiers finishes their reading, Quan says, "Everybody, please pay attention. I'll announce to you all now two things. Firstly, our leaders give us a ration of leave in our country, the following day of tomorrow the one who gets it will depart. Secondly, Captain Van will come to the regiment for his new position tomorrow."

The platoon is once again noisily as a flock of bees losing their beehive. Everyone in the battalion respects Captain Van and was very fond of him too. So this news takes away partly the excitement of getting home letters and leave of absence.

Quan stretches up his arm to interrupt the noisy discussions.

"Alright, everybody keep silent. Anyway, brother Van has to go, so it's in vain to sorrow about it. Now, I would like to explain a little bit: our platoon gets a ration of leave among the three of our battalion due to the consecutive victories in the battles, killing and capturing many enemies, and seizing many arms. Now I give you two ways: the first one is to choose by lot among the '83 soldiers up, and the second one is all of you will cast lots. Now give your opinions, please."

Gia Huong looks around, smiles and says, "There is some thing which I think I must talk to you all. Why, it's usually the man who directly capture enemies will be on leave. That day, it was Quan who rushed forward alone to overpower and capture the two enemies, with our support. So, it's certainly the credit of the whole platoon, yet we would return with bare hands without the men who were daring. On the other hand, Quan is the most senior here. So I suggest that Quan will be on leave, no need to draw at all. Do you all agree?"

The soldiers nod in unison, showing their agreement with Gia Huong's suggestion. Quan holds up his hand and says, "Thank you. But I've lost both my mother and father, and have no relative. So it's useless for me to come back the country. It's truthful. So, please choose a way as I just said."

"To say frankly," Thien says, "I myself very long for taking a leave. But I think that the '82 soldiers are about to be demobilized. So, it's should be only the '83 and '84 soldiers who draw the lots."

"We're fighters who get battles as daily meals," Moi opposes. "It's not me who want to say unlucky things, yet we're maybe alive now and die at another minute. Why, we can only be sure that we're really safety to come home when we've stepped across the border gate. So, for me, it's only fair in case that everyone will draw."

Moi enlisted in 1983. If the ones who enlisted in 1982 are added into the draw takers, his probability to win the draw would be reduced. But he feels that it is necessary to do this. He does not want to forget his comrades due to his own interest. The soldiers keep silent and think over it; feel that Moi's opinion is reasonable. Perhaps, except Quan, anybody also very longed for a trip of return home to see his homeland and his own people again – Oh! Homeland! Where their old mothers, younger brothers and sisters live! Where there are nice wives and good children, and their dear lovers. So much fond remembrance and love have piled up and stagnated in their heart in these months and years.

"Well, then we'll choose the first way," Quan looks around and nods. "I'll write a ballot with a word 'GO' inside, and the rest are blank ballot. Do you agree?"

The soldiers speak their agreements in unison.

Quan opens his notebook and tear off some sheets of papers, then tear them into small pieces, writes down on a piece, folds all them up and puts them together into the inox mug, shakes it strongly for a while. Then he says loudly, "Now, you'll see your luck. One at a time!"

Each soldier eagerly comes near to draw his ballot, and then tremblingly opens it. The faces are full of excitement and eagerness. Abruptly, Ly jumps to his feet and shouts and laughs loudly, "Hahaha! I win it! Mother! I'll meet you again soon!"

The rest is a bit of disappointment. Yet they immediately shout loudly and rush toward Ly, hug him, lift him up, and throw him into the air many times.

"Congratulation! Congratulation, Ly!"

When Ly is released again, his face still reddened and bewildered as if he cannot believe that he is about to come home. Then his eyes too are reddened.

***

In the afternoon, the soldiers come to the phum to buy chicken and liquor to hold a party. They invite some friends from other platoons. The party starts so early, from three o'clock, and ends at four. They drink only a bidon of liquor because Lieutenant General Nam Nga, Front Commander-in-chief, has forbidden drinking liquor after the last campaign.

The party finishes, and the guesses saying good-bye to them. At last, there are Ly, Moi, Gia Huong and a few other fellows sat drinking tea and chatting. The rest of the platoon concentrated in writing letters to ask Ly to post them to their families.

The stories are nearly exhausted soon; the soldiers sit silently and thoughtfully. Outside, the air is strangely quiet. The twitters of the flower-peckers catching worms on the mango trees are heard clearly. The bright yellow light of late afternoon cover the leaves gaps and jumps through the holes on the wattle, forming many sparkling and stirring spots on the ground.

Ly sits with his arms folding around his knees. He looks absently at the front yard lighted up by the late sunshine, as if he is imagining of his future merry days in the city. Suddenly, he turns to Huy. "Huy, you write your letter, and I'll bring it to your family," he says.

"I wrote it already," Huy tells him. "I'll draw a simple map on the envelope so that you can find my house easily. If you have spare time, just visit my house; otherwise, you can post it… If you come and my Ma asks you about my life here, you remember to say that I am very healthy and joyful, and that there is no danger at all. Remember that, please."

"I know, needn't to tell me what to do," Ly says and turns to Moi. "And you…?"

"You go to Cau Ong Lanh Market, find the vegetable area and ask for Mrs. Nam." Moi gazes at Ly, "It's easier to meet my mother there. The way to my house is too difficult to go, and my house gets no address too. By the way, Ly, you bring me some storybooks. My "films store" is empty now. I'm afraid that if I keep telling over and over again the old stories, I'll lose my audience."

"Well, I know," Ly nods and smiles and then he turns to Gia Huong. "Did you write letter to your wife," he asks. "I'll post it for you."

Gia Huong stands up. He walks hastily to the other house, saying, "Just a moment, I'll bring you this thing."

A moment later, Gia Huong comes back. He sits down and opens his hands. His bearded face stretches widely with an easy smile. In his larger, callous peasant palms are two little wooden dwarfs, one made of yellow jackfruit wood, and the other of some unknown dark purple one. Both these dwarfs are polished due to sweat absorbing and many times of rub. He has worked hard again and again at these dwarfs for a month. So, these are the invaluable gifts of a father. They contain much of his love in each carve line and vein of wood.

Gia Huong is the eldest and most solemn and reticent in the platoon. He loves the younger soldiers as if they were his own brothers. Yet he is a serious eldest. Different from Quan who often softly encourages and consoles them, he is easy to lose his temper and usually scolds them, yet he soon forgets all their mistakes. It was unknown how, but the communal detachment did not called him up when he was a single man. Not until twenty-six was he conscripted, when had had his wife and his children and had to earn for their living. He indented to evade his military service, but his wife who is descended from her revolutionary parents encouraged him. She swore that she would be loyal and wait him and take good care of their children. She did not want to have a husband who had to dodge hither and thither, feared of anything. So he went with discontent. Then he slowly felt better and secure with the letters from his wife and his family. He compared himself with the others and realized that he was more luckily than some of them. "Sometimes, seeing Quan just expects to read other's letters, I feel so pity for him," once he told Huy. "I am much happier than he is. If I die, I've got wife and children already!"

Perhaps due to his children, Gia Huong likes to go to phum Chan Dai. He usually holds the sunburnt hair Khmer children in his arms, buys them little packs of candy and gently strokes their hair or tease at them to relieve his fond remembrance of his own children.

"You take these things to the city, put them in a box together with my letter and post it for me," Gia Huong tells Ly. "I wrote to divide them in the letter already. The yellow one for the eldest and the purple one for his younger brother... Surely they'll be overjoyed with the gifts."

He sits gazing at the wooden dwarfs for a long while then he pulls out of his coat pocket the letter and gives them all to Ly. "Well, Ly," he says abruptly. "Maybe a moment later Sa Pien comes here to meet you. I informed her about your leave when I came to the phum this morning. She looked very sad."

"I suppose I'd better see her tomorrow at the phum," Ly frowns. "She'll only make a mess here."

The sun is lowered at the west. The shadows of mango trees stretch out on the ground. Sa Pien and Soun arrive at the house as the last sunlight spot on the floor reduced into a tiny fading out streak.

Sa Pien cannot hide her sadness and worry, though she tries to smile to greet the soldiers. And Huy realizes in her an indescribable fear too. "She must take all of her courage to come here; she must fear of encountering Quan. Fortunately, Quan has come to the other house a long time before," Huy thinks.

On one of Sapien's arm is a full bag of something wrapped by a krama. And, there Soun is! She timidly hides herself behind Sapien. Sa Pien puts the bag on the table, looks at Ly, "Here is a little present, you help me bring it home to your mother… You return home and come back here early… I'll pine for you."

Ly stands up, comes toward Sa Pien, puts his arms around her slender shoulders, "Don't be so sad, Sa Pien, I come home and come back here soon. We should go out there, dear."

He leads her to the mango tree at the corner of the house. The two lovers sit down at the tree foot and gently exchange their confidences.

Inside the house, Soun stands bewildered. She is very embarrassed and scared to death because this is the first time she enters the soldier's house, though deep in her heart, she has expected to get a chance like this one. And Huy, since the moment she just comes here, just keeps his smile and says no word. She does not know what to do. It is impossible to go out to Sa Pien, and it is too difficult to stay here. She feels that her legs suddenly become weak. She looks at Huy, hums and haws, "Sa Pien asked Soun to go with her…"

Gia Huong and Moi look at her, smile with sympathy. They notice that under the cloth of her sarong, her legs are trembling. "Come to sit here, my little girl," Gia Huong tells her. "Huy often says of you. He said that you're charming and very kind… Well, your fruit gave us that day was good. Everyone liked it."

Soun smiles shyly, her bright black eyes glister. She tiptoes toward the table and sits down on the bench. Huy winks at Gia Huong and Moi, "It seems that you two will go to the other house for some task, isn't it?"

Moi smiles broadly and taps on Gia Huong shoulder, "Aha, we go now, Gia Huong, hehehe, this young imp surely cursing at us inwardly that we're his killjoys!"

They nod their heads at Soun and walk out.

Soun looks up at them and then bends her head again; her hands twiddle the sarong lap, her cheeks flushed. Huy gazes at her, feels his heart so warm. After a while, Huy breaks the silence, "How is your Mae, Soun?"

"Yes, Mae's well. Mae said of boong Huy all the time, saying for so long you aren't to come my house." Soun replies.

"I have many tasks at this time. All right, I'll visit Mae next afternoon." Huy says.

"Well," suddenly, Soun smiles and becomes excited. "Mae said that boong Huy like to eat *sâmlâ mchu*[1] cooked with snakehead fish and *ksang*[2] fruit. Tomorrow, boong Huy come and eat with us, will you? Soun will cook *sâmlâ* to serve boong Huy."

Huy is moved; he tries to keep calm and says, "Yes, it's sure that *sâmlâ mchu* cooked by Soun is delicious. Long time I have no meal with Mae and Soun, I miss *sâmlâ mchu* so much."

Soun comes back again to her shyness. Her heart, for a long time now, has been no longer of its innocence and calm. It was just like a windy water surface, with thousands of wave circles. At times, it was indescribable tenderness and sweetness; and at times, it was vaguely worried and fearful. In the late afternoons, she often strolled out along the wild bushes near the pagoda, where lay the little lotus lake. Sometimes, she wandered to the far spring at the hill foot. She liked to pick up the wild flowers and pinned them upon her hair, then looked eagerly at her reflection shadow in the blue water. On the limpid and glistening water surface, a charming little girl was looking questioningly at her: "*Are you really charming? Your smile looks so foolish! Does boong Huy like your foolish smile, that girl in the water? Yes, boong Huy surely likes it. He often smiles and looks at you... Soun, you love boong Huy indeed now! But he doesn't love you. He often teases at you to make you shy to death, teases at you to make you embarrassed from head to toe and then laughs loudly with satisfaction... Yet why is any word from him also sweet and good? Why any word from him just printed into your mind?...*"

Soun has been sat dreamingly in all such afternoons. She talked to herself; asking herself and replying herself. Then she talked to the trees and the grass and the spring and the lake. In her heart, they were friendly and mild and full of sympathy like her closest friends.

To her, and her friends at same age, the Vietnamese koongtops are friendly and easy to approach. They babble Khmer language with a funny accent, but they speak new and strange things. Their uncommon descriptions are full of colors and sounds. Soun and her friends listen to their stories bewitchingly, and the young girls' minds are flooded with strange and remote images. She often images the scenes of the "phums" in Vietnamese cities. There are lots of houses that are many times higher than the pagoda's roof and look like a long box and stand side by side in hundreds of them. Those phums are very crowded, as crowded as the populations of many "*khums*"[3] here, and this population lives in an area as big as a half of phum Chandai. There are the wide and beautiful streets, on both sides of them stand tall and big trees. And the nights there are lighted with many colorful light-tubes, much brighter than the full moonlit night here. She has by chances seen the pictures of Phnom Penh in the books, and their stories are just like in the books. So, Vietnam is just like Cambodia. Yet it is only so in the big cities, but here, in these "*sre-sroks*"[4], just the tiny, thatched roof houses; just the narrow paths which are dusty in the dry season and muddy in the rainy one; and just the deserted and solitude hills and forests. So far, and perhaps until their deaths, she and her friends will not go further than the poor small district market. And the Vietnamese koongtop's stories have drawn strange wonderful pictures. The soldiers make the young country girls surprised and curious, and with the stories, they become secret and attractive. Naturally, they are better in any way than the villager fellows. The fellows are so familiar and simple and they have a small sight and knowledge just like Soun and her friends. And, perhaps due to this, most of young girls here have dreamed of having a lover who is Vietnamese koongtop. There are many bad rumors about these loves: the fellow returns to his home and never comes back here, and the girl would alone take care of her child. It often happens like that. But there are exceptions as well. Soun knew a girl living at the district market, she has married a koongtop, and he stays here for good. The couple went to live at Sisophon and became rich. So, these loves are not always brings misery. Furthermore, when the heart is in love, it isn't afraid of trouble. When Soun met Huy the first time, she felt her heart somewhat strange. And slowly, she knew that she loved him indeed. It was not of her to want that. She feared and felt worried too. But her love was so big and so strong. It pulled her and pushed her toward him and captured her, and she found no way to escape it.

All of a sudden, she is startled and released from her rambling thoughts at Huy's voice, "Soun, what are you thinking of? You look so sad."

"Ye-e-es," Soun shakes her head bewilderingly.

"I'll take the picture of my Puk, Mae and younger brothers and sisters for you to see. It was just sent me from my Mae."

"Yes," Soun nods, her eyes glitter. "Boong Huy bring it here, I do want to see it."

Outside, the sunlight is fading out and giving way to the twilight. Huy lights the lamp on the table and steps toward the top of his bamboo bed, opens his rucksack. He comes back to Soun, gives her the photo sent to him at the beginning of the month. In the photo, his parents are older and thinner. His younger brothers and sisters stand in a semi circle behind his parents, each one tries to make a quaint smile. Soun leans toward the lamp, bending her head down, looks carefully at each person in the photo. Having looked at each one, she gives comments or asks Huy again and again:

"Your Mae's too thin, thinner than my Mae…"

"Is your Puk tough, and did you often got his blows when you were a kid?"

"Is that your eldest younger sister? She's so charming!"

"Your family's so crowded. One, two… eight of them all, and if you come back, your family has nine people. It's sure merrily. You see, in my family there's only Mae and Soun, it's so sad…"

Huy smiles and replies her, looks lovingly at her. Her face now looks really innocent and charming. She is very beautiful with her eyes lightly wink at times; her head lightly bending sideway; and her long eyelash cashes shadows under the lamplight.

Soun looks once more at the picture and then gives it back to him. She looks over around and her eyes lands on the lamp on the table at last. It is a self-made lamp from a crystal medicine pot. "Wow, what a wonderful lamp!" Soun giggles, "Who made it, boong?"

"I did," he replies.

"Boong Huy's so skillful, can make such a beautiful lamp."

"I'll make for you one when I have spare time, you like it?"

"Yes, I like it very much," she smiles.

Sitting some more time, Soun looks out over the yard and cries softly, "My God, it's too late. Soun have to come back now, boong Huy."

"Just sit for a little while more, Soun," Huy says. "Sa Pien has many things to talk to boong Ly."

"It's impossible. Let me call Sa Pien."

Soun stands up and reaches the doorway. In the dim light at the corner of the yard, the shapes of Ly and Sa Pien carve a dark figure. "We come back now, boong Sa Pien," Soun calls gently. "It's too late."

The young couple stands up. They are still too attached to leave. Their hands weave to each other's. A few minutes later, they walk toward Soun. Sa Pien turns her face toward Huy who is standing at the door and looking out. "We come home now, Huy," she says and nods to good-bye Ly, and then turns her back, holding Soun's hand and stepping along the path which is only a grey line in the dark now. Ly reaches the doorway, his face is thoughtfully.

"What time will you be at the regiment tomorrow?" Huy asks.

"Eight o'clock."

"You try to return here soon. Sa Pien will be so sad without you."

Ly says no word. He puts his hand on Huy's shoulder and slightly crushes it, and then he turns around and walks to the other house.

CHAPTER 14

The autumn of 1985 comes, with the cool breezes in the afternoons; the bright yellow sunlight is dreamy and gentle; and the sky is clear and immense. Flocks of migratory birds fly from the northeast southward, leaving behind them their calling sounds echoing in the winds. And in the late autumn afternoons, over the plains, flocks of dragonflies hover and mark the blue sky with so many little rocking yellow spots.

An October afternoon, more than three months since the day Ly was on leave, Huy visits Mae Sa Rinh.

The deadline of Ly's leave is over long ago, but it is no trace or news of him. Moi often tutted his tongue, shook his head and all of a sudden burst out a curse, "Damn him! If he wants to run away, it's just need to tell us a word! If only I come home, I'd teach him a lesson!"

Mae Sa Rinh and Sa Pien were very worried. Sa Pien often visited the base to ask about Ly's news, though Huy himself visited her house every double of weeks. She asked Huy to help her to write a letter for Ly to remind him to come back here early. Huy wrote the letter after her words; they were innocent, simple and ridiculous words, yet showing her deep love and big nostalgia. But Huy began to have doubts about his return. His desertion was eighty percent now. Sometimes, Huy felt very sorry for Quan and wished that if only Ly had not been transferred to the Third Battalion; if only Sa Pien had been still in love with Quan, the two would have been happy together. He knew that Quan still loved her so much. But how can things be changed? Her heart and her mind were completely belonging to Ly now. Soon after the day Mae Sa Rinh had gave him the bracelet to give it back to Quan, the two comrades talked to each other for a long while, since afternoon to deep night. That day, Quan looked so sad, the bracelet reminding him of the past, breaking again the wound from which he had tried to heal by the tasks. Yet that day, he also told Huy so much about himself, about his ideals and points of view about life.

He hears Puk Ho's angry shout when he just climbs up to the top of the wooden ladder. He hesitates and stops there for a while, and then enters the house. Puk Ho slightly nods his head at Huy, and he goes down out of the house, his face is in both angriness and grief mood. Mae Sa Rinh and Sa Pien are sitting huddled at a corner of the house. Sa Pien leans her head onto Mae Sa Rinh's chest and sobs. Huy is embarrassed and does not know what to do – go off or stay there. He is still indecisive when Mae says, "Come here son. I want to tell you something."

He comes near and sits down in front of her, looks questioningly at her.

"Did Ly write letter to you?" she asks.

"No, Mae. We don't know why…"

"Huy, Sa Pien has been pregnant for some months now. And Ly is without a trace… Mae just told Puk Ho the matter. You've seen, he was furious and wanted to kill Sa Pien… What can I do now, son?"

Huy sits stone-dead, his mind is confused. How can a young fellow somewhat boyish like him know about such complicated matters? He blames Ly inwardly for his indifference and pitilessness and looks at Sa Pien with pity. She looks so much pale and haggard, and under her eyes there are black rings for many sleepless and worried nights.

"The lads in this phum scorned Sa Pien and spoke behind her back," Mae Sa Rinh continues, her voice choked with emotion and she almost moved to tears. "And she dares not go any where now. What a torment for Mae and my daughter, son!"

"Don't say any more, Mae!" Sa Pien winces.

He looks out at things in the front yard. They are sinking into a yellow sunshine. The sour fruit tree whose fruit Mae Sa Rinh once picked to cook samlo mchu with chicken to serve him and his friends is rocking in the wind, its leaves still fresh with an indifferent greenish. A slender misty smoke is rising up from the smoky fire to drive away mosquitoes at the corner of the yard. The two water buffaloes are lying to chew leisurely the cut. Now and then they lazily wag their tails to drive away the flies. The old ragged-feather hens are searching hurriedly the last worms under the dump; the little chickens run hovering around the hens' legs and chirp noisily as if they want to urge their mothers to go for a sleep. The spruce white-dotted cock has just jumped onto the lowest branch of the star-apple tree, where he reserves as his bedroom. He leans his head sideways, looks down at his wives and children on the ground and clucks in his throat. All of a sudden, he stands up, jerks his crest aside, stretching his throat and crows in a flat, haughty way. Everything – the sunlight, the trees and bushes in the yards, the chickens, the buffaloes and the faint bluish smoke – is just like any other afternoon, but in the still air now there is something so heavy that Huy feels his heart clenched by anxiousness.

He remembers once he heard the two siblings Kromum and Khla talking to each other. The former was about thirteen, and her younger sister about nine years old. They chatted with innocent, funny words. They were screening rice and Huy was pounding rice near them then. He was thinking something when he suddenly began to notice at their conversation.

"Boong Kromum," Khla asked. "Do you like to go far, very, very far, to lots of places when you bigger?"

"What for?" the older sister asked.

"To see everything, to know everything and all." the younger replied.

"Well, I do like that, but how, why, you can only go so far like that if you were very rich, Khla."

"I wish I can go," Khla said. "I'm so bored to see everyday just like everyday, and I just see the old and familiar Svay Mountain when I look out over the distance. Is there any mountain bigger than Svay Mountain at the far places? Oh, boong Kamum, do you know what's the biggest thing in the world?" she asked.

"The earth's biggest, surely. There're so many people and pigs and cattle and mountains and rivers and all, them all lying on the earth." Kromum said.

"It's not true," Khla opposed. "I heard *Luc Ta*[1] Sa Gong said that Love's the biggest one."

"How can it be? Love's in our stomachs and our heads, how can it be biggest?"

"*Luc Ta* said that all long rivers and big mountains can be measured, boong. He said that even the earth, though it's very, very big, can be measured, boong. But Love's very much bigger, and nobody can measure it. Thing can't be measured surely the real biggest thing."

"How can it be? If it's so big, you'll get stomach-broken and head-broken if that Love creeps into your stomach and your head! Nonsense!"

"Yeah, it's right! Don't know why *Luc Ta* said like that. But *Luc Ta* never tells no lie, so why, boong?"

"I don't know! You go to ask *Luc Ta* himself!"

At this, Khla turned toward Huy and asked, "Boong Huy, do you see that *Luc Ta*'s right? Luc Ta never tells no lie, doesn't he?"

Huy stopped pounding. He leaned his chin onto the pestle's top handle. He scratched his head, and grinned at Khla, "No, he doesn't. But it's too difficult to explain. You just need to know that it's right to say Love's bigger than the earth. All right now?"

He just answered them cursorily then. But now, he suddenly feels that there is something like the simple truths in the pointless conversation of the kids; and in *Luc Ta* Sa Gong's answer too. "Does man always craves for far trips; crave for knowledge of new and strange things? Is Love really the biggest one?" he wonders.

***

About half an hour after Huy leaves Mae Sa Rinh's house, Quan gathers the whole platoon for an urgent meeting. He too has just come home from a meeting in the battalion headquarters.

"Phai cook and prepare compressed rice," Quan announces shortly. "Everybody prepare rice for five days of operation and ammunition of full base. Our battalion will go on the sortie right at eight o'clock tonight. Regiment's scouts have found a very larger enemy power going southeastward to the inland from the borderland. We'll gather at Kralanh Stream area, more than twenty four miles away from here. And our fighting plan is as follows: Two companies will go across the stream to the other side, cut the way of east- northeast direction to block the retreat way of the enemy to the eastern forests. When the enemy is driven away by the regiment power and runs to our ambush, No. 11 Company will attack its flank, No. 12 Company goes around for diversion. Our platoon will be attached to No. 13 Company to cut the way crossing the stream of the enemy. I assign Gia Huong and Bui staying home to protect our base and only one AK is left at home, all other arms will be out for the battle. Fighting assignment for the positions is as usual, fighting plan of A level."

The soldiers hastily disperse to prepare for the operation. Afterward, they gather again to have their meals, and noisily chat to each other in a high spirit because of the exciting battle.

It is a sultry night. The soldiers' uniforms are soaked with sweat within ten minutes after their departure. The crescent moon begins to appear on the horizon, casting down a sort of milky, dim light onto the plain along the Ang Trapaing Thmor edge, where the soldiers go by. When they come by the 1st Battalion's base, Huy sees that a long formation is moving toward the north, following an angle of 30 degree from his battalion. "So the whole regiment is on sortie tonight. For a very long time we have had no battle with such a larger power," he thinks.

His battalion arrives at the gathering place at about three o'clock. Captain Bao orders the companies to cross the stream to deploy the fighting formation at the other side. The platoons such as mortar, DKZ, communication and transportation stay at this side of the stream to support.

Kralanh is a big stream. Even its narrowest bed is more than twenty-five yards wide. And, sure enough, it is a deep stream too. A soldier of the 1st Battalion drowned here while crossing the stream in the flooding season of last July. Along both sides of the stream, there scatter many bushes of catclaw mimosa (mimosa pigra). The soldiers hate and fear most this kind of wicked plant. The only way to do if you encounter it is to avoid it and go another way; it is only waste of time and of a little of blood to involve in this plant. Under the moonlight, such huge dark bushes of catclaw mimosa stand loomed larger as if they want to menace the soldiers.

In turn, the companies cross the stream and spread over after the combat plan. Lieutenant Thu, Head of No. 13 Company places the 12.7mm machinegun at the front, between Platoon 8 and Platoon 9 at the left-hand side and Platoon 7 at the right-hand side, all of them spreading evenly and forming an arc along the zigzag streamside.

On both sides of the stream, running oblique toward the southeast is a grassy plain spreading out over to the horizon, and there are only a few bushes and low trees. Opposite to the streamside and more than three yards away at the north stands a thin forest. Having finished formation arrangement of his platoon, Quan looks around over the terrain and heads toward Thu.

"Hey, Mr. Thu," he says. "This streamside is too low and flat and gets no thing for shield, so you should remind the soldiers to dig shelters, otherwise, our brothers will be easily wounded or killed when the enemy overflows here."

"No problem! Don't worry. We'll move in fighting and not lying at just a place, so it's no need to dig shelters. It's had better to let them have a rest and they'll fight well."

"It's impossible, Mr. Thu. We're to move when we attack, and this time our main task is to prevent the enemy to cross the stream. It's too clear here that you'll expose your soldiers to the guns of the enemy. Please think it over again. We would rather be a little more tired than to waste our brothers' blood." Quan tries to convince Thu.

Thu makes a wry smile and shakes his head, saying no word. He begins to feel offended, but trying to control himself, partly because of his respect to Quan. "Hm, just want to teach me, don't you?" he thinks. "This Thu has fought hundreds of battles and became a head of company from the position of a private; he's not a wet-behind-the-ears scholastic officer!"

Quan feels that Thu is hurt, so he says no more. He sadly come back to his own platoon and has his soldiers to dig shelters.

The ground along the streamside full of pebbles, and the hoes hit strongly to it just breaking out a thin layer of small pieces. Quan has to dig together with his soldiers. It is early dawn when they stop.

About half an hour later, while the soldiers are devouring their handful of compressed rice preparing since the last afternoon, the gunshots begins to be heard at the north, about five miles away. B40 rocket launchers and mortars and other guns are fired repeatedly for a while and then there comes a dead silence. Half an hour more, the enemy begins to appear at the thin forest edge.

Never have before, even in the big battles at the borderland, the soldiers seen so many enemy gunmen at a time. Thousands of them, moving to and fro behind the trees and bushes, teem in a whole forest edge like a larger flock of ants.

Everybody waits no more. The enemy is attacking them, and they fire immediately. The gun smoke soon covers a larger area around the battlefield. The enemy has much more casualties, but it is so crowded and trying to open a way to escape the pincer jaws of the regiment coming down from the upper land, so when the front bodies fall down, they become a layer of shelters for the rear to creep forward. The distance between the two opponents is more and more shorten. Many soldiers of No. 13 Company have died and wounded. The mortar and DKZ shells firing from the back streamside fall behind the enemy's back, or stuck in the bushes at the other streamside if they lower the range of shooting.

The battle is dragging more than an hour; the disadvantage now inclines to the Vietnamese soldiers. Their formation is split up into small groups which are to be broken soon.

Now the soldiers just fire their guns at will, without any instruction. Each time the 12.7 machinegun spits a salvo, a layer of enemy bodies falls down again. At the beginning of the battle, Thuan fires the gun. But a small piece of a broken B40 shell nearby hits his shoulder and throws him down. Quan hands Huy his AK, carries Thuan to the back and returns to continue the fighting. Huy lies at his left-hand side, shoots short salvos into the dark blue uniformed shadows. At both wings of the machinegun, all AKs of the platoon are fired now. The enemy soon fixes the location of the big gun. They aim some of their B40s to the target, trying to destroy this dangerous battery. The B shells continuously break out near around the soldiers. Huy's ears are in a tinnitus mood and almost stone-deaf soon with the gunfire of the machine gun and the Bs broken shells. Luckily, they have the shelters so hardly to be defeated. The sunshine is so tense now, casting down a hot and bright light onto their heads, but nobody caring of it. In their mind now, the upward blood is many times hotter than the sunlight. The dust is so tense that the soldiers get many convulsive coughs; their throats are dry, bitter and choked up.

Huy fires some shots toward a Pot's soldier when he rises up, intending to fire a B shell, the shots miss, but still force the enemy soldier to lie down motionless. Suddenly, he hears somebody's vague shout. It is from Quan. He seems to shout something, but Huy cannot hear it. And he sees that Quan creeps back toward the hiding place of the cartridge carriers. He understands at one that the gun is out of cartridges, and Quan has to creep back to get some more. Huy turns again to the front to fire. He has fired four cartridge magazines and half of the separate bullets of the AK ammunition base, though he has tried to save them. He manages to put the bullets into the cartridge magazines when the Pot's soldiers lie down.

The enemy now takes advantage of the silence of the big gun; they pours plenty of volleys and move forward to the battery; one guy at the left-hand side, and two or three guys at the right-hand side. Huy takes the grenade hooked on his hip, undo its safety pin and wait. When the Pot's soldiers at his right-hand side approaching within the range, he throws the grenade toward them. His opponents are thrown back away with the bang. Then he turns to his opponents at the other side.

In a short moment, Quan creeps back to the gun. Two cartridge belts around his shoulder and his hands pull two other cartridge boxes. "So, all cartridges of the ammunition base number are brought here now," Huy thinks. He dares not think about the aftermath of this. The enemy shots still plough up the ground around them. The bushes and small trees are cut short or broken into small bits.

Quan finishes fixing the new feed belt into the gun and begins to cock the gun. Suddenly, his body slightly jerks, and then he bends down forward. On his left forehead, blood comes out in a spurt, and his nape now is a mix of doughy blood and brain. Thuan who is lying behind him tries to sit up, and then, ignoring his own wound, he bursts out a painful scream, rushes forward and hugs Quan's body. And just a few seconds later, he lets loose the dead body, grasps the puller to cock, his face soaked with tears. The 12.7 mm machinegun shakes strongly. The barrel blooms out fire-flowers and begins to be red hot. The hemp cloth wrapping up the barrel end behind the bead begins to raise smoke. In a moment, Huy spots all those spectacles. Whether he himself screams or cries or does something else then, he does not know. His latest actions then are beyond his control. When he tries to recall it afterward, he just remembers that he still kept fighting. As for how he fought and how long did the battle come to an end, and how they returned to their base, those are like a dark cloud of mist in his consciousness.

The situation of No. 12 Company then is equally tragic. Its formation is in great disorder. Heads of Platoon 7 and 8 are dead, two third of the troops are wounded or died as well. The survivors try to weakly resist the enemy, and are forced to move backward to a place behind the machine gun battery. The enemy soldiers flood in from all sides; at the front, at the right, at the left, anywhere the attacking enemy is seen.

At a place some hundred yards from the battery, Thu, head of company, with a bloody wound on his left shoulder, is firing his AK gun half-heartedly. Lying near him is a communication soldier and Duy, his liaison. They are separated from the formation and try to fight now like the worms falling into a nest of brutal red ants. Thu is firing and shouting into the PRC25 walkie-talkie, ignoring all coded words, "Thirteen is surrounded! Thirteen is surrounded! Do give us urgently support!..."

His shout is interrupted half way. A B40 shell breaks out right in front of him. When the clouds of dust and smoke have dissolved, there are only three dark burnt and broken corpses on the ground.

The battalion fire powers, which have moved backward a short distance then, are firing on a larger scale to support, but can only drive the enemy toward a wing of the streamside at the lower of the battlefield. The enemy has crossed one-third to the other side. And the rest at this streamside attacks loosely now lest it should miss the chance to escape. The gunshot sounds reduce, and a moment later, only the mortars shells are heard broken after the enemy's back.

The regiment power reaches the battlefield near an hour later. They does not expect that the enemy gathers at this place, much more important, the ambush power is too thin in comparison with the enemy's, so it has almost been cleared out. No. 11 and No. 12 Companies have encountered some smaller enemy troops at their direction and pinned down right there, not be able to support.

This late afternoon, as the last red glows are fading away, a few peasants who still linger in the fields see some dozen of ox-carts passing by their places, drawing a cloud of grey dust on the red-purple horizon; on each one are two or three Vietnamese coongtop corpses which are covered by a thin bright blue nylon coat.

The nearby villagers soon know that many Vietnamese koongtops died in the battle of that autumn morning. They tells and retells the story to each other, and each one even adds some details about the characters and face of this soldier, and love story of the other one. The battle becomes a tragic legend, and each villager fancies that he or she has had some acquaintanceship with one or another among those soldiers who have past away.

In this battle, thirty-nine men, including officers, non-commissioned officers and soldiers, became the martyrs. A battle brought a heavy loss on both human resource and fighting spirit to the whole regiment. Very long time afterward, the nearby villagers still recall of the sight of that day, as if it is a never fading accident in their memories – the memories of quiet lives, with simple sadness and happiness, and almost nothing to remember.

CHAPTER 15

Time still passes quickly as ever. And Huy has been away from home for more than two years. His homesick is no longer strong, and he rarely writes letters. Some four or five months he has just sent home a letter. He has also receives less home letters than the time before. Sometimes, he even fancies that he has been a soldier since his birth; and that he has lived this life for a very long time, and then suddenly, a home letter reminds him that he has a family in that far away country, and that there are still invisible yet firm links between him and his intimates at his homeland.

There have been so many changes in the platoon. Quan died long ago. The old soldiers such as Nam, Bui, Qui, Thien, Moi, Gia Huong, U Moi have in turn been demobilized; and there are many new comers such as Vu, Kien, Quang, and so on. Huy is the platoon leader now. Time passes, and it also brings him many changes. He is no longer in hot temper and eagerness, easy to be sad and to be happy like before. His temper now is calm down, though his nature is unchanged. Huy is a sensitive person, not at its normal but special meaning. He is overly melancholy and sentimental. His thoughts and way to see the life are both of superannuation and silliness. He is a sort of person that is often called mockingly as a "daylight dreamer". The people like him do not looks at the life with its real colors and lines, but with an invisible filter through which everything is covered with a romance, uncommon aspect, whether much more complicated or absolutely simplified; the sort of person that unconsciously prefers to living in his dreams than in his real life.

A very long time after Quan's death, his sadness still remains. Many nights, he has been laying restlessly, tears rolling down on his cheeks as he thought of Quan. Quan's relics, which were given back to the platoon, consisted of his diary notebook, the poem notebook that Huy had read once, and the jade bracelet. Huy has read the two notebooks again many times, and then fired them as Quan's wish. In his diary, right at the first page, he wrote, "IF I DIE AND SOMEONE

GET THIS DIARY BY CHANCE, PLEASE FIRE IT RIGHT AWAY!" Reading the diary, Huy has felt that its owner was still enigmatic and strange as his first feelings toward him. The more he knows about Quan's thoughts, the more he finds that they are so vague and far away from his people, just like something beyond human awareness. He himself has many thoughts, but they are close and attached to the everyday life. As for Quan, such thought are very, very far away things. Nevertheless, in his mind, Quan is still a noble man. A star that just flashes in a short moment, yet left in the witness' memory a wonderful and forever being light.

As for the bracelet, Huy has buried it under the ground in front of Mae Sa Rinh's charnel house. Sa Pien did not want to keep it, but it still forever belonged to her anyway. So, just let it be saved by Mae, and she would have given it back to Sa Pien some day, as their souls met each other's again at the heaven, if heaven and the world of the dead could have really existed.

Mae died later than Quan's death about two months. The grief caused by Sa Pien's situation, and then, the death of Quan, these two occurences have taken off her the remaining little old health. When he got the bad news of Mae, Huy sat stone-dead, his throat choked, and his mind stupefied and puzzled. He could cry out loudly no more. Some days after Mae's incineration, Sa Pien left home to somewhere no one knew. Some time later, there were humors that she was seen to live in a little inn alongside the provincial road of Battambang Town, together with a middle aged man. The house where once has been cozy and happy, with Sa Pien's cheerful and gentle voice, with the spinning sounds in the late afternoons, is very desolate and quiet like a graveyard now.

One day, Huy paid Puk Ho a visit. He sat looking at Puk whose hair had been once shiny black but almost whole grey now; looking at his gloomy face and his moist, spleenful eyes; and he almost shed tears after the old man. Puk seldom left home, except the times he came to sit for hours in front of Mae's charnel house, where her ashes were kept. He sat huddled on the ground, his head bending down, his arms folded up around his knees, as if he was embracing his grief and regret.

For a very long time later, sometimes Huy wonders again that whether what happened and concerned so many fates of which he has known during that time is really casualness, or has been wrongly and awkwardly fixed by some unknown supernatural power. The life converges the people from many difference departing points, links them together in invisible connections, and then, just like a callous and brutal wave, it sweeps away, clears out everything. The sole remains are memories. And might be, at this one, they cling to him, root in him like the roots of wild trees on the cliffs, but at the other, they are just like a passing by wind. Sometimes, he tells himself that those are just his fancies. He tries to keep away from them, to forget them. But, all of a sudden, in a short moment, like a lightning, they flash in his mind, and cause him a sharp pain in his heart, so short, but almost unendurable.

Huy still does not forget Quan's words in their conversation a midday at the borderland, never forget it – *"...you are so sensitive and have so many illusions. That is no good for you. Due to it you will suffer so much."* That Quan has felt this by his thought, his experience, or just a casual intuition, Huy can never know exactly. He just realizes that Quan's words are strangely right toward him. The more he lives, the more he has deeper thoughts and knowledge about people and things around, and the more he judges matters exactly. But besides things belonging to reason, there is also in him a strong control of sentiment. The conflict between reason and sentiment makes him confused and indecisive. At last, his actions often follow his sentiment than his reason – it guides him and instructs him, and if he does not obey its deep orders, he will be always in torment and restlessness. Reason just keeps its role as a historical critic; it will criticize and judge what right and wrong, but just only afterward, when things come into the past. Sometimes he asks himself if there is anyone in his shoes. Worst of all, he realizes so clearly his weakness, but cannot overcome or even deny it. Or, it is just a sort of self-conflict that everyone has, though in one form or another?

CHAPTER 16

In early rainy season, the battalion is ordered to build its new base at another place. Captain Bao strictly forbids the soldiers to take along anything from the old base; the houses and stores will be reserved in whole to hand over to a battalion of the 74th Regiment. The new place is a thin forest, far from the villages; the nearest phum is about six miles away. So once again the soldiers have to do everything from the beginning to build the houses and fortifications: cutting down trunks for the posts, making thatches for the roofs and so on. Everyone is rather sad. They are not afraid of hard works. They are sad because they have had so trong attachment to the old base and the villagers. The paths in between the squads and platoons are so familiar that they cannot miss the way even if they go along it with shutting eyes. The clusters of Ten O'clock Flower (Moss-rose) and Thai Magic Carpet planted last year along the paths or in the ground basins in front of the houses are at their most beauty now, with verdant leaves and blooming flowers being seen everywhere in warm sunny days. The houses just have been renewed. The sparrows and starlings have become familiar with the soldiers; they have often landed down in crowded flocks at the meal times waiting for some handful of redundant cooked rice from the soldiers. Everyone has his intimate family at the phum and has adopted mother, father or adopted brothers, sisters. All such things, though little or big, important or not, have formed the Sentiment and Intimateness that soothe them and help them to lessen their homesick. But what else can they do now? Soldier life is a succession of journeys, a succession of casual meeting and separation. So to be regretful is only to make one's heart heavier.

The platoons are hastily to cut bamboo trees and make thatches so that they can build immediately their houses after the arrival.

After two weeks of preparation, they depart on a fine day of April. Each platoon has managed to borrow some ox-carts to transport their stuffs. Huy meets Soun's mother while he is in the phum to take the ox-carts. He stops and asks after her, and tells her about the removal of his battalion.

"Where do you go again, son?" Mae asks surprisingly.

"To a place near the deserted phum, about twenty miles from here, Mae. And there'll be another army unit coming here to stay," Huy says.

"Why don't they go there, and you all are still to be here?" Mae asks.

"It's impossible, Mae. This is the plan of the leaders, and we must follow it."

Mae shakes her head sadly. Huy says good-bye to her, sends his regards to Soun, and then goes hurriedly to the ox-cart owners' houses. He encourages himself that he should not be so sad, that he will certainly come back here to visit Mae and Soun and other people when it is possible.

Yet as soon as the ox-carts leave the base, he spots Soun standing among some dozens of women and children. They come there to bid farewell to the soldiers. Soun does not see him yet because he is mingling with the crowd of soldiers and the heavy loaded carts. She is looking for him, eagerly, embarrassingly and sadly.

"Hey, Soun!" he waves his hand and calls her loudly.

"Boong Huy!" she shouts jubilantly and then shut up. She is almost shedding tears and does not know what to say.

Huy looks into her red eyes, feel very touched. He too does not know what to say now. So many things have happened continuously – No.13 Company was cleared out, Quan's death, Mae Sa Rinh's death, Sa Pien left her home, even Chip, the pet starling which U Moi has given him as a souvenir caught cold and died long ago – All those things made him plunged into deep grief. He has rarely come to the phum, rarely met Soun, and worst of all, has forgotten his promise to make a lamp for her. "Why do I just remember it right now?" Huy shouts inwardly, and feels angry with himself. He steps unconsciously following the carts, yet he keeps looking back at her over his shoulder without a wink. He can only shout back when he goes so farther from her, "Don't be so sad, Soun! I'll come back to meet you again. I'll make you a lamp, more beautiful than the old one!"

He cannot help looking back at her little dear shape until it is hidden behind the clouds of dust and the green mulberry tree shades. Her sad red eyes still obsess him until he arrives at the new place.

The soldiers reach the location at midday. They look depressedly at the catclaw mimosa bushes with lot of hairy fruits on them. The fruits are rocking in the winds as if they want to threaten silently: "Get away from us, or you folks will be miserable!"

They quickly unload the stuffs, say thanks and see the villagers off, then immediately set to work.

They work hard until dusk, save the rest time for meal in the afternoon. Anyone is very hungry and tired out. Their faces and hands are torn scratched by the thorns. Their bodies are terribly itchy though they dare not take off their coat to prevent the hairy fruit. The itch is less tense while the soldiers are working, but it begins to persecute them now. The more they scratch, the more their bodies are itchy, and it is ineffective even though they scratch until their skins are bloody torn. At last, they build a fire to dry their bodies and feel that it was better. Afterward, they come to a spring some two hundred yards away to take a bath and then return for the supper.

The following day, when they are clearing the bushes, Thuan discover a big hive of honeybees. He fires a torch made of dry twigs and grass and put it in front of the hive. The disturbed bees fly out and attack the soldiers. They run to the spring, jump into it and dive, and are released only after a long while.

Nevertheless, Thuan still gets near two bidons of yellow honey. He is handing Huy a bidon for tasting when Captain Bao approaches.

Bao has partly changed his temper recently. He is gentler, and hits or curses at the soldiers no more. He drinks much less alcohol too. And he looks even open and cheerful now. He smiles at Huy and says, "Wow, 12.7 platoon's lucky, eh? Got honey and a noisy attack from the bees!"

"So terrible, sir!" Huy replies. "We'd have got great trouble with the bees if there's not this spring." He gives Bao the bidon of honey, "You try it."

Bao takes it, tries a small gulp and says, "Good," he gives back the bidon and looks around, "All right, continue your work. Try to finish the houses and dig the trenches early. I'll go to DKZ platoon now."

He goes off. Huy passes the bidon to the others so that each one can taste it, and then they continue to work.

About midnight, a rain begins to pour heavily. The soldiers just hang their hammocks under the trees because they have no time for camping. At first, they are too sleepy and tired to wake up, so they cover the hammocks with the nylon pieces and try to sleep again. Yet the rain is more and more heavily. And the rain water soon follows the hammock strings down and makes the soldier backs soaking wet and cold. Not be able to sleep again, they sit up reluctantly, take off their clothes, wrap themselves up with the nylon pieces and sit close to each other, chatting and waiting for the dawn.

The rain threads its way down through the leaf layers of the trees, tapping upon the nylon coats and making an evenly monotonous sound. The water soaks into the rotten leaf layer, meets the warm air of the ground and pervades a cloud of mist. The whole platoon sit shoulder to shoulder, looking at the pervading mist around, chatting softly and sometimes one or another burst out again a sporadic cough or a peal of giggles. Their stories are as rambling endlessly as the rain. The night seeming endless is over at last, but the rain is still prolonged.

All next day, it is still raining, at times heavily and at times slightly. The soldiers work under the rain, but with a slower speed. Luckily, it is sunny and warm on the following days. Yet everyone tries to work harder because they are afraid that it may rain again and their work would be slowed down. Huy devotes himself to work – paring wood, digging trench, roofing the houses, etc – without a rest. His body now is steel-like; whatever you curve or hit or stretch it, its steely nature is unchanged. Not only steel, but fire also is in him now! The fire in him is burning, more and more strongly. Sometimes, when he stops working to roll a cigarette, he misses Quan very much. Quan takes a big place in his heart. He did not realize this when Quan was alive, but he realizes it now. Whenever he thinks of Quan, he feels an unendurable sadness. A losing and painful feeling, almost a pain of body, makes him exhausted and want to cry madly so that the heaven and his own pain would have dissolved into tears. But that crying just happens silently in his heart. Tears do not come out upon the eyes. They turn into black blood and bitter gall and flow back to the heart.

Everything is well done at last. Houses and paths and trenches are all fine and neat. And the battalion is allowed to rest for a month. In the spare time, Huy and his comrades go fishing at the spring. At first, they sit leisurely on the streamside like Jiang Ziya[1] waiting for his good king, soon later, they use their mosquito nets as fishing nets, but although they come to and fro, stirring up a long distance in the spring, only some little fishes and shrimps which are not enough for a mouthful are caught. The fishes and shrimps and crabs are all gone soon because there are hundred of men hunting them daily. "We have to grow vegetable and raise chicken to get good meals; we must stop abusing the nature excessively like that," Huy thinks, "but until then, just have only salt and dry fish sauce!"

A few days later, the soldiers begin to weed and make vegetable beds and melon trellises. They have water spinach seeds enough for five big beds and some green pea seeds that Mae Sa Rinh has given Quan long ago. About half a month later, they begin to have vegetable in the meals.

Gradually, they become fond of this new place. Their houses are built along the streamside. In front of the houses there are many bushy trees dropping their roots upon the water. There is always a wet steam pervading in the air. In the mornings, the space is melodious with many singing birds. Sometimes, a nightingale would come to perch right at the gable and sing its songs over night. Its sweet songs helps the soldiers to forget their sadness in their watch, pouring down soft and gentle tunes into the sleeping soldiers' ears and brings them peaceful nice dreams.

Unexpectedly, the soldiers feel as if they were some hermits or poets who conceal themselves here to lead a leisured life.

One day, Huy meets Thai, deputy head of scout platoon, when he comes to the spring to take a bath at midday. They talk ramblingly for a while, and then Thai says, "We'll go to reconnoiter at the east of Chandai tonight."

Wandering in his mind, Huy is suddenly startled as he hears of Chandai. Suddenly, a hungry nostalgia floods up his heart. He misses Mae Sa Rinh; misses Puk Ho; misses Sa Pien; misses the two brothers Kan and Lum; misses the two siblings Kromum and Khla; misses Soun's Mae... But the one that he misses most, more than anyone else is Soun! Huy suddenly realizes that now. He interrupts Thuan, "Well, let me go with you. We'll pass the phum when we return. You all wait for me outside. I come in the phum to visit a friend."

"She is Soun "the black eyes", isn't she?" Thai grinned broadly. "Huy, the whole battalion knew your story already! All right, this evening you come to my house, we'll get supper and drink tea before departing."

Huy is eager all this afternoon. Since his coming here, he has seldom thought of Soun. Yet her image is very dear to him already, and it has occupied a small but so significant place in his heart. Each time when he thinks of her, his heart is strangely warm and tender and agitated. He realizes the first time now that he can never forget this girl. The first time he admits shyly to himself his sentiment, "So, I really love Soun now. Oh, Soun! I love you indeed, don't you know?" He takes no rest this afternoon. He chooses one among the medicine pots and carefully makes a lamp to give Soun as his promise long ago. This is the most beautiful lamp that he has made so far. Previously, he has simply made a lamp for use. Yet today he makes it with love and great happiness.

The scouts and Huy go through that night, cutting a zigzag trail toward the coordinate place at the eastern forest. They arrive at the place at about three o'clock, taking a short rest, eating the compressed rice, and laying ambush to the end of next day. They find out nothing. A very long day passes slowly. The evening clouds change from bright red into yellow and then dim purple behind the mountains. A little while after nightfall, they begin to cut a short trail to the top end of the phum. Having arrived at the old tree standing at the phum's edge, the three scouts stop. They scatter toward three directions and forming three tops of a triangle, hiding themselves behind the bushes. Huy steps sneakily from one to another tree or bush to enter the phum.

It is early night, but the air is very quiet in the phum. The soldiers of the 74th Regiment have just come here, still being strange to the place, so they dare not come to the phum at night. Very few houses are lighted; the phum is almost dark and dull. Huy carefully goes across the wooden fences, listening to the sounds. It is not at all useless to be so careful. Almost in every house in those remote phums there are men following the enemy. Although the villagers still have good sympathy toward the Vietnamese soldiers, but as for their relatives who join the enemy army, certainly, he and they cannot treat each other with sympathy if he encounters them. He recalls once he and Gia Huong visited Ta Nuok's house, the old man told them when it was twilight, "You two sons come home now and come here another day, it's no good to stay here now."

Huy realized something enigmatic in his attitude because he had been often very happy to have the soldiers as his guests. When the two were some distance from his house, Gia Huong explained, "He did so to avoid an encounter between us and his grandson. The kid ran to Pot's army a few years ago. Sometimes, he returns home to ask the old man for his money or rice."

"Isn't he afraid that we'll lay ambush and arrest his grandson, brother?" Huy asked.

"He knows that we're not such kind of mean soldiers, sure enough. It'll be different if we meet the lad in the battlefield, but in such times like this, he comes home not for fighting with us, so we had better ignore him." Gia Huong said.

Huy understands completely now what Gia Huong meaned as he is in the same situation. He sneaks into the phum in order to meet Soun, so he does not want to fire his gun or even has an unnecessary noisy encounter. But he has to fire in compelling situation. And to avoid such situation, it is not overly at all to be careful a little bit.

Reaching Soun's house ladder foot, he stands still for a while, looks up to the house. The lamp has been put out inside, and he cannot guess if Mae and Soun are awake or not. He claps slightly upon his trouser pocket; the lamp is still there safely. He creeps gently up the ladder and then stops at the highest step, leant his back against the wooden bar and sit as still as a statue for a long while. The time is of a standstill then. "How long does it last, some minutes, some hours, or some centuries?" he asks himself. His sense of time ceases to work now. In his mind, there are only Soun's images.

Soun, with her simple white shirt and her big round eyes, like an angel, looked stealthy at him at the wedding. Soun, who was coy when he invited her to dance ramvong. Soun, her face reddened listening to his teasing words, spoken out by Chip, the starling. Soun, her eyes casting down dreamily, her long beautiful hair hanging loosely down to her shoulders, and her long curl eyelashes moving gently the day she and Sa Pien came to his base. Soun, her sad red eyes looked after him when he left the old base... He is startled and wakes up from his dream by a sound of body turning inside of the house, and then Soun's voice – gentle and clear and sweet – resounded in the quiet air of the night, "Mae, did you sleep?"

"No," Mae says.

"I'll go to the district market with boong Myun tomorrow. I want to buy for you a new krama, Mae. Your old krama is torn out."

"Don't, my dear. Just buy for yourself whatever you like, I need nothing. My krama can be used for some time more."

"I like nothing, I just like you'd be happy. Say yes to me, Mae."

"Yes, well, just do as you like. Get your sleep now, dear."

The body-turning sounds again, this time of both mother and daughter. Then silence. Huy sits for a long while more but he hears nothing more save the soft breaths. Soun and Mae are soundly asleep already. He pulls the lamp out of his pocket, puts it near the doorway.

Soun will see it tomorrow when she opens the door. She will know who put it there. And she will be very happy then, sure enough.

"So long, dear Soun!" he murmurs, and quickly, but still carefully, returns to the old tree at the phum's edge. The scouts must be so anxious now, and might have cursed inwardly at him too!

CHAPTER 17

The months pass silently, and no special thing happens to the platoon until one late autumn night.

It is so late. Now and then, the cold winds blow by. The leaves above the soldiers rustle in the winds and countless dewdrops fall down wetting their coats. The ambushing night is half over. It will be dawn soon. Tuan and Thuan sit leaning against two big trunks, asleep. Huy stretches out his legs, changes his sitting posture to feel easier. "Just let Tuan sleep a little while more then I'll change the watch," he thinks. A few verses occur to him some moment ago have pushed away his sleepiness. He looks up to the sky. The moon, as thin as a white porcelain sickle, has moved toward the southwest, casting down upon everything a dim light. Suddenly, he thinks that he just hears some vague sounds from the north of the forest. He lies down on his stomach; put one of his ears upon against the ground and listens carefully. It's right. There are sounds of steps and of the ox-cart wheels grinding on the tough surface.

The crackling sounds of the wheels are nearer and nearer to the ambush site. Then from the forest corner, the shapes of a group of people and five or six ox-carts appear under the crescent moonlight. There are also shapes sitting on the carts and walking hastily behind them. Huy waves his hand up to give signals for the rest to be ready for firing. Those people are not civilians, sure enough; they must be enemies, or smugglers, because the people at this unsafe borderland never go out in the dusk. The carts and people are so nearer now that Huy realizes there are women's shapes on the carts. He turns to Tuan, shakes his head slightly.

In the ambush nights like that, the soldiers often encounter their enemy. But they are often a group of Pot's soldiers sneak to the nearby phums to take rice or to make a raid on the Vietnamese bases, and Huy has never seen women in such groups before. "How will we do? Let them go off? Fire?" In Huy's mind, the two opposite thoughts are still fighting with each other yet the men go ahead have passed the site where he had put the DH10 (orientation) mine. It is absolutely sure that these people are enemy now. The shapes of the AKs and Chinese B40 rocket launching guns are seen clearly under the moonlight. In a flash of moment, Huy makes his decision. He presses lightly on Tuan and Thuan's shoulders and points his forefinger toward two directions – the secret signal to spread out the fighting formation, and then he opens the safety pin of the gun. There are about ten gunmen among the enemy group. And there are only three Vietnamese soldiers who lay ambush here. But they have the advantage of hiding themselves in the dark and can fire in advance to take initiative.

Huy decides that it is no need to turn on the electric detonator of the mine but just fire their guns. He estimates that in the first salvo, they can kill a half of the enemies. And the rest will be resolved soon. The main matter is they will not shoot the women. The men walking ahead are about a dozen of yards from them now.

The enemies are carrying their guns on their shoulders. They will waste at least two seconds to hold down their gun to fire back. The leading man is six yards from Huy now. Huy holds up his gun and fires continuously some double shots. Tuan and Thuan also fire simultaneously right after his shots. The oxen are scared and run hysterically away, bring with them the women on the carts. After the first salvo, four men are knocked down, and two among them are B40 gunners. The rest runs scattered to the trees on both sides of the path and fires back. They seem to know that their opponent power is so small through the shots. These enemy soldiers are really the warlike and very experienced gunmen.

The sound of gunshots rouses up the forest corner for a long while. Obviously, those enemy soldiers are very bull-headed, they fire back in moderation, waste no bullets, and seeming to set their mind not to retreat. Huy thinks for a short moment and realizes that they want to take away the corpses of their comrades. Having decided to approach nearer to put to an end their lives, Huy shouts loudly, "Fire more strongly to help me to charge!"

Thuan and Tuan fire a few long salvos. Huy takes advantage this moment to creep ahead. The trunk where an enemy is hiding and firing back is only six yards from him now. Huy rolls his body over toward another trunk and pours a short salvo to the man. The gunshots from him shut up. The other enemies smoothly retreat into the forest after some more salvos. A minute later, the battlefield is quiet again. Huy waves his hand and calls out Thuan and Tuan to come to gather the arms of the dead soldiers. He approaches the trunk where the enemy gunman has hidden previously. The dim moonlight is enough for him to see a motionless dark mass. He comes nearer. Suddenly, there comes a flash of light and sound of gunshots from this dark mass. Huy feels his thigh frozen cold in a shot moment, and his body becomes very weak. He falls down onto the dew-wetted grass; his ears still hear some short salvos of gunshot.

The enemy soldier is heavy wounded already but still alive, and he has waited for him to come near to deal him a revenging blow.

Right after Huy falls down, Tuan dashes toward and fires a salvo into the man to see him off to the hell. Huy pants heavily, touches his hand to his thigh, the blood is flowing out and wetting his torn out trouser leg.

***

Huy sits on a bench under the cool shadows of the trees outside his hospital room. On the branches above his head, the flower-peckers are twittering and hopping to look for worms.

The spring is drawing near.

Together with the changing season, the nurses seem more beautiful with a thin scarlet lipstick coat on their lips. Huy smiles and looks at them. There are only the wounded soldiers here. Not to mention the sick soldiers, the lightest wounded soldier just of his case – with a broken thighbone. There are men who have lost one of his leg or both two legs or got some heavier wounds. "To make up seems not appropriate to the situation here. But it doesn't matter," he thinks. "They make up themselves to help the soldiers to have more love of life, to have more courage to live a new life, with their human conditions as the handicapped. These nurses are really charming and noble. They too, have to be apart with their homeland and their families, have to suffer so much here. Yet they are till love the life and always keep gentle smiles on their faces."

In this season, the Military Hospital is crowded with wounded and sick soldiers. From the combat units, they are sent here to be cured or to wait for transferring to the country. Lying on the nearest bed from Huy's is Binh, a scout. Binh has got a heavy wound at his chest, but he recovers now after six months of curing. His unit set up commanding position at the Angkor area. He has invited Huy to visit there for a few days when they two can come out of the hospital. Luckily, Doctor Toan, in charge of wounded soldiers, has recently said that they would be allowed to come out simultaneously within a few days later. And he is very eager with this unexpected journey. He has heard lots of things about Angkor, a grandiose ancient works in the world, and often wished that he would get a chance to come there.

Binh is coming near. On his hand is a bamboo stick threading through many grilled scorpions. Huy smiles and greets him, "Just come back from the market, huh?"

"Yeah, I met that charming girl who sells grilled scorpions, I spoke to her some things and then she gave me this one. Try a little, don't you?" says Binh.

He sits on the bench, breaks in halves the bamboo stick and gives Huy one of them. They eat the grilled scorpions in silence. Having finished it, Binh wipes his mouth with his sleeve. "You've sure rarely seen scorpions there at your area. At Angkor Wat, they are of millions, teaming at the old trees' roots, rock slots and stonewall slots of the temples. But we never ate them. There're lots of birds and wild animals there. You just have to go around for a bit of time to get fresh meat," he says.

"Yes, there're some of them, but not so much there. When we stayed at Ampil, we often saw the very big ones in the ground holes when we went out to dig sand lizard holes. But we never ate them too. These are all of shells and of a little of meat, not enough for a bit of mouthful. But I must say that, he he, them that we just eat today are rather delicious," Huy says.

Binh turns his body away to look after a nurse at the distance for a while, and turns back to Huy, "Hey, my old chap, Xuan looks very beautiful today, doesn't she?"

"She's always beautiful, she's sure the belle here," Huy winks at Binh. "You're really smart to choose the belle for your love. And I found that she's very fond of you too. Why, have you two exchanged your promises to each other yet? Oh, I would drink a glass of wine to give you my blessing wish."

"There's no promise," Binh frowns. "Our soldier's life is of much more unluckiness and of much less luck. I think I am just lucky with this wound, but I don't know if I would get some more of them since now to the day we can return home or not. Huy, I'd like to talk faithfully with you that I love Xuan so much. But I can't say anything to her. Beautiful like her, she will never be short of courters. You see the doctors, who are driven crazy about her, don't you? What am I in comparison with them? Giving her my promise and she would be very pitiful if I get some trouble? No, I can't!" he stops, his face looks very sad.

"Well, we can't know how our life will be, huh. So do I. I love a Khmer girl, but just love her in silence. How can I dare hurt her if it maybe…" Huy takes a long deep sigh. Suddenly, he misses Soun very much.

***

Two soldiers and a nurse walk on the path toward the gate of the Military Hospital. The nurse holds a little cloth bag, seeming to be made by herself. They walk very slowly as if they do not want to end early the moment of farewell. And they say no word, just step onward silently. The nurse is Xuan, the girl that Binh loves very much but dared not say to her. Xuan's country is in Thai Binh province, a beautiful and tender-hearted northern girl. She loves Binh too. Her eyes tell this whenever she comes to the room to take care the wounded soldiers. But she is a girl. She cannot say anything once the boy says to her nothing. Many a time, Huy observes their manners and listens to their words and in his mind comes up many questions about life and love and this very war. Binh does not speak out because he loves her even more than he loves himself; because he does not want to make her grievous if any he would die. And Xuan does not speak out because she is waiting for his words. And he too, can he speak to Soun anything?

They reach the hospital gate. Xuan stops. The soldiers stop. The young girl looks at Binh with her passionate eyes. And she still says nothing yet. Still waits.

At last, Binh breaks the silence, "Eh, well, you should come back in, Xuan. Thank you for seeing us off," he pauses for a while, seeming choked in his throat, and then continues, "Do well your tasks here. I wish you will come home soon, and get much of happiness in your life."

Xuan still gazes at him. Still speaks no word. Still waits.

"Thank you Xuan," Huy says. "I too like to wish you to get much of luck in your life." He turns to Binh, jogs slightly his elbow upon the latter's back, shouts inwardly, "Hey! Come on! Say something now, my old chap! Just say something to give her a little bit of pleasure!"

Xuan's eyes begin to be red and swollen with tears. She holds out the cloth bag to Binh, says in a choked voice, "You two return your units and do your duties well and be safe until coming back our country. There are some kinds of tonics and vitamins in this bag, you keep them to use gradually. I come in now."

Binh nods silently. He takes the cloth bag; his hand trembles lightly. Huy looks deeply into his eyes, and sees that in the bright eyes gazing at Xuan there are thousands of words. Yet he still speaks no word.

Xuan reaches out her hand, shakes Huy's hand in a very short moment. Then she turns to Binh. He keeps her small hand in his. The two hands, like two pieces of magnets, stick strongly to each other and seem to be not able to separate again. For a long moment. At last, Binh lets his hand loose, and Xuan withdraws back her hand embarrassedly. She turns around and walks quickly to the opposite direction. Her shoulders are trembling as if she tries to keep her cry back.

She is some hundred yards away already. The soldier stands unmoved, looks at her. Suddenly, Binh seems to lose his control. His face puckers up painfully. Then he shouts loudly, "Xuan! Oh, Xuan!" He dashes toward Xuan. The girl turns her back around astonishingly, happily. They hug each other, for a long while. Xuan leans her charming face against Binh's shoulder. And they seem to murmur some things to each other. The wounded soldiers walking on the path look at them and smile with sympathy. At the hospital gate, Huy is smiling and looking at them too, moved and happy. At last, the two lovers can say things needful to say to each other.

CHAPTER 18

The road to Angkor Wat where Binh's unit locating comes through the dense forests; and there are almost military trucks to and fro only. So seldom, they meet a civilian on his motorbike or some Khmer monks walking along the road.

All the day long after they have left the hospital, the two took many short hitchhikes on the way. The military trucks carried munitions, medicines and military equipments to the units locating in the area. The jolly corporal drivers gave them a lift with pleasure. "To get you two, we have two gunmen more and surely we'd be safer," they said agreeably right after Huy and Binh asked them. There is just one uncomfortable thing: when they left the main road and turn to their locations, the two had to walk again.

About four p.m., after a walk for some four miles, they reach a small pagoda. Binh tells Huy, "We'll spend the night in the pagoda. Last year when we garrisoned near this place, I often visited the pagoda and asked the monks to give me the kitten to protect the rice store. The two old monks in this pagoda are very benevolent."

The pagoda is very small indeed, and falls into heavy decay by the war. The roof is heavy broken and the walls are dotted by bullets. Venerable Sim, the eldest monk is about seventy years old. His body is skinny, but his eyes are still very bright. The other monk, Nasuk, is in his middle fifty and has a peaceful face.

In the evening, after the supper, the old monks converse with the soldiers in a small room at the back of the pagoda. In the conversation, once in a while Huy feels missing Quan again. So many times, Quan have explained to him about Buddhism, about the profound philosophy to get the Way. He lets his mind follow his thoughts, paying little attention to the conversation between Binh and the monks. All of a sudden, one question from Binh draws him back to the reality.

Binh tells the master monk, "*Luc Ta* Sim, as I know, nowadays there are still many people who very fond of Prince Norodom Sihanouk. Last year, when I was garrisoning at this place, I knew that the folks living in the nearby phums are still hiding his picture in their houses. I can't guess how they could save the pictures during the Pol Pot's regime."

"I remember that time, about over thirty years ago," *Luc Ta* Sim says. "Under the Prince's regime, the folks were quite well-to-do. The old people always remember that time. I too can't know how they could save the Prince's pictures. Maybe those are not the old pictures but were taken later and carried here from Thailand. My dear Vietnamese koongtops, Cambodia has to bear this miserable destiny due to her karma. In the time of the powerful Khmer Empire, we have made so much of invasions, massacres and ravages. Our Khmer people have been always proud of this glorious past, but they haven't ever realized that violence would be paid for violence. Khmer people have to bear this fatal calamity; it is unavoidable. But I am both a monk and a Khmer man, so I certainly felt heart-broken with the savageness of Pol Pot and Khmer Rouge. I too escaped the death by an inch under their regime."

Huy looks at the old monk. His way of explanation is strange enough, but not to be unreasonable, because it is in accordance with Buddhism's causal principal. It occurred to him a thing, he asks the monk, "Sir, Vietnamese koongtops come here to drive away the Pol Pot army and save the Khmer people from the genocide. But why, besides the party of Mr. Heng Xam Rin, the other parties, including Prince Norodom Sihanouk's, just treat us as their enemy? Why don't they co-operate with the new Khmer government to build their country but just fight over power with each other? Most of Khmer people I met are fond of us Vietnamese soldiers. But why the other parties' leaders just oppose us, consider us as the invasion army?"

The old monk looks thoughtfully at Huy for a long while. He says at last, "This has its reason. Between Cambodia and her powerful neighbors – Vietnam to the east and Thailand to the north – there was a vendetta since so long time ago. You must know that our old Khmer Empire was very large, including the south of Vietnam nowadays. The civilians pay no attention to politics, but the Khmer intelligentsia and the country's leaders always think that Vietnam and Thailand are the great threatening; always think that Vietnam and Thailand are the tigers who want to swallow up this country. Your Vietnamese army came here to drive away the Pol Pot army, and that is a great favor for us. But a vendetta is always a vendetta. They, the intelligentsia and the politicians, will never forget it, sons. You're soldiers and you have to do your duties. The soldiers of other armies are of the same. They have to do their duties. Unless the Vietnamese army withdraws out of Cambodia, otherwise, they will never stop opposing you and opposing the new government which they consider as a pro-Vietnamese government."

Huy nods his head. Things that the old monk talks to him are very fresh. So, everything has its reason.

Suddenly, *Luc Ta* Nasuk interferes, "You sons must be tired, well, get your rest now and ready to go tomorrow. We will pray for all of you to be always safe, and this country would quickly escape from the mournful war."

***

Two soldiers, their uniform soaked by sweat and covered by the road dust, step onto the stone bridge across the moat surrounding Angkor Wat temples under the fading afternoon sunlight. Five huge towers are burning in the red glow like five huge glorious torches. And Huy stands dumbfounded in an indescribable feel. Of awe, or of admiration, or of stun, or all of those feelings are mixed up together in his mind?

Binh pulls one of Huy's arms. "Alright, we get to have our meal first, I'm so hungry. You keep staying here for a few days and go around for seeing until you feel enough. No need to hurry."

They go toward the direction where Binh's squad is located. There are two soldiers who sit and talk to each other in front of a small thatch roof house. They jump onto their feet as they spot Binh. One of the two is a Khmer boy, about fifteen or sixteen years old. The other one shouts loudly, "You're allowed to come back, brother Binh? It's so sad without you those months." He turns to Huy, looks at him questioningly.

"This is Huy," Binh smiles broadly. "He lay in the hospital with me. He'll stay here for a few days to see the old temples. Why, is there any good food to serve our guest, Bang?" he turns to Huy and points to the two others. "Bang joined this unit at the end of 1985, and this boy is Rai, previously in the Pol Pot's army. We captured him and then converted him to join in our unit. Here, our duty is to keep the commanding position, so we're short of power. It's less of work hard to get him."

Bang and Rai head for the kitchen. Huy and Binh go out to the lake to have a bath. When they return, the supper is served.

After the meal, Binh discusses with Bang and Rai some tasks and then they all come out the yard to drink tea.

Huy sips his bowl of hot tea and asks Rai, "How long did you stay in the Pot's army before joining us?"

"I was taught to use mines, fire AK and B rocket launchers since I was twelve. Then I joined Khmer Rouge army when I was fourteen."

"Is anyone of your family alive?"

"My parents were killed by some very small faults. I was about five then, Khmer Rouge brought me up and I worked for them. Afterward, they began to teach me to use the weapons."

Rai tells Huy about his life.[1]

He was separated from his parents since he was a little child. His father was a teacher. And his father and mother were separated too at two villages locating about four miles from each other. Rai was brought up together with about ten other babies and took care by a grown-up. Since a very little age of six or seven, he had to work in the fields. A group of children had to pull plough instead of cattle. Food was so short and almost rice gruel. Each week, the children were taught a Khmer letter. And they thought that the world around them existed just like themselves, knew only violence and hard works, always in starvation and there were only weapons around.

Khmer Rouge taught them that the enemy was so near to them, so they ought to be very carefully. They had to learn the songs such as *"Victory, Power, New Government New Power, Strive to Kill the Enemy"*, and *"Everyone as One"*. Rai could keep a gun the first time when he was ten. The gun was almost as tall as him and he got many difficulties to keep it on his shoulder. He practiced to fire by shooting at the fruit, small animals or fish in the rivers. Khmer Rouge had plenty of kinds of weapons and allowed the kids to choose among the AK47s, M16s, M60s and Kalashnikovs.

He was taught to swim by a very simple way. That was to be thrown into the river. And he was near to drown if one of his friend did not pull him to the rive bank. For Khmer Rouge, life was cheap and they did not care of anyone's life.

The kids were given uniforms including black shirt and trousers and a red white striped krama. And they wore sandals made of tires.

The Vietnamese army approached Siem Reap in 1983. The two armies fought to take control the temples in the Angkor area.

Khmer Rouge took control Ta Prahm and Preak Khan, and Vietnamese army Angkor Wat, Angkor Thom and Bakain Mountain.

At the time Vietnamese army came into Siem Reap, Rai stayed at a Khmer Rouge's camp in the forest to learn using mines. Khmer Rouge told the kids that Vietnamese soldiers were the giants with big teeth and long beards. The kids were so frightened. Afterward, Rai was very glad to find that the Vietnamese soldiers were of the same size of him.

When Vietnamese army just came, the powers of the two were similar. But after a few days of fierce fighting, the Vietnamese used tanks. Khmer Rouge's soldiers had never seen a tank before, so they did not know how to fight it. They tried to shot at the tanks, and found that they were motionless. Khmer Rouge soldiers thought that the tanks were destroyed and came near to them. Instantly, a Vietnamese soldier hiding in the forest gave signals, and from the tanks, fierce salvos killed all of Pol Pot's soldiers. That time, Rai was lucky because he did not come near to the tanks, but he was captured by the Vietnamese soldiers laying ambush in the forest.

And then, with their kindness and sincere treatment, the Vietnamese soldiers have convinced Rai to join their unit.

Huy sits listening to Rai's life story, feels that Pol Pot's regime was really a terrible one and beyond anyone's imagination. A regime that has turned human beings into animals that knew only to eat and kill.

He asks Rai, "Do you love these Vietnamese comrades? Do you see that we're very different from the Khmer Rouge soldiers who knew only to threaten and kill?"

"Sure. I love boong Binh so much, and boong Bang and the others too. They treat me as their youngest brother, take care of me when I'm sick and never be cruel or merciless to me like the Khmer Rouge." says Rai.

That night, Huy cannot sleep and he hopes that it will be dawn soon to see Angkor Wat's temples. He falls asleep at last because of being tired when it is near to dawn.

***

Thus Huy has stayed at Angkor Wat for three days, but he still feels that he does not see enough. He still feels that his heart is trembling with the gigantic and mysterious scenery of the temples.

"Do the unfathomable smiles at Angkor Thom that I have seen in photographs conceal a premonition of Khmer nation destiny? Is the howling of the winds through the ancient trees the lament of great souls who have built the ancient urban area of Angkor? Is the glistening fire-liked sunlight burning on each ancient tower of Angkor Wat the teardrops of King Jayavarman II, King Suryavarman II and King Jayavarman VII for regretting a lost golden age – the age that the Khmer Empire once spread over immensely through Southeast Asian regions? Now and then, the elephant packs wandering across the declined temples growled sadly again. Are they too crying for the lost past? Does this devastated but imposing scenery prove for a truth: the crystallization of tear and blood of uncountable amount of human beings must be everlasting with time? Like the Great Wall of China. Like the Egip's Pyramids."

The civilization of Angkor began in the IX century and prolonged to the XV century. The ancient Khmer urban area of Angkor spread all over 1,150 square miles, located at the north of Tonle Sap Lake, province of Siem Reap nowadays. Over 100 stone temples which have been devastated but still existing under winds and rains, and they are the remaining of the biggest ancient city in the pre-industrial time, including the palaces, public works and wooden houses which were absolutely ruined by the time.

After being occupied by Thailand about 1431, Angkor's inhabitants scattered to other places. The ancient urban area ruined gradually and became a lost city. Over four centuries, large dense forests had surrounded it. Once in a while, the monks who walked across those forests found the vestiges of the devastated works. They sensed the holiness and mystery of the ancient temples, but knew nothing about their originals. They invented many fables about those temples, and thought that some gods had built the works in the ancient time. After four hundreds of years those stories became legends. And people just knew by the legend that there might be some lost ancient city in the forests. Until 1860, Henri Mouhot, a French explorer discovered it again. And since then, the mystery buried for some hundreds of years was disclosed gradually.

Later, when he returns to his homeland, with his deep love of the country of temples, Huy will study and understand much more about Angkor; about the rise-and-fall history and a glorious but so painful past of Khmer nation and people. Yet now, he just listens in amazement to the strange and mysterious sounds rose up through the

Angkor Wat temples' gates. He just stands and looks up amazingly to the ancient towers and feels that there is something that is very great and very melancholic flooding upon each fold of stone, each glyph, and each old tree. The Apsara dancers on the stoned-walls seem to be moving evenly with their wonderful dances. And their faces seem to have sad and enduring smiles.

Huy still stands wistfully when Binh comes near. His face is radiant. He reaches out his hand. There is an open letter in it.

"This is a letter which I just write to Xuan. You read and tell me how well it is!" Binh says.

Huy takes the letter, comes to the foot of a thnot tree, sits down and reads the letter with concentration. Binh wrote it with wrongly grammatical sentences and wrong words due to the education of a fifth grade pupil. Yet each of such sentences and words pervades a pure and beautiful and deep love. Having read it, Huy folds the sheet of paper, gives it back to Binh who is sitting eagerly near him to get the comment.

"You wrote so well. I myself am moved when I read it, it's sure enough that Xuan will like it and be moved so much. I like to wish you two will be together forever soon," Huy tells him.

Binh pulls his arm, "All right, I'll put it away then we will go around for hunting. I determine that I will serve you some very good food today and let you always remember your friend Binh."

They carry out their guns and walk around the western forest for a long while, but cannot find any good prey. There are some big birds, but Binh says that their meats are so tasteless, that they better find some deer or boar to be worth of bullets.

All of a sudden, Binh cries in a low tone, "There is a fresh pile of boar dung, my comrade. This boar is not far yet, sure we can kill it."

They follow the faint footprints of the boar on the hard sand of the forest. Binh goes ahead, and Huy is some yards after him.

Suddenly, Huy hears a round of gun-fires so near to them. He throws himself onto the ground, rolls over to a big tree foot, aims his gun to the direction where the gunshot comes and fires a long round. The gunshots are echoed from deep inside of the forest. Then he glances back to the place where he and Binh have stood. Binh is lying motionless on his stomach. One side of his head and his upper body is wet with blood. The blood on his coat still reflects the glistening light, which get through the thin leaves above their head. Huy bursts into crying, "Oh, Binh!"

The air around becomes quiet again, just the rustling sound of leaves and the vague twittering of birds.

Huy lies still, keeps his breath so gentle and tries to listen to any strange sound. About half an hour later, the air is still quiet, only the endless song of the forest. The enemy must have fled away. They must be few of power and just took a hit-and-miss sudden attack. Suddenly, Huy hears three single shots and then the loud voice from the edge of the forest, about three hundreds yard away.

"Brother Binh! Brother Huy! Where are you?" Bang's voice.

Huy shouts loudly, "Bang! I'm here. Binh was shot!'"

About five minutes later, Bang and Rai appear. Huy stands up, runs toward Binh. He turns up Binh's body. His chest is broken. His eyes half close, just the white pupils can be seen. Huy puts his hand onto Binh's nose. The breath has stopped. Tears come up his's eyes. He cries, "Oh Binh! How can you be dead?"

The other soldiers run toward and kneel down at both sides of Binh's dead body. The three soldiers hold Binh' hands in theirs, their eyes dewed with tears.

The spring does come no more. And this winter is Binh's last winter. Oh, Xuan! Do you know?

CHAPTER 19

Once again, the battalion gets a hard dry season. This year drought is terrible. The short of water makes trees and bushes withered. The melon and gourd trellises are dried and died soon. Their bodies are sweaty all the time in the sultry hot weather. And all the streams near their base are dry up too. The soldiers have to come to the nearby phums some five miles away to get water. The lotus pond near the pagoda soon remains a thin water layer on the muddy bottom. The villagers and soldiers have to line up waiting for each one's turn to decant piece-by-piece mugs of water in the small holes dug deeply into the pond bottom. For almost two months, the soldiers can only wipe their bodies with wet towels each three or four days a time.

In the middle of July, the battalion is ordered to march to the Height 182. As regiment scout's reports, some two hundreds Pol Pot's troops have gathered there more than half a month ago, and have been camping around a big lake in the forest. The Height is also the only place having water source within an area of forty miles of radius. On the map, the blue symbol of the lake makes a long streak. Everyone prepares for the operation in depress. For a long time of drought, everyone's nerve is so tense and uneasy, and their bodies are exhausted; they can only wait for rain. To fight in such a condition would get no good result, but the military orders are as firm as mountains, to be soldiers, they have to execute them anyway. They try to get enough water for the operation, but each one can only at best fill up half of four-litter-yellow can of water. So they can only hope that they will drive away the enemy, take the lake and can drink at their will.

The Height is about forty miles from the base. The battalion tries to cover this distance at night to avoid the hot sunlight, but due to the very sultry weather as well as their short of water that their speed decreases gradually. They are one miles and a half away from the lake when it is dawning. Captain Bao lets his unit take a rest. Each soldier pulls out his dry rice bag, fills it with water and chews it to relieve his hunger. Nobody dare touch dry compressed flour. Such food is for the moonlit nights, when they sit chatting and drinking tea; eating such food in operations can only make them heavy-stomach and not able to walk.

About an hour later, they reach the Height. Fighting formation is deployed and they slowly approach the lake. But they soon find that the enemies have left the Height a few days ago, leaving the marks of cooking stoves dug around the lake edge. And the lake is just a big hollow now, as dry as the sky and earth. It is now just a corpse of the lake which is still marking a freshly blue streak on the map.

Captain Bao is furious and bursts out his curses, but his fury quickly falls down. He begins to worry to think of their return. If they follow the old way, they have to cross a forty-mile long plain under the heat. It is the shortest way. And if they go roundabout a little westward, they will meet the nearest phum, about twenty miles away, and can get something to drink. But the way is much farer, and there is much more possibility to encounter the enemy. Everyone is tired out now, they almost cannot lift up their legs; how can they fight if they encounter the woe?

Bao decides to choose the farer way at last. The battalion returns like a defeated troop, even worse than being defeated. The groups of soldiers drag their feet on the grass plain, keeping in order no longer. Many soldiers faint away and fall down onto the ground, especially among the gunfire platoons. Kien and Vu, two new comers of Huy's platoon cannot help falling down when they are about three miles from the phum. Huy pulls a bidon of water out of his rucksack. Since the time returning from the borderland, he has never forgotten to save a bidon of water in his rucksack in each operation. Many times, he has carried it away then carried it home again, without using it. Yet his habit proves its useful results now. He pours the water into the bidon cover, let Kien and Vu take small gulps, and just allows each of them to drink only three times like that. The two young soldiers are better now, so they continue to go. Gradually, all of soldiers groups come in the phum. Luckily, there is no enemy there.

The battalion never comes to this strange phum before. Rows of fruitful coconut trees stand along the main road of the phum. The soldiers throw themselves at the feet of the trees, looking hungrily at the big green coconut fruits above their heads. After little while of rest, they scatter into the houses to beg for the fruit. The villagers are unwillingly to give them the fruit. They shake their heads and say that they do not know who the trees' owners are though the trees stand right in front of their houses. A man says, "Don't know nothing; maybe those trees belong to the house in the north." And when the soldiers go to the house in the north, they are told that those maybe belonged to the house in the west. The soldiers get angry. They aim their guns at the fruit and fire; green and ripe fruits fall down like raindrops. At this, the old women run out and cry, "Don't fire, young men, don't fire! You'll kill the trees. Well, well, just climb on to get fruit and stop firing."

Huy watches the scene, feels ridiculous and pitiful for the soldiers. Anyway, we are only the youngsters, who suffered so much, yet those villagers treat us so badly. Or, they have also their own sufferings? Are those coconut fruits their means of living? Are their rice, their chicken and pigs and cattle and fruits robbed many times by the Vietnamese or Khmer Rouge troops? So, as a result, for them, there is just a fear and resentment. Then who are wrong, and who are more pitiful now? These perverse soldiers who are firing and robbing, or those villagers who are living in a time of war and chaos?

***

The drought drags along until the end of July, and seeming content with its actions, it suddenly disappears at last. One evening, a gale rises up and lashes violently against the bamboo hedges around the phums, break the big rotten branches on the old trees; and dark clouds come covering the sky. The rainstorm pours down, fills up the streams and little springs and the lower grasslands in a moment. The rain falls heavily over the night. The next day it is sunny. And it is raining again and again after two or three days for a few months afterward.

The trees and bushes and grass in the phum and plains and forests begin to be verdant again with the rains. Bamboo shoots sprout like caltrops at the feet of the old bamboos. Many kinds of mushroom vie with each other to come to the surface at the streamside or on the rotten trunks. However, the villagers in Chandai do not call each other to go into the forest for getting bamboo shoots and picking up mushrooms as usual. This year, so many new training enemy powers from the border penetrate into the interior. The Vietnamese small units are surrounded and raided, and some companies have to leave the base and open a bloody way to retreat. The battles occur like daily meals between the Vietnamese and Khmer Rouge armies. Even the paths and trails in the forest are full of mines. A few villagers in the nearby phums have been wounded and killed by enemy mines on the paths or at the streamside.

A fine sunny day, Soun goes into the forest alone to pick up mushrooms. The dear forest does not prevent her; does not warn her. Soun goes into the forest alone. And never comes back.

In fact, Soun knows about the dangers lurking in the forest. But she feels so regret to think of the fat round fresh mushrooms. Moreover, she is very fond of wandering to pick up mushrooms and to murmur to the butterflies, or to tease at the squirrel puppies who always stare at the stranger then scream and run away; and to think of Huy too. That morning, she was the first one who saw the lamp that Huy had put sneakily at her door the night before. She was startled with amazement at first, and then understood how it was soon. She held the lamp upon her breast. Naturally, sweet romance folksongs burst out her little mouth. She was thrilled with joy. A strange joy and happiness and even nostalgia of Huy flooded up her heart, made her almost breathless. Soun gaily showed off it to Mae, then, she poured the oil from the old lamp into it, lit it, sat looking at the little fire and talking merrily to it, as if it could listen to her and could answer her, as if it was Huy himself. Soun had the endowment and innocence of most of the girls who lived near the nature and forests and mountains – they saw everything as the human beings, and liked to talk to them in their fancies, though in fact, they just talked to themselves, and listened to themselves.

"My dear lamp, you were lay here over night, so you surely felt very sad and very cold... Sister Soun's so bad, sister Soun didn't know nothing. Come on, stop be angry with me! I'll love you, wipe you and always fill you up with oil, you like it?

"What a pity for boong Huy, my dear lamp! He must be very strenuous to come here last night. Yet, I didn't know and didn't talk to him. I was just asleep. Your sister Soun's bad, so bad!

Soun just chattered such innocent words before Mae's smile and tender eyes. Mae too was so joyful.

Yes, Soun wants to go into the forest to pick up mushrooms, then dry them up and send to boong Huy. She begged Mae to allow her to go. Mae did not agree. She wanted to have something to send boong Huy as well, but Soun absolutely should not go into the forest. No matter what Soun plead for her permission, Mae insisted shaking her head. Yet early this morning, Mae went to Ta Nouk's house to help him to cook for a death anniversary. Soun stays at home and after finishing her homework, she takes out the lamp again and talks with it for a while. Then a strong desire occupies her, and she cannot resist it any more. She takes the rattan basket and leave home.

The forest seems to be smiling merrily and singing her songs to welcome Soun. The grass and low bushes are glistening with their wet leaves in dew and raindrops of last night. They rustle as Soun's sarong lap slightly touching them as if they wanted to coddle themselves, *"Bend down to us for a bit, boong Soun, smile upon us!"* And Soun bends down to them, smiles upon them very tenderly. The little and spotless lilies of the valley try to pervade their fragrant as Soun steps by them. The long thin leaves waggle, and the flower buds rock slightly to greet her. The ancient keruing trees hunch their backs to look at her, shudder themselves to release the reddish dry leaves down upon her shoulders and her hair as if to fondle her, and discuss rustlingly to each other, *"Wow! The more this little girl gets older, the more she's beautiful!"*

Soun walks through the old trees and the verdant bushes, receives their greetings and praises, and replies them friendly and merrily. When the sunlight crossing the jade layers of leaves dries up the early morning dews on the trees and bushes, her rattan basket is haft filled up with the sweet mushrooms already. Soun begins to be worried when she recalls that she did not obey Mae's words. "Well, I should stop picking up mushroom and go home now. Mae's maybe worrying for me so much," she thinks. Soun comes back, walking along a little stream. She almost tumbles when she crosses a swampy plot, but she tries well to keep her balance immediately. Being calm again after the slip, Soun laughs loudly to mock at herself. Her merry laughter does not stop yet, all of a sudden she hears a lower click right at her feet, and then something rebounds up in front of her stomach. An ear-tearing explosion throws her down. Soun lies on the ground, so small and so lonely; her white shirt is torn out and bloody. The rattan basket rolls away from her some yards, the little mushrooms splash around, and many of them are reddened by Soun's blood.

The trees and bushes above and around Soun are still rustling in the winds. But they turn again now into insentient things, being unflinching without knowing that a little girl has died right at their feet.

***

What's the date to day what's the month and year now is the universe still being there is this sky and earth still being there or has broken up is my heart still being there or has been broken into thousands of sharp crystal pieces which are tearing me out it was dim and immense dark outside what for the winds wail and scream and cry outside where does the night hide my dear where do the winds drive my dear please give her back to me please give Soun back to me am I still being aware or have lost my mind so that I suddenly hear hundreds of insane screams and cries in my head dear Soun where do you go so that Mae sits crying and missing you here so that I sit stone-dead missing you here is someone outsidethere in the dark please answer me where does my dear go don't tell me the ugly terrible word death what is death I don't care to know it I just want to get Soun again I just want to see Soun again I want to believe nothing more I want to hear nothing more say to me nothing more dead **dead dead**, *oh, something stabs my heart...*

No, you didn't die, my beloved Soun. A little angel like you can't die. I never want to believe that I've lost you. I believe that you've flown away. You've flown away with your light transparent wings, with your loving and benevolent heart. You've flown away. To a place where there is no animosity and discrimination; there is no gun and war. And, from that high and far and eternally peaceful place, you're still smiling upon me very tenderly. Your shirt is no longer reddened by fresh blood. Your shirt is absolute white like fine clouds, like sunlight, like your innocent pure heart.

(Extracted from Huy's diary)

CHAPTER 20

Once again, a new year comes and is half over in Huy' soldier life. One day in May, a very heart-broken incident happened. It made all of the Vietnamese soldiers sorry and grievous; made the nearby villagers furious and frightened and outraged; made even the thin afternoon smokes and red clouds behind Svay Mountain tinted with a mourning color every afternoon now. The story had originated from a previous point of time, as the later narrations of some comrades of the culprit and of the victims' intimates.

Last spring, the battalion X moved its base from a southern commune to Kandal, a big phum stood at the northeast of Svay Mountain, about twenty miles away from Chandai. It was a public relational battalion. Its main duty was not to fight, but as its name, to do public relation tasks, in order to strengthen the union and sympathy between the Vietnamese army and Khmer people, give advices and training to the Cambodian administrative and militarily local leaders. This unit consists of soldiers who were very good in Khmer language, some among them could even write Khmer letters finer and exacter than many villagers. They divided into many three-soldier groups to stay in each peasant's house to live and work and eat together with them. They were trusted and loved soon. There was a man named Z in the battalion, whose character was somewhat abnormal. He was seldom to speak and be cheerful with anyone. He was addicted to alcohol, and often sneaked away to drink by himself.

Z was very fond of May, a young girl in the phum. He often tried to flirt with her, but she did not like him and always dodged away from him. In fact, there were no girl who isn't feared when she saw a man who always drunk like a fish, with his blood shot dull eyes and his taciturn, unfathomable face.

Days and months passed thus, he would attack and she would dodge from him. Maybe the girl's attitude even made his conquering blood more excited and decisive at first. But when he found that so much of his time and labor was in vain, he became disappointed and embittered. In his mind, a feud and jealousness germinated. He was extremely miserable, his anger came up to his throat when he saw May spoke to and smiled with his other comrades. Many times, he just wanted to shout out, "Why do you treat me like that while I always love you and do good things to you? What can I do to make you please?" The more he was lovelorn, the more he was drunk, shutting his ears to the dissuasions and deterrence of his superiors and comrades. And, it was unknown when it occurred to him a mean and barbarous revenge plan.

The fatal day came.

It was a fine, sunny day. The villagers called for each other to go to the grassland at the forest edge to cut thatch. They started at dawn, altogether about fourteen or fifteen people, including old men, old women, girls and children. They went out, with the sickles and shears in hands, laughed and talked merrily to each other.

A pair of red winking eyes stared at the folks as they went out of the phum. A wicked smile appeared on his face, Z looked after the people until the last one was hidden behind the trees. He came back to the phum to look for alcohol.

About two hours later, Z staggered to his residence. He took the AK gun and wore a belt of three cartridge magazines on his chest, and went sneakily along a short cut to the forest, took a roundabout route to the place where the folks were cutting thatch. His comrades who lived with him in the same house seeing him took the gun out, but they paid no heed to this, just thought that he went out to hunt birds or do some task.

The forest was at its most beauty and verdancy then. Little green buds of leaves and sprouts were seen everywhere after the heavy showers, trembling in the breezes. Flowers were blooming on the trees and low bushes. All kinds of white and yellow and purple orchids were also showing their graces. Even the dwarfish lily clumps at the foot of tall old trees, nestling behind the curved, rough and mossy roots were also showing their light purple and white little flowers. The red turtledoves, black-necked grackles, starlings and nightingales were singing to call for their lovers. The rustling sounds of falling leaves and water flowing in the little streams wove an endless forest air. The forest was beautiful like a virgin. But Z was like a blind and deaf man. He did not hear and see anything but the dark savage thoughts in his mind.

He appeared suddenly in front of the folks, his black barrel pointed straightly to them. The people were startled as they saw the queerness on his face. They stopped cutting, stood still gazing at him, worried and feared.

"Old people and kids sit down there, take no move until I allow. The girls follow me," said Z, pressed and crunched his teeth at each word.

The folks looked amazingly at each other. Then Son Ke, an old man, gathered all of his courage to ask Z, "What do you want, koongtop Z?"

"Shut up!" Z shouted furiously. "No question at all. I'll kill right away anyone get to move or open mouth! Sit down!"

Old Son Ke looked at the other people, made a signal for them to obey Z. He looked very terrible now, just like a demoniac. None could guess whether he only threatened or would shoot really. They sat down reluctantly.

Z seemed pleased with the obedience of the folks. He turned to the girls, pointed his forefinger to the forest. "Go!"

Among the folks there were three girls: May, Sori and Chun. They walked on hesitantly. Z walked behind, his gun pointed straightly at them.

When they were some dozens of yards away, Z turned around and looked out. The people still sat quietly there. He commanded, "Sori, you use the kramas to tie hands of the others."

Sori looked at him fearful and shake her head. Z scowled at her. She resigned herself to do after his command, unfolding tremblingly the kramas on May and Chun's heads to tie their hands. Z came near, pushed so brutally that the girls fell down on their backs. Then he wore the gun on his back, snatched Sori's krama, and pulled her to a middle size trunk, where he could see the folks outside and the other two girls. Z pulled her arms toward behind the trunk and tied her hands together. Sori burst into crying, she begged, "Don't boong! Don't do it! It's so pitiful for Sori!"

Z's upper lip was dragged on with a wicked smile. He tore Sori's dress and then her sarong, and began to rape her right in front of the other two. May and Chun lay curled up, bent down their heads, trembled because of shyness and fear, then they burst into a convulsive sob as they heard Sori's cry and groan. About two minutes later, May decided to run, she kicked lightly Chun's leg to give a signal. They suddenly jumped to their feet then ran tottering out of the forest.

Z roared furiously. He hastily put on his drawers and ran after the girls. The folks outside began to run dispersedly when they saw May and Chun ran out. Z open the safety lock of the gun, shot at the girls and old people who ran slowly. Then he chased and continued to shot at the other ones.

Five people were killed that day, among them there were May and Chun, and five or six other ones were wounded. Sori was luckily survived because Z just ran after to shoot the other ones and forgot her there.

When the soldiers of battalion X heard the gunshots and came to the place, they were very stunned by the scene of the bloody bodies of the old people and children and girls lying on the ground of grass plain. Z was trying madly to shoot at a little boy. The soldiers quickly surrounded Z, called him to put down his gun and surrender. But Z was very excited and mad now. He shot back at his comrades and tried to escape. At last, a shot which broke one leg bone of Z stopped his overbold resistance. Afterward, they took Z to the hospital of the unit to cure his wound and waiting for his trial.

The incident was unexpected and terrible, beyond anyone's imagination. Yet it happened already. Everyone in Battalion X was heart-broken and sorry. They did not know how to explain to the villagers about the sins of their comrade. The folks were very indignant. They called down curses upon the Vietnamese soldiers, asked to get right of sentence Z themselves to revenge for their intimates. The air in the phum was heavy and dull. So much merits, so much sweat and blood of the Vietnamese voluntary army units become meaningless in a moment because of a single individual. A separated gap, which was difficult to heal, appeared in the previously close sentiment.

The occurrence was urgently reported to the highest leaders of the Front. The reports pointed out the villagers' requirements and petitioned to hold a special Military Court to judge and execute the sentence right at the place of action to mollify people's angriness. The Front Military Justice Council immediately made its decision to judge Z at Kandal. The open trial was announced to the units in the neighboring areas. Each unit was asked to send representatives to watch the trial.

The trial is carried out at the large yard in front of the pagoda. Since early morning, hundreds of folks from nearby villages have gathered there already, noisily discussed and gave guesses about the sentence. The soldiers came there a little later.

Because their base locates nearby, so many officers and soldiers from Huy's battalion also come there to watch the trial. Huy leads

Thuan and Kien coming there with him. He observes quietly. Though the place is very crowded, the air is rather quiet. The people speak to each other in a very low tone. They murmur the curses upon Z, and guess that he will certainly be condemned to death.

About eight o'clock, the Front Military Justice Council's officials, the criminal and a dozen of gun-hands come there on two Zil trucks. Z is taken down of the truck with his hands in handcuffs. His left leg is still in a plaster band. He looks helpless and his usual aggression and taciturnity disappeared. He is now like a refractory just received a good slap and is aware of nothing but a dumbfounded fear.

The crowd, which was so quiet before, suddenly becomes to be helter-skelter as the trucks arrive. And then the screams and cries rise up suddenly at a corner of the crowd. Some women try to get loose from the keeping hands to rush toward Z to attack him. They are the victim's wives or daughters or sisters.

An over middle aged grey head justice official holds up the loudspeaker to his mouth and speaks loudly in Khmer, "Please calm down and keep silent, ladies and gentlemen. This Z is guilty. The military court will judge him strictly and clearly. Now, please take your seats and keep order to watch the trial."

At this, he and five other military justice officials come and sit down at two tables, which have been arranged by the head of phum. Z is helped to get his seat at a chair in front of the tables. A middle-aged official stands up and reads the indictment. He reads slowly, stops at the end of each sentence. The interpreter, an officer of battalion X translates the words into Khmer language for the folks.

The indictment narrates the happenings of the criminal behaviors and concludes with a suggestion of death sentence, which will be executed right at the phum. Next, the judge who presides over the trial, and who is the grey head officer, begins to interrogate.

"The accused, is the indictment right in narration of your evil deeds?"

"Yes, it's right, sir." Z replies inarticulately. He has bent down his face right at the beginning of the trial; there is no trace of blood on his face now.

"What is the reason and motive of your homicide toward the innocent folks?"

"I don't know, sir."

The judge frowns, "Is it really that you shot and killed dozen of folks and do not know why?"

"I did not intend to kill them... I... I just wanted to rape the girls because I hated them... I shot them just because they ran away."

"Why did you resist your comrades when they came there to prevent you?"

"Well, I feared... I... I did not be aware anything then... I was like a maniac then...

"Do you repent for your sins?"

Z is silent. Then he weeps; mumbles and moans some vague words.

"I ask you again, do you repent for your sins?"

"I was extremely rued... extremely rued..."

"Do you want to say something to the victims' intimates?"

Z shakes his head with helplessness.

The judge waits for a moment and then repeats the question. Z hesitates and then speaks tremblingly, "I am sinful. I beg to be dead for my sins."

The judge nods and waves a signal at his secretary. The young man asks everyone to stand up to listen to the verdict.

"...The Front Military Court declares to sentence to death the accused who named Le Van Z, born___, enlist ___, rank of corporal, position: deputy head of squad of X battalion, Y corps due to his sins of rapes and murder savagely many Khmer innocent folks, driving a wedge between soldiers and people of two countries, destroying the Vietnamese volunteering army's honor and prestige. The sentence shall be executed today,_____, right at Kandal phum, district of Svay Chek, province of Battambang. On behalf of Vietnamese' People Army, the court would like to admit its fault to control without strictness the soldiers, so that the heart-broken incident could take place. We would like to ask for your forgiveness. There was short and long fingers on a hand. Z is an evil man. He will pay for his sins. But there are still many good men in the Vietnamese volunteering army, so I hope that you all still love and help them. Your loss could not ever be made up sufficiently, but to soothe and help the victim families to do the funerals and cure the wounds, on behalf of the Front, we would like to send to each family four quintals of rice and two thousand Riels. Please stay here to receive it after the sentence is executed."

He pauses for a short while, then presses his voice, "The executive team arrange for the sentence now!"

During the trial, some soldiers have gone out to the field at the north to prepare for the execution. A stake has been fixed on the ground. Z is helped to come there; a soldier ties a strip of black cloth above his eyes and ties him to the stake. Everyone stands round in silence and waits in palpitation. Three executive soldiers stand in a cross line, hold up their guns and wait for the order of the team leaders.

Z's body trembles tremulously. He cries. It is unknown that under the black cloth his eyes still open or close now.

"Fire!" the team leader shouts loudly.

Z's body bounces and twitches for one second and then bends down after the salvo. The team leader comes near to check if he died for good and then nods his head and waves at his subordinates to clear away the corpse. The execution seems to end so soon. Everyone stands astoundingly for a while. The sun is at its zenith then. The red light casts down upon the field. The executive site is very quiet in a moment. The sound of breezes rustling on the grass is suddenly clearly heard.

The people gradually go away. Huy stands still. There is neither sadness nor joyfulness in his heart but it becomes so heavy with an ambiguous feeling. The bright sunlight makes his eyes painful. Suddenly he feels extremely tired out. Suddenly he wishes that he could lie down and pillow his head on the soft sweet spring grass to fall asleep. And when he awakes, he would be glad to realize that everything in those past years is just the happening in a delirium-like fugitive nightmare. But that very wish is only a fantastic hope now. His thoughts seem to have nothing to do with his will. His mind seems to be cut off from his tired out body that is asking to have a rest. It still moves evenly in some strange orbit. A succession of far-away images and memories suddenly comes back in his mind – the plays and games of his childhood; the people who have almost disappeared from his life so long ago. He remembers them emotionlessly as if they have nothing to do with him – a warrior who is in a strange place now. When he is startled and free from those memories and looks back around him, everyone has left the ground of execution. The soldiers in the executive have also brought away Z's dead body. There are only Thuan and Kien who sit waiting for him under a tree shadow. A rain is coming. The sky darkens with grey heavy clouds. And the wind begins to blow strongly and becomes an eddy, whirling the dry grass and leaves all about upon the field.

***

In a battle at the end of May, a B40 shell broke out near Huy's trench. He got no piece of the broken shell, but its pressure and shake so great that he fainted away. He found himself lying in the division's hospital when he awoke again. He stayed there for a month. Afterward, he received the decision to be demobilized.

One day before returning home, Huy comes back to Chandai the last time to say farewell – maybe for good – to the place and people.

Anyone of his acquaintances whom he meets again is very glad to know that he will return his homeland, yet also feels sad to be parted from him. Soun's mother hugs him and weeps. He bends his head on Mae's shoulder, and his tears, which seem dry long ago, suddenly overflow like a flood. Her shoulder is soaking wet with his tears. And his chest is soaking wet with hers. He also drops by to see Puk Ho and sit drinking with him some glasses of liquor. The liquor now gets an extremely bitter taste.

When the late afternoon glow is almost fading out, Huy comes alone to see Mae Sa Rinh's charnel, and Soun's too. His most beloved people in a stormy season – his away-from-home season – have gone one by one away and left him alone. And it is his turn now to leave his beloved people here to come back to his old place where his fresh and blood people live. But his comrades still stay here, with so much difficulty and trouble and misery. The soldiers' sweat and blood will still flow down and absorb into each wild tree fallen leaf and each grain of sand here. A question ripples in his mind, "Where's my homeland?" His homeland is in South Vietnam where he was born and grew up with so many sweet memories; where he has had his family and friends. His homeland is also a place in Northwest Cambodia now, where he has lived and fought and loved; where he has learned the lessons about love and life. "I will be parted from you tomorrow," he tells himself, looks up to the incense's smoke flying sluggishly in the faint yellow sunlight. "I'll be parted from you tomorrow, oh, my dear homeland! But I'll always keep in my heart an immense nostalgia."

And what about his own melancholy? Just the sighs are swept into endless space.

AFTER WORD

RECOLLECTION

In memory of Tan
and my other comrades

Tan,

I recall the winter days of 1985; we would all day long tramp in a stream at phum Pou Roam Bon, Phnom Srok, back and forth to catch fish by hand. I carried a bamboo basket, splashing along in the shoulder-deep water, treading on your heels, just only to help you to keep the caught-fish.

I recall the cold nights at the end of year. Putting on one more uniform coat, I would sit cross-legged by a lamp, which was fueled by melted fat in meat-cans. With a piece of carton from the cartridge chest on my ankles and a tiny piece of pencil in my hand, I drew Tchiete. I do not know now how many pieces I have drawn of her. I only remember that with the simple, clumsy lines, my heart would be so warm, my blood would excitedly and heatedly flow in every vein. I have forgotten the cold air and my lonesomeness in those winter nights. I did not sleep because of being in love. It was a clear and normal thing. Yet you did not sleep too. You lay restlessly on the hammock, looking silently at me, at the smoky fire from the little lamp, being sleepless with me. You understood and loved me then, maybe the most. I recall the day you paid me a visit after transferring to the company. You looked sorrowful seeing me in an old uniform coat, worn and fraught with awkward hand-sewed lines on the back. In fact, we had no longer to wear worn clothes then, hadn't we? However, my new coat was given to my Khmer sworn-brother. A few days later, you sent me one of your new coats.

Then soon after that day – the last time we met each other – you passed away. During those days away from home, I've lost not only you but many other friends, among them, some who were very close to me and some whose faces I was just familiar with.

My dear Tan! My dear comrades! Your tombs have been covered with many layers of dead grass. Your names, your images now just remain in my memory – the short memories would suddenly appear in moment, and then again plunge into the chaos of everyday life. What that matters is I have no right to forget! The heart still beating in each of our chest has no right to forget!

Tan! It is almost the eleventh anniversary of your death. I am writing these words to burn a joss stick of my heart to recall you and other old friends. Pray God for your souls will be peaceful.

Saigon, November 1997

Nguyen Thanh Nhan

A LETTER TO SANLY

Saigon, November 1997

Dear Sanly,

Writing the first lines of this story, I would frequently remember you. I recollect now the day we have run across each other at an art gallery in Saigon; and the things we talked about. This book has been written partly because of our argument then. I hope as you read it, you will find out some thing that in our conversation I could not point out clearly. Also, I hope you and your friends too – the young intelligentsia who would be in the future the main riders of the nation-boat of Cambodia – would have a new vision, more understanding and more sympathetic toward the Vietnamese volunteering soldiers.

I would like to remind you of what happened. You remember that day, don't you? A late afternoon at the end of 1995, at the gallery, in front of a painting, you were standing quiet for a long moment.

The painting showed a Vietnamese soldier who was holding a bowl of milk in his hand, his other hand holding a spoon to feed a Cambodian baby, and around them were some other soldiers. In the background, a desolate and collapsed phum, some burning stilt houses with curls of smoke rising, and, some scattering corpses on the ground. The artist, who made this painting and many others for that exhibition, was a friend of mine. That was the reason for my presence. I did not understand fine art so much then, but I really loved it. And, I too, at the time, was standing behind you, looked at the painting. It brought into my heart some feeling, which I cannot recall and express exactly now if there was no our talk. It was a deep sorrow, neither so violent that makes one feel painful nor a light, momentary one. Over the years, the sorrow has been sticking in, sinking down my heart-bed, and becoming an unvarnished memory. It was the sorrow of the most woeful, ugly, and painful thing to the humankind: the sorrow and the helplessness due to the aftermath of war. That is what I felt of the painting then. But you, dear Sanly, you only noticed that it was a mediocre, rather exaggerated praise on what is named as the sentiment between the army and people, the united friendship between Vietnam and Cambodia, and the common humanity.

At that moment, you mumbled, in Cambodian, "It's deceptive, dishonest..." I just caught fragments of what you said. I had acquired a smattering of Cambodian, but forgotten a lot, so I could not understand all of your words. I only felt that you were annoyed and dissatisfied. I stepped forward to face you, smiled and asked, "Do you know Vietnamese?"

You shook your head, and then nodded, "Just a little!"

"Would you please go out for a drink with me? I have something to talk to you about," I said.

"Yeah!" you replied so sweetly, and smiled, continued in Cambodian, "I can't say much in Vietnamese. Could you talk to me in Khmer?"

"My Khmer is just like your Vietnamese!" I smiled. "I've forgotten a lot. You speak English well, don't you?"

"Yeah, my English is better than my Vietnamese. I've just been in Vietnam for two months."

Then, we sat and talked for a long while, sometimes in Vietnamese mixed with a little Khmer, sometimes in English and, at other times, we tried to understand each other through gestures and facial expressions together with the languages. We understood what the other talked about, though, and expressed our thoughts so well, didn't we, Sanly?

You told me your name. You were a student abroad in Hanoi, being on your Lunar New Year vacation, and, just stopping by Saigon to meet some compatriots studying there before going back to Cambodia. You were just nineteen years old, and loved the arts so much. In turn, I told you a little about myself: I was a veteran who had been living in Cambodia for years. Then, I asked you what did you mean about the painting a moment ago.

(The conversation, as mentioned, was so confused. Therefore, to help the readers to follow it easily, I would like to narrate according to the logical occurrence of the story, ignoring the interruptions and difficulties made by the language barrier.)

You answered straight away as if you had been considering it for a long time, "I said it was deceptive because the soldiers in that painting seem to be a symbol of rescue and the heroic Knights to our Cambodian nation: an ugly, ridiculous and excessive self-assumption that hurts our national pride. I'll tell you why. The Vietnamese army intervened too deeply in our internal struggle, made it become more serious and difficult to bandage. Had the Vietnamese soldiers been for the unity, for the impartial support only, they would have left right after we had our own strong army. Yet, not until the early 1990s were the shades of Vietnamese uniforms really absent. And as I've been told, the Vietnamese soldiers did many bad things too. Then, how do you explain to me its motive and meaning?"

I tried to arrange my thoughts so that I could express to you at my best. Then I said, "What you just said was also the questions that have distressed most of us soldiers. Firstly, I temporarily ignore it, to tell you the true meaning of the painting. It is misunderstood, and you're wrong in your sense of it. I know exactly that you're wrong, because I am a close friend of the painter. I used to talk to him many a time during him creating this piece. In addition, I used to be a soldier too. It doesn't highly praise the Vietnamese army as you think. Did you notice the look in the eyes of the work's characters? The baby's eyes are somewhat frightened, although her lips innocently opened to receive the spoon of milk. And the eyes of the soldier who feeds the baby: He doesn't look at her; he gazes worryingly at some undeterminable point. How will the orphan be? Who'll look after and bring her up in the later days? Would she live to grow up? – No one can know! His eyes are carrying those thoughts; and the others' eyes too. They are looking around, this one at the main characters, that one at the burning houses. They are stunned and dazed because of the terrible destruction of the war. They do not know how matters can be so bad like that. They seem to be painful and helpless too, with their hands hanging down, their fingers loosening surprisingly. They are still not used to the woe, the loss, and will never be used to it, though their uniforms have been worn and faded after many fighting years.

"No, the painting does not separately praise any person or nation. It only praises the universal humanity. Mainly, it tries to show us the ugliness, the hideousness of war, dear Sanly!"

I stopped and looked for your reaction. Your face remained the lines of innocent youth. The dark, big round eyes looked sensible and intelligent. Your hair was not curly as many other Cambodian women but smooth, black and thick, falling down onto your shoulder. Your eyes and your hair reminded me of another girl...

I tried to restrain a sigh and made my mind return to the present. You nodded softly, seeming to show agreement, and then your eyebrows rose up, as if you wanted to say something. I set my hand out to stop you, and continued, "Please let me finish what I am saying, Sanly. Now, I'll talk about the way you look at us Vietnamese soldiers... I don't know if there are many Cambodian young people who share your point of view or not, but it is a real pity and dangerous thing if many of them would have the same idea. Perhaps I'll try to talk, but I'm afraid that with some words only, or even with our conversation in this whole evening, I still can't say enough, can't express completely what has turned over and over in my own mind and my comrades' during the years of separation from our homeland to hold arms in another's country.

"We used to wonder for whom and for what we were fighting and killing and may be killed. We could not always answer these questions ourselves. Sometimes we felt our explanations reasonable, and sometimes we felt them quite absurd. You say that if we were really not self-seeking, we would have withdrawn from Cambodia long before that time. You don't know that the war in your country then was not simply a civil war between the parties who had different political point of views. Cambodia then was merely a chessman on the strategic chessboard between two powers, two doctrines competing to take control of Supreme Commander in the international arena. In fact, what I tell you now, was figured out so long afterward.

"So, we only felt confused then. We weren't like our former generations who held arms to liberate their motherland, in the time of resistance against the U.S. army. We even weren't like the soldiers of the years 1978-80. They fought to drive away the cruel Pol Pot's army who was burning and killing the innocent people along the Vietnam-Cambodia border. They all absolutely understood the meaning and purpose of their works. They deserved to the volunteer title. For us, the soldiers since 1980 forward, things weren't as clear and simple as that. After all, as an unavoidable matter, we were bound to involve in the Cambodian war. We grew up, full eighteen years old, took our military service, and then were sent to Cambodia either we liked it or not. We are not the men who chose the army as our career. We just took the citizen's responsibility toward our homeland. And, as soon as learning what was war and death, we all just wished that it would come to an end early and let us return back our home soon, peacefully and happily."

"I'll go back to the beginning to explain why I said it would be a regrettable and dangerous thing if you and many other young people looked at us with such a prejudice. You young intelligentsia would be the people who bear the burden of your country in a near future, and some among you would take the highest positions in the government. If the majority had such an unsympathetic view, the danger of war would have been like a piece of ember, just smoldering forever. I really hope there'd be no one like that. I knew many others – the old people, the youths and the children, who lived in the resort, poor phums in the northwest of Cambodia. They didn't think like you. They loved us. They had sympathy toward us – the very young men who had to be away from home, suffered so much. They really treated us as their sons, their brothers…"

I paused and felt that the more I said the more I could not express completely many thoughts that flooded into my mind.

You stared at me thoughtfully for a long moment, then said, "Everything you say sounds very nice, and reasonable too, but I still find some thing not sufficient. You seemed to exchange fraudulently the concept here. I say, you Vietnamese soldiers have covered yourselves with the fabulous wreath of the knight, but your army has done lots of bad things. Had the soldiers had the same conscience and sense as you say, they would not have done those deeds. There were cases of rape, robbery and oppression to Cambodian soldiers and people. You can't deny it. The most ridiculous thing is all of those actions were laid under a rather noble coat."

"You are too young, Sanly! You have not yet learnt how complicated and contrary humans are. And, the war – with so many contrasting sentiments: love, hate, resentment, fury and craziness – can cause everything; can seriously change anybody. On the other hand, what you say is true, but only the rare and personal cases. Those cases cannot be considered as the ground to judge our soldier's nature. I'll tell you a story that is quite true."

I paused, remembering things that seemed so far away now. You just sat staring at me, still and patiently. You understood my feeling. Then I began. "Many years ago, early one winter, a Vietnamese volunteer battalion came to phum P, a poor small village in the northeast of Phnom Srok district, Battambang province (now of Banteay Meanchay). It encamped there for some months to take the dry-season campaign in the vicinity. The captain settled himself in a house at the top end of the phum. Beyond his residence, the platoons scattered about. The 12.7mm machinegun platoon encamped at the north, where a little stream flowed by. The head of this platoon was a young, rather romantic fellow. He loved the good natured and simple

Cambodian peasants, and was trying to learn more of the Cambodian language so that he could talk to them more easily."

"Early one morning, he was sent for to the captain's residence for some tasks. The dawn was misty. You know, it was so cold that winter. In fact, it was the coldest winter of my years in Cambodia. The young man walked quickly and kept his hands on his cheeks to get warmer. He was ten yards from the porch when he found a young girl about sixteen years old in the garden. She was pounding ripe rice under an old coral tree covered with the late red flowers. She wore a plain, thick white cotton shirt, with a purple scarf around her neck. A soft black hair fell down to her shoulder, and her cheeks were rosy with the cold and hard work. She looked really charming and adorable. The young man took a few more steps then stood still and looked at her. She stopped pounding and looked up to find his steady gaze. She then stood still too and looked straight into his eyes. So, both sides were looking at each other for an uncountable moment. Then the girl seemed to awake and turned her head away, shy and embarrassed. The young man asked her where the captain was, but she said nothing, just pointed at the house. Then she turned back through the garden. The fellow just caught a glimpse of a smile flashing across her blushed face."

"It sounds very romantic, just like a novel!" you remarked, smiling.

"Yes," I replied, "but such a sad one, I'll continue. The army unit stayed at the phum for three months. On days off, the young man often went out to sit by the streamside waiting for the young girl who came to fetch water. After a couple of days, he came to her house, had a chat with her grand mother and her mother. Three months passed quickly. They had just become more familiar when the unit was ordered to withdraw. Six months later, the unit returned to that area. This time it set up the post at the foot of Svay Mountain, three miles away from the phum. The young man continued to visit his girl friend. They had now begun to fall in love with each other but the girl was still very shy. When they met each other, she just sat quietly, smiled and listened to his loving words.

"Winter was about to return again. Yet in that year the air was so heavy. Neither the soldiers nor the peasants in the nearby phums could escape from the tense, anxious mood: The Khmer reactionaries' army revived after a shutting year. Dozens of divisions and battalions from the training bases in Thailand border began to burst out for action along the frontier line. The posts of single Vietnamese volunteer companies were surrounded and attacked fiercely. Even the innocent peasants too were involved in misfortune. Many local dwellers were wounded or killed by mines when they went out to the springs or the woods. One day, the little girl went out alone into the forest to pick up mushroom. She stepped on a mine and died, near a dry stream some miles away from the village. The villagers found her bloody body that late afternoon, with her tattered rattan basket nearby and the mushrooms scattered about..."

I had to pause, felt my throat choked and bitter. My voice was so tremble you could realize it easily. You gaze at me in astonishment. I lifted up my head, took some deep breaths, tried to calm down, and continued.

"The fellow was heartbroken as he got the news. He was like a maniac, dejected for months. There came a day, the soldiers just got allowance, so they bought some meat and strong spirit to relax. During the party, he went out suddenly. He missed the girl, and so panic, he wanted to commit suicide. He took a grenade, went back to the phum, intending to see her house where they had taken acquaintance the last time. Reaching the house, he sat down under the old coral tree, burst out sobbing under the compassionate eyes of her grandmother and mother. Then he climbed the ladder into the house, searched for the lamp that he had made from a crystal medicine pot to give her as a gift one year ago. He leaned back against the wattle wall, holding the lamp in his hands, dreaming about the bygone days, and fell into asleep unconsciously.

"It was sunset when he woke up. He reached down his hand to his hip, where lay the grenade: it had disappeared. He went out of the house and found X, one of his comrades, who was talking to the mother. His comrades had realized his strange mood, so they sent X and Y to follow and protect him if necessary. Y had come back the post already, taking along with him the grenade. The fellow managed to reach X, pretended to say something and then clutched X's neck in his arms, trying to get the gun. They were fighting decisively when the head of phum brought away the gun for hiding, afraid that he might take risk. X still tried to hold him tightly. The latter now was crazy and not to be conscious of what was wrong or right. He hit and kicked X, and shook himself loose, ran to the head of phum's house to take again the gun. The old man, meanwhile, tried to hold him and console him, but he continued to be aggressive. Eventually, the young villagers had to force him. This one held his arms; another held his legs, pushed him down the ground and tied him on. He madly shook and tried to get himself loose, until he fainted from exhaust.

"He was on his own narrow bamboo bed in his house when he woke up. The head of phum had sent an oxcart to carry him back. He lay quietly in the darkness recalling what had occurred, feeling it to be a terrible nightmare. He was near to death, a sort of no meaning death that would make heartbroken to his close people. He didn't know why things were so bad. It wasn't because of drunkenness, since he just drunk just a little, could not be so affected. But why, he would always wonder for a very long time afterward."

"Is it you who was the fellow?" you asked suddenly after a long time of silence.

"Yes, it's me," I said. "Up to now, Sanly, I still can't know whether I really understand the reason of it or not. You see, such things have happened. It was incredible things, but it has happened already."

Then I was silent. So were you. I thought that maybe you had some sympathy with me then. Outside, the sunlight had faded out. The night fell. The gallery had closed. In the bar, the tiny red and green bulbs on the bonsai pots were flickering. Sitting some more moment, we said good-bye to each other. You wished me well. And I gave you the same wish.

Dear Sanly! This letter, I send it to you and to your friends as well, as a non-detachable part of this book. To say clearer, it is a prelude of the story about the days I lived. To write it is to pay partly a spirit debt that I would bear with all my willing to my companions, among them now some are still alive, struggling to find their happiness and some sleep forever.

I hope you read it with sympathy. In fact, I am not a writer at all. I am just a simple man, with my own simple words, telling again a story that many people have known.

To Sanly everyday of peaceful and happy youth.

Yours truly,

Nguyen Thanh Nhan

NOTES

CHAPTER 1

[1] *Tet* (Vietnamese): the New Year.

[2] Named after Chi pheo (His nature is aggressive but not cruel), a character in a short story of Nam Cao - a famous Vietnamese writer.

[3] B52: slang word of Vietnamese soldiers refers to a sort of army big tin bowl.

[4] A famous Chinese poet who lived in Tang Dynasty (AD 618-907).

[5] A detail about character Chi pheo in Nam Cao's story: he often cut himself his face to claim damages.

[6] This is a sentence in the Declaration of independence from China by Nguyen Trai (1380-1442), the great Vietnamese poet and politician: "Generals and soldiers were like fathers and sons. A bowl of liquor mixed up with river water also became good wine."

[7] *trà quạu* (Vietnamese): very strong tea

[8] *bidon* (French): one littered water bottle used in the army.

[9] *bánh tét* (Vietnamese): traditional cylindrical glutinous rice cakes cooked for the Lunar New Year days in the South of Vietnam.

CHAPTER 2

[1] Vietnamese folk verses; *ba hương* banana, *nếp một* glutinous steamed rice and *mía lao* sugar are the symbols of the most deep sentiment of the children to their mothers.

CHAPTER 3

[1] *tiến lên* (Vietnamese): a popular kind of card game in Vietnam.

[2] *hà thủ ô* (Vietnamese): a kind of pharmaceutical weed which was very often used for drink by Vietnamese soldiers in Cambodia.

[3] *varma ati* (Tamil language): hitting vital spots (martial art)

[4] *prâhok* (Khmer language): a kind of traditional salted fish of Cambodia.

CHAPTER 4

[1] This is an old folksong often sung by Vietnamese children in the old days:

> *"We pray God for rain*
>
> *To get water for us to drink*
>
> *To get the fields for our planting*
>
> *To get full of our cooked rice bowls*
>
> *To get the straws for our cooking..."*

CHAPTER 5

[1] *giông* (Vietnamese): a kind of lizard lives on the sand

[2] "Hurt the stork kids": This is a phrase from an old Vietnamese folksong saying about a stock mother who must go out at night to find food for her kids. It fells down into the water and is captured. The stock mother begs the man not to cook her with dirty water but with clear water, so that her children would not be heartbroken. The meaning of this folksong is deep and multi-aspect.

[3] *linh lác* (Vietnamese slang words): literally means the most subordinate soldier; *lác* in Vietnamese also means tetter.

[4] *ramvong* (Khmer language): a popular dance of Cambodian people

CHAPTER 7

[1] *antiques*: slang word of the Vietnamese soldiers refers to the booties.

[2] "wrapping one's body with horse leather": Chinese proverb, words of Ma Yuan (14 BC - 49), a famous Chinese general in Eastern Han Dynasty, meaning that the noblest soldier's death ought to be at the battlefield.

CHAPTER 8

[1] *thnot* (Khmer language): sugar-palm tree

[2] *phum* (Khmer language): village

[3] *koongtop* (Khmer language): soldier

[4] (Khmer language): Vietnam and Cambodia are united!

[5] (Khmer language): Good health brother soldiers!

[6] (Khmer language): Vietnam, Cambodia are united, eating *prâhok* will have good health, go away remembering *prâhok*!

[7] (Khmer language): Young girl, do you love me? I love you so much!

[8] *guava fruit*: slang word of Vietnamese soldier refers to a grenade

[9] *l'khol* (Khmer language): a kind of Cambodia folk play

CHAPTER 9

[1] *Sơn* (Vietnamese): a popular Vietnamese first name; this word had some various meanings such as paint/ painting or mountain…

[2] *bánh tét, bánh ít* (Vietnamese): two kinds of traditional glutinous rice cake in Vietnam.

[3] *hò* (Vietnamese): a kind of folksong often sang on boats

[4] *krama* (Khmer language): scarf; can use in lots of way.

[5] (Khmer language): Thank you so much, Smak!

CHAPTER 10

[1] *Mae* (Khmer language): Mother

[2] (Khmer language): White shirt! White shirt! I miss you and can't sleep! White shirt! White shirt!

CHAPTER 11

[1] *phở* (Vietnamese): a very popular kind of noodle soup in Vietnam and all over the world now.

CHAPTER 12

[1] *Ovpuk* or in short *Puk* (Khmer language): Father

[2] *Mia Huy* (Khmer language): Uncle Huy

[3] *khang cheong* (Khmer language): the north

[4] *boong* (Khmer language): older brother/sister

CHAPTER 13

[1] *Sâmlâ mchu* (Khmer language): sour soup

[2] *k'sang* (Khmer language): a sort of fruit in the northwest of Cambodia; it has sour taste and is often used to cook sour soup.

[3] *khum* (Khmer language): commune

[4] *srok sre* (Khmer language): the remote areas

CHAPTER 14

[1] *Luc Ta* (Khmer language): old Buddhist monk.

CHAPTER 16

[1] Jiang Ziya (dates of birth and death unknown): a Chinese semi-mythological figure who helped King Wen of the Zhou to establish Zhou Dynasty (1046-256 BC).

CHAPTER 18

[1] Character Rai is based on Aki Ra's life story – the founder of Land Mine Museum in Siem Reap. For more information about him, please visit:

http://www.talesofasia.com/cambodia-akira.htm, or
http://www.cambodianselfhelpdemining.org

About the Author

Nguyen Thanh Nhan was born in 1964. He used to be a Vietnamese volunteer soldier who lived and fought in province of Battambang (now Banteay Meanchey) and Siem Reap, Cambodia from December 1984 to July 1987. He got his bachelor of laws degree in 1994, but did not want to pursuit this career. Since 2000, he began to work as a writer and freelance translator. His published own works include a novel, a short stories collection in Vietnamese, and short stories, poems and articles in some Vietnamese newspapers, magazines and websites. His published translations includes: *The 7 Habits of Highly Effective Teen* by Sean Covey; *Weird Tales From Northern Seas* by Jonas Lie; *The 33 Strategies of War* by Robert Greene; the *Demonata series (so far 3 books)* by Darren Shan; *To the Lighthouse* by Virginia Woolf, *Three Junes* by Julia Glass, *Collected Stories for Children* by Walter de la Mare, *Growth of the Soil* by Knut Hamsun; the *Barsoom series* by Edgar Rice Burroughs (forthcoming); *The Resurrectionist* by James Bradley (forthcoming), and so on.

He lives in Saigon, Vietnam, continuing to write his own books and translate good works all over the world into Vietnamese.

Made in the USA
Middletown, DE
28 September 2017